Melissa Manning is a Melbourne-based writer and lawyer. She grew up in southern Tasmania and has lived and worked in London and Hungary. Her writing has been recognised in awards and published widely, including in *The Best Small Fictions* (US), *To Carry Her Home* (UK), *Award Winning Australian Writing* and *Overland*. *Smokehouse* is Melissa's debut collection.

www.lissmanning.com
@lissymanning
facebook.com/melissamanningwriter/

SMOKEHOUSE

MELISSA MANNING

UQP

For Paul
The life I choose

First published 2021 by University of Queensland Press
PO Box 6042, St Lucia, Queensland 4067 Australia
Reprinted 2022, 2023

uqp.com.au
reception@uqp.com.au

Copyright © Melissa Manning 2021

The moral rights of the author have been asserted.

This book is copyright. Except for private study, research, criticism or reviews, as permitted under the Copyright Act, no part of this book may be reproduced, stored in a retrieval system, or transmitted in any form or by any means without prior written permission. Enquiries should be made to the publisher.

Cover design by Josh Durham, Design by Committee
Map and illustrations by Josh Durham, Design by Committee
Author photograph by Paul Manning
Typeset in Bembo Std 12/17pt by Post Pre-press Group, Brisbane
Printed in Australia by McPherson's Printing Group

 This project is supported by the Queensland Government through Arts Queensland.

  University of Queensland Press is assisted by the Australian Government through the Australia Council, its arts funding and advisory body.

A catalogue record for this book is available from the National Library of Australia

ISBN 978 0 7022 6302 6 (pbk)
ISBN 978 0 7022 6455 9 (epdf)
ISBN 978 0 7022 6456 6 (epub)
ISBN 978 0 7022 6457 3 (kindle)

University of Queensland Press uses papers that are natural, renewable and recyclable products made from wood grown in well-managed forests and other controlled sources. The logging and manufacturing processes conform to the environmental regulations of the country of origin.

The characters and events in this book are fictitious. Any similarity to real persons, living or dead, is coincidental and not intended by the author.

Smokehouse: Part One   1

Boy   85

Leaven   95

Stone   113

Chainsaw   125

Faal   147

Bruny   159

Nao   171

Smokehouse: Part Two   185

Smokehouse

PART ONE

They'd been living in Bellerive for eight years when Tom showed Nora the ad for a property down the Channel.

'I think Kettering's too far,' she said.

'It's only half an hour's drive,' Tom countered.

'No.' Nora shook her head.

'I'll drop the girls at Mum's.' Tom stood at the chipboard bench and poured coffee into a thermos.

It had been a long week at work, and she couldn't be bothered to argue. 'Fine.'

It was one of those clear winter mornings. The snow-capped peak of Mount Wellington was visible as they drove from the Eastern Shore across the Tasman Bridge. Tom turned the car heating on full and when 'Coward of the County' played on the radio he sang along loudly. Nora couldn't help laughing.

They drove past the Hobart regatta grounds and down by the docks. It was slow going as people made their way to Salamanca Market, crawled in search of somewhere to park. Tom drove on, tapping his fingers on the steering wheel and sounding out the rhythm of their day. Between songs, he stopped to press a palm briefly against Nora's thigh. She tried to remember how long it had been since she'd welcomed those gestures of tenderness.

They pulled in at the shops before the entrance to the Southern Outlet.

Nora had her seatbelt off before the car stopped. 'I'll go in.'

The smell of herb-coated barbeque chicken filled the small supermarket. She stood in front of the glass-fronted cabinet and watched the chickens turn on steel posts, juices dripping.

Back in the car, she passed Tom a bottle of ginger beer and, as they drove down the outlet, Nora poked holes in hot-dog buns with her index finger, furrowed tunnels for the bananas she'd bought. She handed a filled roll to Tom and opened her chocolate Big M.

'No chicken then?'

'Wasn't ready,' Nora lied.

She had intended to enjoy the drive and close her mind to Tom's whim. She focused on the warmth in the car, the texture of squashed banana in her mouth and the taste of it mixed with chocolate milk. She moved the radio dial, pushed through static, gave up and turned it off. Tom opened his window and threw Bob Marley lyrics into the air, let them fly away on the wind.

They drove beyond Margate, past knee-high grass and makeshift roadside huts selling apples, leatherwood honey and eggs – honesty boxes and signs advertising the price of produce. She was beginning to get comfortable when the view shifted. Vegetation fell away, bands of forest clear-felled, the road scraped wide and flat. A thick, grey blanket hung in the air like a horizontal curtain; it hid the true sky as they drove into Electrona.

Neatly ordered boxes with small gravelled yards lined the road. The desolation, Nora thought, must be caused by pollution, by the plumes of charred smoke that wound from the chimneys of the aluminium smelter. It occurred to her that the boxes were the homes of shift workers, men driven by money rather than aesthetics, none of them interested in gardening. Squares to sleep, eat, wash and shit in. In the thirty seconds it took to pass through the tiny township, she felt oppressed.

Then, at the edge of Snug, she noticed the sign for Snug Falls. A trickle or a proper waterfall, she wondered. Perhaps they could stop there on the way back. Maybe if she gave this a chance things might change, they might become that kind of people.

They went by the turn-off to Coningham and snaked down the steep hill into Kettering. A knuckle-shaped cloud drifted across the fierce blue sky, blocking then unblocking the sun at the beckoning of the wind.

'It's somewhere near here,' Tom said, as he eased the car beyond the gravel road that skirted the bay around to the left. Ahead, a corner shop sat elevated above the main road, the awning over the narrow concrete verandah supported at each end by thin, green paint-chipped poles.

He parked at a petrol station across the road from tennis courts with sagging nets then went inside to ask for directions. Returned with a Freddo frog for each of them, the kind with a strawberry cream centre. Nora ate the head of hers first then sucked at the filling before letting the rest of it melt away in her mouth while Tom drove back the way they had come until they reached the gravel road they'd passed earlier. He drove onto it as though he'd never driven on that kind of surface before or was trying to build suspense.

'It's at the top,' he said, with the authority of first-hand knowledge, as if the man behind the counter at the petrol station hadn't told him which way to go.

A wide, metal gate blocked the entrance to the property. Tom stopped the car and Nora got out, left her door open and undid the looped chain. She swung the gate all the way back and stood waiting until Tom had driven past, her car door closing with the momentum.

The end of the road gave way to tussocked pasture. Tom walked ahead and, despite the expanse of the property, Nora felt compelled to follow him. She avoided the cow pats and walked where the grass lay flat, pressed to the ground under Tom's boots.

Tom strode to the far boundary fence and they followed it to the bottom corner then turned and walked along the fence line that separated the property from the one below. By the time they had walked the entire boundary, Tom was smiling as though he had the measure of the place. Nora was captivated by the smell of eucalyptus and freshly cut pine, felt a sense of freedom she hadn't for a long time. She wanted to know more about the space, to understand what lay in the middle. But Tom rubbed his hands together and asked her what she thought in a way that meant he had already decided.

'What do you think happened to the cows?' she asked.

Tom shrugged. 'Been moved on. All that shit has to be good for the soil though.'

'Yep.' Nora shielded her eyes with her hand and looked down towards the river. She tried to see the bay, but it was obscured by trees.

Tom stood behind her, resting his hand on her shoulder, and pointed. 'We could take out the tops of a couple of the tall ones. Open up the view.'

She felt her opposition drop away.

On the way home, Tom talked nonstop about the kind of house they could build, the crops they could grow. 'We'll need a tractor,' he said.

She could think only of the moment when he had read her

mind. Knew no matter what he suggested now, she would agree for a view of the bay.

Tom parked on the grassy reserve adjacent to the caravan yard and the four of them crossed the road, hands strung together like paper dolls.

'Right.' Tom broke the chain. 'Let's do this.'

There must have been fifty vans jammed onto the corner lot. The largest and flashiest ones at the end nearest the intersection, and the cheap ones packed away at the far end, which was canopied by a line of wattles in full golden bloom.

'Can we look by ourselves, Mum?' Trudie asked.

'Yeah, Mum, can we?' Lara said.

Nora laughed. 'Go on then, see what you can find.'

'No point looking up this end.' Tom nodded towards the huge vans with signs advertising showers and toilets.

'How small do you think?' Nora asked.

'It won't be for long. Let's see what they cost.'

They stepped in and out of caravans, pressed buttons to open drawers and cupboards. Nora marvelled at sneaky storage nooks. She pumped taps, visualised cooking in one of those miniature kitchens, imagined all of them held tight in such a tiny space: a swaddling reassurance, or claustrophobia?

She and Tom lay on a bed, and she felt outside of herself when he slid his hand into hers. Was this the life she was choosing? Where she was headed now?

'Come on,' he said and got up, went to look at the next one.

But Nora stayed, stared at the bunks where a beige concertina door was tucked against the wall. She could walk away now, tear down the 'for sale' sign outside their house in Bellerive. Make the choice she'd been thinking about for months. But there was something in Tom's enthusiasm, something of the man she'd seen that very first day on the pier. And there were the girls to consider. Maybe, Nora thought, this was the life they were meant to have. Maybe this was the life in which she could feel complete.

Her colleagues at the museum complained about their partners, but their grievances seemed minor. Small disturbances about dishes and bins, disciplining children. Nora joined in but she knew the fractures in her relationship with Tom were different, deeper fissures, and she wasn't even sure how much of it sat with Tom. Perhaps the dissatisfaction was her own fault; perhaps she wasn't attentive enough, grateful enough. She had never expected to feel so absent, as though her identity had bled out into the fabric of their family. She longed to feel the margins of herself. She rolled over on the bed and wondered if this new life in the country could give her that.

They went to Tom's mother's for dinner. Marjorie cooked chicken breasts, placed them in segments of French sticks and tied each one with a length of kitchen twine, arranged it all on a platter in a manner supposed to convey haphazardness.

Nora sipped riesling from a chilled glass. The girls told Marjorie all about the van they'd bought, and Marjorie nodded, oohed and aahed, said things like, 'Well, doesn't that sound lovely' and, 'Gosh, bunks, how grown up you two are getting.'

'It's not big but it won't be for long.' Tom leant against the kitchen bench and drank beer from a stubby. 'Driveway first then we'll excavate the site. After that, it'll be the water tank and the slab. Before we know it we'll have a toilet and bath.'

'Sounds like it's going to be fast progress.' Marjorie lifted her glass, tilted her head to cheers their new life and drank.

While the girls tore sections off their gourmet rolls, Nora thought about the bathroom in their current house – floor ripped up, no vanity – still half done after three years. Tom had promised to sort it out soon, when things at work calmed down. He'd become annoyed when she suggested they pay someone to do it. She tried not to think about what that meant for the new house, tried to let herself believe that it would be different.

'A fresh start will be good for all of you,' Marjorie said.

'Mmhmm,' Nora agreed, and the cold wine at the back of her throat went down the wrong way.

The caravan and portaloo had been delivered, and Nora drove the girls down to the property. Let them pick at the edges of the excavated bank between the new water tank and the van. Trudie and Lara added to the collection of fossils they'd been putting together with each of their trips there, put themselves in stories from a time when creatures swam in the places they now stood. All while Tom and the concreters finished screeding and smoothing the freshly poured concrete, and Nora made the beds in the caravan and set up the camp shower.

After the workmen left, Nora, Tom, Trudie and Lara pressed thumbprints into the slab, side by side, a set for each room. Tom, with crusts of concrete on his face, in his hair, seemed content, and Nora was captured by the girls' excitement, by the sight of Tom putting plans into action.

They went to the pub for dinner. A two-storey brick building perched on the curve of the bay. The public bar patrons turned to watch them as they walked across the tacky carpet.

The barman paused mid-pour. 'Food's that way.' He nodded at a sign that directed them to the bistro. Single file, they navigated a doglegged corridor lined with pictures showcasing the faded glories of the Kettering cricket team.

The bistro was a large room at the rear of the building. Floor-to-ceiling aluminium-framed windowpanes and, beyond, the terminal where the ferry docked on its constant trips between Kettering and Bruny Island.

A woman poked her head into the room. 'Pop into the bar when you're ready to order.'

They were the only people in there. The girls ran between faux timber laminate–topped tables, picked carnations from vases and slid the pale silken blooms behind their ears, while Nora and Tom studied the menu on the chalkboard. Tom gave the girls some money for the jukebox. Then he went to the bar and ordered: fish and chips for the girls, and crumbed calamari for the two of them.

Nora walked out to the lawn, wanted to be close to the bay.

'Here.' Tom returned with beers, stood close behind her, his chin perched on the top of her head.

She leant back into his chest, as though it were something that still came naturally, as though in doing so she could conjure the depth of former affection, but her head felt flat against his body. Unnatural. Outside in the warm summer sun, she was vaguely aware of the girls dancing to Kate Bush in the bistro.

'Imagine what you could do with this place. They have no idea what they've got here,' Tom said.

'Mum,' Trudie called.

The waitress had delivered their food, and as they ate Tom talked about how great their new life was going to be, promised the girls ponies, mini bikes – things he and Nora hadn't discussed. Between bites, she observed the small road to the ferry clinging to the edge of the bay. Noticed the worn carpet in the vast room: pink roses faded to puce and vines entwined, all on a background of grubby grey; threadbare tracks leading to the jukebox.

They were immersed in their meals, in Tom's plans, when there was the sound of running in the hall; two young girls similar in age to Trudie and Lara flew into the room, stopped just short of Nora and Tom's table.

The girls turned from them, yelled in unison, 'Muuum?'

A couple followed. The woman looked at Nora and Tom, then pointed to another table by the window. 'We'll sit there.'

'But, Mum,' the taller of the two girls objected.

Self-conscious, Nora wondered if she should offer them their table, move to another.

'But, nothing,' the woman replied. 'This table is fine.' The couple sat, sipped their drinks and talked to one another as their children – dressed alike in denim overalls, floral shirts with puffed short sleeves, and thongs – stared at Nora, Tom, Trudie and Lara.

'Is it true?' the woman said.

It took Nora a moment to understand that the woman was speaking to them. She swallowed without properly chewing her food, felt it thick in her throat, and had to pick up her glass to drink before she could respond. 'Sorry?'

'Mudbrick. We heard you're building with mudbricks.'

Tom beamed. 'That's the plan.'

'I'm Sally. This is Darren. These two are Becky and Ava.'

Tom introduced Nora and their girls.

'Can we go outside?' Becky asked, thick ponytail swinging as she stood.

'Go on. I'll call you when the food arrives.'

'Mum?' Trudie was already up.

'Just stay where I can see you.'

The four girls raced outside, huddled for a moment in the centre of the lawn before beginning a game of chase. Tom got up to close the door on their shrieking.

'Would you like to join us?' Nora asked.

Sally and Darren dragged their table across the carpet.

'When will you move down?' Darren directed the question to Tom.

'Actually, tonight's our first night.' Tom glanced at Nora. 'We can already tell we're going to love it, so much better than the suburbs. Right, babe?'

Nora nodded, shifted her chair to face Sally.

Darren clapped Tom on the back. 'Got that right, mate.'

'Are the girls starting at Woodbridge next month?' Sally asked.

'Yes. Trudie in grade five. Lara in grade three.'

'Same as ours,' Sally said, and the four of them slipped into comfortable conversation, made plans for Darren to come over with his backhoe, dig out a dam.

Outside, the girls rolled down the sloped lawn, and Nora wondered who she might become, whether this place, these people, might change things. Might render this life enough.

At the end of the night, when the meal was finished and the men had drunk too much beer, they all left with promises to arrange for the girls to play together, to have dinner again. Trudie and Lara fell asleep in the back of the car as Nora drove.

'See how easy it is? I don't know why you were worried,' Tom said.

'They seem nice,' she agreed, as she pulled into the driveway, the sweep of headlights panning across the bare concrete slab, settling on the caravan. She eased the car to a stop next to the portaloo.

Nora was roused from sleep by the crunch of tyres on gravel. She rolled over, was confused. She must have dreamt she was still in their old home, was dislocated by the unfamiliar cream-and-beige swirled walls of the caravan. Tom was gone, and she remembered him saying the night before that he'd be up early to check the paper and head out to buy a tractor.

She peeled back the sheet and stepped into her thongs then made for the portaloo. As soon as the disgusting thing had arrived she'd sprinkled lavender oil on every surface, but the odour of urine pervaded. It was worse as the day wore on, with the full summer heat. But the portaloo was temporary, she assured herself; it would be gone soon and they would have a proper toilet in a real house.

When the girls woke, she walked with them to the paddock below the slab, and they started dragging sticks and branches into a pile. She'd promised a bonfire as big as the girls could build. Now they had the space, these were the kinds of things they would do, the kind of childhood the girls would have.

She and Lara were tugging at a stubborn branch that was hooked under a fallen tree trunk when Trudie shrieked from nearby, 'Mum, Mum, Dad's got something. What's Dad got?'

Trudie was already running back up the hill by the time Nora let go of the stuck branch and turned. She could just make out Tom unloading something from the trailer. Lara ran after Trudie and, as she followed them, Nora could hear the girls' excited babble.

'Oh, Dad, I love them. Thank you, thank you, thank you.'

'Daddy, you're the best.'

Nora arrived to the three of them standing between two goats: one large with huge horns, the other smaller with shaggy hair. A smile broke across her face at the sight of the girls hugging the goats. 'Nice tractor,' she said.

Tom winked. 'I drove down to Garden Island Creek but the bloke wanted way too much for a piece of junk and he wouldn't bargain. I bought these two' – he gestured at the goats – 'at a property at Nicholls Rivulet. Turns out the guy who was selling them is a stonemason. You should see his place, Nora. You'd love it. Anyway, he might come to the mudbrick course and we're going to make plans and then he's going to build our fireplace. We're talking a monster of a thing with openings into two rooms. How great is that?'

Caught up in Tom's enthusiasm, she laughed. 'That does sound pretty great.'

Darren's cousin was coming over. They'd arranged it the night before, at the pub. Andrew would show them how to milk the nanny goat, Nancy. Nora had refused the offer, told them it was too kind, but Sally, looking at the hoof-shaped bruise on Nora's cheek, had insisted.

Now Tom was getting up and leaving, taking Trudie with him. He'd seen an ad for a tractor in the *Trading Post* and reckoned he needed to get in fast.

When Andrew showed up, Nora and Lara were playing hopscotch next to the van. The young man climbed out of his car, walked easily towards them, rolled-up flannelette shirtsleeves revealing muscular arms. He extended his hand, first to Nora and then to Lara. 'How you liking it?'

'So far, so good,' Nora said.

He nodded towards the property below. 'You've met Ollie?'

She shook her head.

'Must be away still. You will. Everybody knows Ollie. He's German. He smokes stuff, salmon mostly. Also possum, wallaby.' Andrew pointed at the building on the lower property. 'That's his smokehouse – you can just see it next to the A-frame.'

Nora could barely make out the small structure through the trees.

'So where are you hiding her then?' Andrew asked.

The three of them walked across to the side paddock gate. Andrew took one step to every two of Nora's; Lara had to almost run to keep up. As they approached the gate the billy goat, Henry, lifted his head, paused, then flew across the field towards them, head down as though ready to charge.

Andrew didn't flinch. 'Now that's a big boy.' He reached through the gate and scratched the place between Henry's horns.

'Yep, Henry's huge,' Lara agreed. She pinched her nose between two fingers. 'And he smells.' She cocked her head to the side. 'Actually, he stinks.'

'They usually do,' Andrew said, and smiled at Nora. 'It's a boy thing.' He opened the gate. 'Make sure you latch it,' he told Lara. Then he pushed Henry out of the way and walked up the lumpy paddock to Nancy.

'Trick is to make her comfortable. You want her to feel secure. If she thinks you're afraid or worried, if she reckons you don't know what you're doing, she'll be off and you've got Buckley's of getting the job done.'

He hauled Nancy to him and straddled her before running his hands along her body. Nancy threw her head about, shifted her feet then settled.

'How long's it been since she was milked?' He stroked Nancy's face, moved crusted hair away from her eyes.

'We've been trying every day since we got her but we can't seem to make it happen. So it's been a week since someone's done it properly,' Nora confessed.

'Right. She's going to be a bit tender, might carry on.' He scratched under Nancy's chin. 'I reckon we'll get Henry outta the way for a bit. He doesn't look like the protective kind, but with horns like those you wouldn't want to be wrong.'

Andrew strode down the paddock to Henry, grabbed him by the collar and led him out the gate. Nora wanted to call 'stop', to ask what would happen if Henry ran off, how they would get him back, but she wasn't the expert.

Andrew clipped the gate closed behind him, and Henry shuffled about, butted his horns against the steel a couple of times then lost interest and began chewing at the grass alongside the driveway.

'Okay, this is how we're going to do it. I'll show you first. We'll get her used to it. Then you can have a try.'

'Really?' Lara beamed.

'You do know it's an everyday thing?'

Lara stared Andrew straight in the eye. 'Uh-huh. Even when it rains.'

'Right then,' he said, scratching the goat around her horns. Nancy leant into him and rubbed herself against his dark-blue overalls.

'Have to go to Sydney again next week. Just for a few days. Should be back by Thursday, Friday at the latest.' Tom tore the ring top from a can of Cascade Blue.

Nora was steaming vegetables and stirring a pan of marinated beef strips on the tiny cooktop. She'd wound the van windows all the way out to try to let some air in, tucked the curtains back against the wall and velcroed them in place. 'I thought the travel was meant to ease off.'

'It was.'

'Right.' She poured teriyaki sauce into the pan. 'When?'

'I'll take the early flight on Monday.'

She burnt her face taking the lid off the vegetables, stepped back.

'You alright?'

She nodded. 'Fine. Yeah, I'm fine.'

When the logs arrived, Nora was home alone. Tom was off on yet another work trip, and the girls were staying in town with Marjorie for a few days before the mid-February school start.

'Where d'ya want 'em, love?' The bloke from the timber yard climbed down from the cab of his truck.

Nora had no idea, told him to leave the logs at the end of the slab, watched as he tilted the tray and let them tumble into the semblance of a pile then drove off, his hand stuck out the window in a half-wave, half-salute. 'Good luck to ya.'

After he left she stripped down to her underwear, tied her hair in a ponytail and laid a towel out on the paddock. Restless she turned over every ten minutes until it was too hot to bear. She should be enjoying her time alone, but without work, without Tom and the girls she didn't know what to do with herself.

For the next few days Nora cleaned and tidied the van, drove to Kingston to buy groceries, and picked up the last of the girls' school supplies. By Friday everything was done so she took the ferry across to Bruny Island and lay on the beach at Adventure Bay eating icy poles, reading, dozing and swimming. She tried not to feel guilty for doing something for herself.

That evening she walked the boundary of their property, stopped to look down on the German's smokehouse and wondered how it worked, then climbed the hill behind the van to get a glimpse of the bay. When the earth turned away from the sun, she sat in the van with the door clipped back and drank wine while hemming the girls' new school dresses.

Tom collected the girls from Marjorie's on his way home from the airport. Nora had been reading on the bed, had fallen asleep. She opened the door to find Trudie walking the length of a log, pivoting and performing an arabesque before executing a piked dismount.

Tom ran his hands over each log and got down close to check for straightness. Nora waited for his opinion, for the logs to fall short, but he stood up and put an arm around her shoulders.

'Not bad, not bad at all.' He hugged her tight and kissed her forehead.

In the morning, the four of them got started on peeling the bark away. The smooth flesh like freshly exposed skin. The girls competed to see who could remove the largest sheet of bark. Trudie tunnelled her fingers under a thick section, tore it back then ran shrieking, arms covered in baby huntsman spiders. She slapped at herself and flew across the paddock and into the dam, let her head go under where normally she wouldn't. After she climbed out, a lace of spiders floated across the surface.

The next week, while Nora got the girls settled at school and Tom went back to work, tradesmen arrived and bracketed the skun posts to the slab like totem poles. Nora tried to imagine what came next but was distracted by the beauty of the newly arrived bath, a plumbed-in toilet and the sheer joy of the departure of the portaloo.

In the evenings, when Tom and the girls got home, the four of them played chase, running the perimeter of the slab and weaving around the posts as if they were witches hats on an obstacle course. In the sweaty quick-breathed huddles that came after, Nora was buoyed, saw threads of this imagined life made real.

'I'm going to have to stay at Mum's tonight.' Tom was emptying his dirty clothes from his last business trip onto the bed and putting clean ones into his bag.

Nora sat on the bottom bunk. 'You only just got back. So what's it now – one week here, one week in Sydney?' She could hear the girls playing hopscotch in the gravel next to the van.

'It's a new client, Nora. He wants to meet the team. His office booked the flights and of course they've got us up in Sydney for an early start. It's not like I want to go.'

'Right.' Nora picked at the satin edge of Lara's Sherpa blanket.

'Thing is, if I stay here I'll have to set the alarm for five o'clock. But I won't need to leave Mum's till six. And you know Mum, she'd sleep through a hurricane.'

Nora stared straight ahead at the pile of Tom's dirty clothes on their bed.

'Sorry, babe.' He kissed the top of her head. 'You smell good.'

She shook him off. 'Course I do.'

'Come on, you know I'd rather be here with you, but we've got to pay for the dream home somehow.' He took her chin in his fingers, tilted her head up and kissed her. Then he winced.

'It's only one night. I'll be back for dinner on Friday. Promise.' He caressed her breast.

As Tom drove off, she could hear the girls shrieking, 'Faster, Dad, faster.' She knew they were hanging off the roof rack, having the time of their lives. Soon they'd come running back down the drive, wild with excitement.

Later that night, after they'd calmed down and finished the egg and bacon jaffles she made for dinner, Nora boiled the copper and filled the bathtub for the girls. While the girls shampooed their hair and made stacks like soft-serve ice cream on top of their heads, she sat on a stool drinking red wine from one of the two-litre casks Tom had started buying. She noticed a light in the trees from the A-frame on the property below and could just make out the silhouette of the adjacent smokehouse.

When the girls were tucked up in their bunks, Nora added more hot water to the bath, peeled off her clothes and sank beneath the warmth. Above her the navy sky was decorated with more stars than seemed possible. She tried not to think about Tom, tried not to wonder who he was with, what he might be doing. She imagined herself at the phone box: coins dropping into the slot at the sound of Marjorie's voice. *Yes, of course, love, I'll put him on. We're just finishing dinner.* Or perhaps, *He's already asleep.* Or, *He's just popped down to the shops to pick up some wine.*

She lifted her head above the water and listened to the sounds of the night. Leaves whispered against branches. Her nipples tightened as they touched the cool air, then warmed again as she exhaled, dipping back beneath the filmy skin of water.

When she and Tom had originally planned things, it had seemed reasonable that she'd take extended leave. Tom would have to work to fund the build, but someone needed to look after the girls and be around when materials were delivered. Between holiday, long service and unpaid leave, she took nine months off.

'Just enough time to grow our new baby,' Tom had joked.

But now it seemed ridiculous. With Tom working and the girls settled at school, doing gymnastics twice a week with Sally's girls and Hannah, a gangly girl from Trudie's class, Nora couldn't imagine how she'd fill the next five months, could hardly wait to get back to work. She yearned for a point of focus in her days, a purpose that wasn't driven by Tom or the girls.

She started to think about an earlier return to work, but Tom was travelling more rather than less and couldn't be relied on for the promised sharing of drop-offs and pick-ups. Even when he wasn't travelling, neither of them had factored in the later school starts, or the need to get the girls to and from the bus stop every day. If they were still in Bellerive it would be easy. The girls could catch the bus right outside their house, and they could always stay at Marjorie's or at a friend's place. In Kettering, there was only Sally and Lynn, Hannah's mother, but Sally was often stuck at the shop and Lynn worked shifts, so there was no chance of a reliable routine. She'd have to find another way.

She sat in the van, next to the place where the house should be. She'd been sure, though she couldn't now think why, that the house would be beginning to take shape by this point, was sure that she would have her promised view. She wanted to get the chainsaw out and do the job herself but she didn't know how. Felt stupid and weak.

~

Tom had returned from his latest trip to Sydney the night before, just in time for Easter. He was lying on his back with an arm hanging off the bed. The girls were in their bunks only centimetres away, with their sleepy buzz breath, the concertina door between the sleeping sections of the van peeled back to let the warmth from the fan heater fill the space.

It would only take a couple of months for the shell to be finished, Tom had promised. But the cold weather had begun to set in and, almost six months after they'd moved, the house was only bones: slab, posts and a roof, with no skin to bind the parts together. Nora was still climbing across Tom and sidling along the thin bank of wardrobes filled with angled clothes hangers.

As she got up she considered treading on his hand, if only to make him see this wasn't working. She slipped on her ugg boots and closed the door behind her, walked over to the slab, tucked her dressing-gown tight and yanked her pants down. She sat on the new toilet, elbows resting on knees, and looked out at the navy sky, but it didn't soothe her. It was no longer okay. Tom had promised a house. He'd promised a view. The caravan was supposed to be fun and it had been for a time, but they were starting to get on each other's nerves.

She longed for the nights before the posts had been fixed to the slab with ugly, thick brackets and covered with the roof. Before the roof went on, Nora had still felt the possibility of the place, had almost been able to grasp the life Tom had planned, see it mapped against the sky. But since the sheets of corrugated iron were secured to the beams she couldn't help but feel hemmed in.

She wiped herself, tugged her underpants back around her hips. Then she changed her mind, removed them and left them beside the toilet. She padded across the slab to where the front verandah should be, slipped out of her ugg boots and rotated her feet on the ice-cold concrete into fourth position, lined up with the edge of the slab. She raised her arms in a curve in front of her and let the crisp, clean air assault her skin.

When she returned to bed, Tom woke. He rolled over and spooned his body around hers, placed one leg over both of hers. She tolerated it for as long as she could, for as long as she was able to convince herself that it was not a trap. She did not go back to sleep

They'd left it too late, should have made the bricks in summer, but there'd been too many business trips and so the date for the mudbrick course kept getting pushed out. Tom said it would be fine. They'd get the other parts done first, worry about the bricks later. Finally they'd pinned down a date in early June, and Nora had been sure it would rain, thought they were destined to live in the van for years.

Tom was up early. The door between the sleeping and living sections of the caravan was clipped shut. She kept her eyes closed, pretended she could go back to sleep, but she was hungry and the smell of food was too much.

She got up and slid the door open.

'Hungry?' Tom asked, flipping eggs.

'Yeah,' she replied, and shuffled across to sit at the end of the table where she could watch the novelty of Tom cooking. He slid an egg onto a piece of toast and put the plate in front of her. He buttered his toast while she ate, runny yolk slipping down her chin.

'What's the weather like?' she asked.

'Perfect.'

'That's lucky.' Nora couldn't believe it. 'What time will the class start?'

'Not for a while but I need to get things ready – run a hose from the tank, take the wheelbarrows across, line up the frames. I want to get all of that done before Darren gets here to dig out the clay.'

The mudbrick expert from Adult Ed arrived first, introduced himself as Jack. He was smaller than Nora expected but appeared strong, and she was strangely pleased with him. Jack and Tom stood around chatting, Tom pretending at a level of knowledge he didn't possess. But when Darren arrived with the backhoe and Jack began to direct him, Tom seemed happy to defer, busied himself with arranging the moulds, removing straw from bags.

Nora made coffee and, when enough clay had been dug out, she carried a tray with mugs and biscuits across the paddock. The three men stood waiting.

She walked back across the uneven ground to check on the girls.

'Has it started?' Trudie asked. She and Lara were leaning out the door of the van in their nighties.

'Put some clothes on. I'll make you breakfast.'

'But …' Trudie objected.

'It won't start for ages. You're not going to miss anything.' Nora pressed them back inside.

'Can I put my name on a brick, Mum? Dad told me I could,' Lara said.

Lara's hair was Medusa-like. Nora tried to remember when she'd last brushed it. She sipped her coffee. 'I don't see why not.'

'I'm doing fingerprints,' Trudie said. 'It'll be like code and only I'll know they're my bricks.'

'That's stupid, what's the point in that?' Lara said.

Trudie reached out and dragged her fingers through Lara's tangled hair.

'Don't.' Lara pushed Trudie in the face. 'Leave me alone. Mum, tell her not to touch me.'

Trudie appealed to Nora then elbowed Lara in the ribs. Hard.

'Right, you.' Nora pointed at Trudie. 'Go and get dressed.'

'She started it.'

'I'm not interested.' Nora turned to Lara. 'Sit down. Now.'

Nora finished making their food, closed her eyes for a moment. Soon there would be bricks. It wouldn't be long until they were in a proper house, then there would be room to breathe, to get away from one another.

The mudbrick course attendees arrived. They edged cars tentatively down the steep driveway or left them at the junction, up by the gate, and walked down the gravel drive, boots crunching on grit. Twelve people all up: a husband and wife; the rest of them young blokes with shaggy mullets, football shorts and singlets.

The woman slipped a finger under her bra strap, moved it back onto her shoulder. 'I'm Tammy. Beautiful spot you've got here.'

'Nora. Thanks.' Nora extended her hand. Tammy's handshake was firm despite her tiny stature. 'Where are you planning to build?' Nora asked, making an effort to be polite.

'Oh, we're still looking. Waiting for the right place to call out to us.'

Nora nodded, looked over at the treetops and wondered when she'd get her view.

The work was hard. Shovels of clay with straw mixed through were much heavier than Nora had expected. Sweat ran down her back, behind her knees and into her boots.

Sometime around midmorning, Tom tapped her on the shoulder. 'Could you do the sandwiches?' He said it as though it were a question. Then he leant across with his spade and smoothed the top of the brick Nora was making. 'You have to make them flat, love.'

She watched Tammy sliding her mould from a brick.

'Time to help Mum with lunch, girls,' Tom called out.

Nora let the girls rinse their legs at the dam while she made food and tried to quell her disquiet. When the three of them walked back across to the worksite with a full picnic basket, everyone was sitting on the ground. Tammy had drying mud smeared across her forehead, chunks in the ends of her hair. Her husband, Jim, was sitting next to her, running an index finger along the outlines of the muscles in her thigh.

Nora wanted to stay mad, but there was camaraderie among the group as they sat on the cold earth and ate the sandwiches and cake she had provided, drank cups of instant coffee from thermoses. They lay back on the grass, enjoying the late autumn sun. When Lara farted, everyone laughed.

'Right, siren's sounded, time to get back to work,' Jack said.

Since that first promising weekend, there'd been more rain than seemed reasonable. The Adult Ed courses rescheduled three times before two clear days eventually arrived at the beginning of July. A new group of students and hundreds of bricks made, with extras to be sure. Some would break, Tom explained to Nora.

'Oh,' she said, instead of, 'Yes, I know.'

It appeared as though things were moving forward, as though sometime in the coming months there would be a house. But then the bricks needed time in the sun to cure and the sun didn't offer itself up again, not in proper doses, not in a way that was enough. Six weeks after the last bricks had been made, when the laying of them ought to have begun, the entire property was waterlogged and gumboots were necessary every day, so Tom flew to Queensland for a conference. Boring stuff, he said, but he might as well get it out of the way. He could only take so much time off. Nora fidgeted, tried to keep her expression plain. She was envious of his flight to warmer weather.

That night she lay in the bath, drank wine, stared at the endless expanse of corrugated iron that robbed her of the night sky.

When he returned from the conference, Tom inspected the bricks dotted across the paddock.

The next day he drove down to Nicholls Rivulet to see the stonemason. That night he came back with a scrawny man who had followed him in a dilapidated station wagon.

The stonemason, Walde, began right away, marked chalk outlines of the fireplace on the slab by torchlight and, when Nora questioned the depth of the hearth, he pondered, twisting his ragged beard in his fingers, then rubbed the old line out and drew another in its place.

'I still think it needs to be deeper.' She wrapped her cardigan tight about her body and imagined herself standing in front of the fire.

'No,' Walde stated.

She gave Tom a questioning look, turned her palms out in appeal.

'How about just a bit deeper?' Tom asked.

Walde seemed both embarrassed and indignant. 'When it's done, it's your fireplace. Before that, it's mine.'

Nora almost laughed, wanted to tell the straggly little man where he could jam his fireplace.

'You wouldn't like it,' he said, 'and it wouldn't be respecting the stone but you can ask someone else if you want. People will do things for money.'

'You're the expert,' Tom said.

Later in the week while Tom was at work, a truckload of stone was delivered, and Walde was there to check it over. Some of the stones were huge, and Nora couldn't fathom how they would possibly be moved. But Walde started pushing them around, selecting the best then squatting deeply and gathering them into his arms one by one. He carried several onto the slab and placed them near the chalked-out fireplace. Nora was amazed at the weight he could carry. She put the kettle on in the van and made them coffee.

For the next few days, Walde worked quietly, arriving each morning while Nora was dropping the girls at the school bus and leaving in the early afternoon. The first day she tried staying there while he worked, but being alone on the property with the man who looked like Catweazle was disquieting, as though his tendency to social discomfort was somehow contagious.

When Walde turned up on Saturday, they were all surprised. The four of them were still in bed, the caravan a hothouse of morning breath and stale air. The girls were the first to spill out into the sharp light then Tom got up and made coffee.

Nora stood in the doorway of the van, fan heater pumping warmth onto the backs of her calves, and observed Tom and Walde carrying stones across to the slab, the girls weaving between them firing a stream of knock-knock jokes. When Walde cackled at every punchline, the soles of Nora's feet, clad in bedsocks, relaxed into the vinyl-coated floor. At lunchtime she made tuna, corn and mayonnaise sandwiches, and Walde produced a thermos of soup and two old vegemite jars, one filled with homemade goats' cheese, the other sauerkraut. By the end of the day, exhausted, the five of them had moved much of the stone to the slab, all of it placed in piles as directed by Walde.

On Sunday afternoon, Tom kept replenishing Walde's beer glass as they worked, asking questions about stone, and it was as if a tap had been turned on. Walde was spilling out all of the words he'd previously held at bay. The two men laboured side by side and chatted, stopped only for some afternoon tea or when the girls interjected with another request for Walde's own seemingly endless supply of knock-knock jokes.

In the week that followed, Nora found herself seeking out Walde's company. Every time they spoke, he still went red and hunched in on himself, but eventually he stopped breaking eye contact, and Nora felt, in a place behind her ribs, a deep appreciation for the effort he was prepared to make, and admiration for his connection to his craft and the stone itself.

On Friday Tom came home with six bottles of wine that a client had given him, and the three of them polished off four. It was late before finally the decision was made for sleep. Nora and Tom tumbled into bed, and Walde slept in his car next to the van.

After that Walde spent most nights sleeping on the concrete slab under the roof without walls, tucked deep in a swag. The girls woke him every day with a chorus of, 'Morning, Catweazle.'

By the time the fireplace was finished, the rain had abated and the mudbricks had finally dried out. Tom took a week off in lieu for all of the extended interstate trips. He brought in a couple of local men Darren had recommended and, though Tom had never laid a brick in his life, he mortared and smoothed, tapped and levelled with the brickies while Nora was relegated to lugging mudbricks, and making sandwiches and coffees.

'Better if we stick to our strengths,' Tom said.

Blood pulsed through Nora's veins in bolts. She felt thin, pulled tight, attenuated. The hairs on her arms stood on end with the frizz of anger and, at the tail of each day, after she'd collected the girls from the bus stop and made dinner, she fell into the bath, stared at the corrugated iron roof then closed her eyes and let the water soothe the remaining hiss, ease the aches from her muscles.

As the borders of the house took shape, Nora thought constantly about going back to work, tried not to focus on Tom's attitude to her capacity to help with the build. Tried not to think about the message her quiet acceptance of his directives sent to their girls. She had hoped that the solidity of the outline of the house would bring something to rely on, a stepping-stone to the inevitability of filling it with contents. But Tom was no more focused than usual, moved from one task to the next without any real regard for whether the first was complete. The girls had almost finished their third term at Woodbridge. The people who had bought their old house in Bellerive had probably put in the kitchen benchtop and completed the bathroom renovation. Nora felt foolish.

A week after the last brick was laid, they tested renders. Walde came with a bottle of cheap red wine and more goats' cheese, and they narrowed the render colours down to two options. She and the girls preferred the deeper earthy brown, but Tom talked the girls around and they settled on a creamy tone that Nora thought was insipid. She tried to get Walde on her side, but this wasn't his stone and he wouldn't give an opinion.

'They're both fine,' he said.

Nora longed to go back to work, where people would at least consider her views.

When eventually they moved in, it was almost October; the house largely open space with a few framed-up timber partitions. After so long in the van, it seemed strange to sleep in rooms without walls and, though she'd been impatient for the move, Nora wondered if she preferred the van. But there was the fireplace. Walde had created a masterpiece – the thing was comforting, magnificent and rustic. Opening to what would eventually be the kitchen at the back and the lounge at the front, it was the focal point of the house. It was impossible not to be drawn to it, impossible not to run your fingers across its contours. They lit a fire every night, even on the rare nights that it wasn't all that cold.

Nora dropped the girls at the bus stop early so they could catch up with their friends before school, and drove to Hobart to meet her boss, Cara, at Retro cafe down in Salamanca.

Cara was already sitting at their favoured booth at the rear of the cafe, papers spread in front of her. She peered at Nora over her glasses.

'Is everything okay?' Nora asked.

Cara stood, reached across the table to put an arm around Nora. 'It's good to see you,' she said.

'What's going on?' Nora asked.

Cara laughed, smiled broadly and touched her abdomen. 'I feel disgusting one hundred per cent of the time. Jane and I are pregnant. Well, I am. I feel sick as a fucking dog. And I'm so happy I could die.'

A wash of emotion swept through Nora's body. Happiness for Cara, sadness for what Cara was about to lose, nostalgia for those early days when she was pregnant with Trudie, mad with excitement.

'Congratulations. That's wonderful.'

They ordered coffee. Cara nibbled the crusts of a piece of toast.

'I want to take the full year, so someone will need to step in, run it all.'

Nora sipped her coffee, didn't respond.

'What do you think? You'd need to take ownership of the comms side but Phoebe can help, and I know you're not back yet, but …'

'God, I'd love to, Car.' Then before she'd said more, a tumble of thoughts: who would get the girls to the bus, pick them up? How would it work when Tom was in Sydney? Who would make dinner? What about school holidays? There had to be a way, but she couldn't think what it might be. Cara's job was far from part-time – no short days or flexible arrangements. Nora felt a wave of nausea, a fuller forming of a partially known thing. Without all the supports of their life in town, this new life of theirs was really only a new life of Tom's.

On the drive back south, she tried to map ways of making it work. She could go in early. When he wasn't travelling, Tom could drop off the girls. Nora could be home in time to pick them up. And when Tom went to Sydney, she could take Marjorie up on her offers of help – swallow the martyrdom and endless thanks that it would require.

It was quiet when she entered the house. The girls were still at school, had arranged a sleepover at Sally's, and Tom, having taken an early flight home from Sydney, was watching a game show and drinking port.

'Cara's pregnant.'

'Really? Wow. Is she pleased?'

She scowled. 'Why wouldn't she be?'

'Didn't think she was the type. Seems pretty job focused to me. Bit of a man hater.'

'Seriously, Tom. She's not into men so she must hate them? That's fucking ridiculous.'

'That's not what I said. Geez, what's your problem?'

'Well, it's not like she got pregnant by accident.'

'Fair enough.' Tom eased the cork out of the port bottle and poured himself another glass. 'But you don't have to bite my head off, Nor.'

She took a glass from the cupboard and poured herself a port.

'Guess that puts the office in a bit of strife.'

'What do you mean?'

'Losing both of you. That's got to make things a bit difficult.'

'They haven't lost me.'

'Yeah, but you're not going back. I mean, now that things are settled here. I thought we'd decided.'

The electric pulse of adrenaline shot through her limbs. She slugged her port down in one go. 'Christ, Tom. Tell me when we discussed this? In fact, tell me when we've ever discussed anything?'

'No point talking when you're like this.' He turned the volume dial on the television up.

She spent the night in the van with the girls' parkas draped over her body and legs, curled up and freezing. In the morning, a plume of smoke from their neighbour's smokehouse twisted into the sky.

Nora was standing out the front of the house, hands on hips, staring but not really seeing anything. She was thinking about her mother and what she would have said about all of this. A flicker in the corner of her eye: a bird or some other kind of animal steadied and began to take shape. The emerging form of a man. She was annoyed at the interruption, was affronted by the audacity that would bring a stranger to walk onto her land uninvited. She pretended not to see him, shifted her body slightly so that she looked out towards the other side of the property.

The man moved with a sturdy, deliberate gait, as though he knew the undulations of her land and, as he got closer, Nora could see he had a package tucked under his arm. She wondered if she should feel alarmed, but the man was wearing a hat fashioned from skins. It would be stupid, wouldn't it, to be afraid of a man dressed like Daniel Boone, to be afraid of a man whose appearance was ridiculous?

He came to where she stood, on the edge of the rise, and handed her the newspaper-wrapped package. For some reason she was surprised by the flattened tones of his heavily accented English.

'I brought you some *feesh*.'

She didn't know what to do with him.

'Ollie.' He extended a hand.

'Nora.' Her hand enveloped in his. 'Coffee?' Her voice was barely audible.

Ollie nodded and followed her around to the back. Despite being a large man, he seemed to measure out his steps like a child, careful not to tread on her heels. At the back door, he bent and removed his boots. They were the kind with elastic, slipped off readily against the tilt of his hand. She wanted to reach down and touch their softened insides.

They went into the house and he moved to the fireplace, broad hands outstretched. His socks made small sounds as they caught against the seagrass matting. She stood at the sink, side-on to him, as she filled the kettle, watched him inspect the stones, run his fingers over them. He bent to peer up the chimney. Self-conscious, she turned to the stove, put the kettle on and emptied heaped teaspoons of instant coffee into mugs. Out the window, she saw his footprints bathed in the shadow of the water tank; they had erased each of her own, pressed the trace of her deep into the earth.

'Sugar?' She was sure that he was looking at her, inspecting her. He didn't respond. She turned around.

He was on his knees, feeling the hearth. 'It's Walde's work, yes?'

'Yes.' She poured boiling water into the mugs, added milk to both without asking. Felt compelled to fill the silence. 'All we need now is a view of the bay.'

Passing his coffee, she grazed a stubby half finger. She quickly pulled away, a frisson of electricity up her arm.

He took a sip of coffee. Smiled. 'Now I am careful with the knife.' He waggled the cropped finger at her.

She noticed the possum-skin hat was on the chair by the door where Tom usually put his coat.

The next time she saw him was at the intersection of their roads when she was driving the girls to the bus stop. His car door was open, the engine running. He'd stepped off the gravel, was deep in the blackberry bushes, filling a basket. He grinned and waved, showed them his stained teeth. The air sucked from Nora's lungs. The girls asked if they could stop to pick some, but they were running late. They needed to get to school. On the way back she looked for him.

She started imagining him on the rare nights when she was making love to Tom. It was easier when Tom was behind. But his hands weren't right. His fingers gave the game away. Afterwards she'd feel guilty.

When Tom was at work, she watched for the smoke, imagined that Ollie was signalling her. *I'm here. I'm here.* Smoky words woven into the air as she hung out the washing, when she fed the chooks.

One day she went to the tractor Tom had bought, turned the crank until her arm felt weak, almost gave up when finally the engine caught. She drove it as though she'd done it before – between the potato paddock and the chook run, behind the lip of the dam – her hand vibrating on the gearstick. The scrub was thick at the bottom of the property, the trees still not cleared, and she couldn't even see the wire fence between the properties, let alone the complete outline of his house.

'Becoming quite the farmer,' Tom said, when he saw the tractor had been moved. She couldn't bring herself to respond.

The girls were away on school camp, and Tom was in Sydney. Nora kept checking the sky but the smokehouse hadn't given out signals for days. She needed to make plans, think of ways to pass the time.

Ollie had a boat; she'd seen it when she drove past his house pretending to acquaint herself with the area. She'd got stuck at the end of the road where there was no place to turn. She'd had to reverse a good few hundred metres before she found somewhere. Felt stupid even though it hadn't been her fault.

She slipped on her boots and walked down to the dam, dug cool and supple clay from the side. Moulded bowls and plates, a teapot. With the flats of her fingers, she smoothed surfaces, picked gritty stones out with her fingernails and flicked them into the water where they disappeared, created tiny ripples. Ebbing circles. Her calves ached and she gave up squatting, sat instead in the earthy wetness, dangled her feet in the dam, dipped them up and down, experimenting with how much to make invisible under the murky water. She wanted to ask Ollie to take her fishing. She wanted him to see she was capable, to roll up her sleeves and let him see her poke a hook through bait, remove it from a thrashing fish. Scale and gut.

She pushed her misshapen clay pieces together, made a clump and threw it into the middle of the water. Left after the last of the ripples pressed into the edges of the dam.

That night she tried to remember what it had been like in the beginning, thought about the day she'd met Tom. If the dentist hadn't run late, she'd have caught the bus, would have been home at her share house in West Hobart while Tom was hanging over the end of the wharf.

She remembered those first moments vividly: walking down to the pier, Tom's head and upper body hidden below the thick slab of concrete, a foot hooked loosely around a bollard. She'd been drawn by the sound of metal banging on metal. Tom hauled himself up, caught her watching. Grinned.

'Bit of old pipe kept catching on my mate's boat,' he explained.

'Oh.' She began to move away.

'Don't suppose you're hungry?' he'd asked.

Nora was embarrassed by his friendliness, surprised to hear herself tell him she was.

Tom ordered fish and chips from the punt while she stood on the pier and pretended to be interested in the river. She thought about leaving, but her feet seemed stuck to the spot.

Shiny white package hugged to his chest, he led her across to the old swing bridge. They sat in the sun and let their legs hang above the water, ate potato cakes and fat pieces of flake with crispy golden batter, and crumbed scallops with meaty roes the colour of tangerines. She closed her eyes and savoured the sweet, juicy flavour of the scallops.

They talked, and Nora threw brown-edged chips at a group of seagulls. While the other gulls scrambled for her offerings, Tom tossed a handful of chips to the one-legged gull that had been pressed to the side of the pack.

When all of the chips were gone, Nora and Tom rubbed the white paper, wiping up salt and licking their fingertips. Afterwards they sat in a pub, drank beer to wash their meal down and compared froth moustaches. Then Tom had checked his watch and said he had to go. Nora, feeling possibility slip away, hastily wrote her number on a bar coaster, pushed it into his hand. He ran his index finger across the digits and put the cardboard square into the back pocket of his jeans as he stood.

'I'm only going to the toilet but, you never know, they might have put a phone in.'

Nora felt the mortification wash from her stomach up to her forehead.

Neither of them would remember what they had talked about that day. But they would laugh at Tom's seagull, remember the moment when the bird had scrambled for a chip, almost fallen off the pier before revealing a second leg. Tom had called it a charlatan, and she had been pleased with the word. She remembered that, at least.

Nora shifted in bed, listened to the wind playing in the eaves and let her mind wander. What if she had caught the bus? She wouldn't have met Tom. She wouldn't be living here, wouldn't have told Cara she didn't see how she could take her role, wouldn't have extended her leave by another year. She might have travelled, met someone along the way. Perhaps she would be living a different life in another country. She might be single; she might not have children. But then Trudie and Lara wouldn't exist.

It was a guilty thought, but the girls bound her to Tom in a way that seemed unnatural, in a way that had seemed good and right in the beginning but, as the years fell away, had begun to feel oppressive. If they hadn't been born she wouldn't need to feel so guilty about all of this.

The petrol station had rods on sale. Nora stood them on the floor next to her, checked for length and examined the flex. She bought a packet of yellow-and-pink striped floats and a plastic box filled with sinkers. She kept the sinkers in her pocket, for the promise of their weight.

On the weekend, instead of going to Marjorie's for lunch, she told Tom she had a migraine and went to lie in bed. After he and the girls left, she drove down to the petrol station and bought three rods, sifted through packets of small silver-streaked fish in the bait freezer.

The woman who had just moved in down the road was there, her arms filled with packets of chips. 'Planning a fishing trip?' The woman's dog, tied up outside, barked.

'Thinking about it,' Nora said.

It was hot in the car, as though summer was trying to show itself early. Nora had to edge her skirt down to stop the skin on her legs from burning. She lifted the bottom of her T-shirt and placed it over the steering wheel then wound down her window.

She decided the next time Tom went away she'd take the girls on a trip. They'd get the ferry across to Bruny Island, camp at Adventure Bay, collect periwinkles. They'd catch fish with their new rods, and make necklaces from hat elastic and shells.

'I could help cut the trees, carve out a view of the bay.' Ollie was bending down, looking in at her.

The girls were at Sally's, and Tom and Ollie were working at the trees. Nora watched Ollie lift his chainsaw, coil the rope, sling it across the back of his shoulders. Had the sense that Ollie had been born knowing things. An innate set of practical skills that others needed to learn and practise. She liked the way his ponytail swung behind his back. She found herself thinking of the old photos of Tom at university, with his dreadlocked hair. The one at a party where he was looking at a girl in a particular way, a way that Nora was sure he had never looked at her. She'd once asked Tom who she was, but he'd dismissed the question with a wave of his hand.

'No-one. An old high school girlfriend. We broke up. She moved away.'

'Was she your first love?'

'Suppose so. In that kid sort of way, I suppose she was.' Then he'd changed the subject, asked Nora about something else, and she hadn't pressed for more, though she'd wanted it.

She wandered down to get a closer look at the men's work, had the idea of offering help of some kind, but she arrived at the bottom of the property as Tom reached up to pat Ollie on the shoulder.

'Nice job. Thanks.'

'We should finish. Cut logs.'

'Nah. You've done enough, mate. Let's have a beer. I'll finish it up tomorrow.'

Ollie shook his head. 'It will only take a few minutes.' And he started his chainsaw and began carving logs from branches.

'Right then.' Tom started his chainsaw too.

Nora walked back up to the house and took food from the fridge and, when the chainsaws fell silent again, she drank a beer and lit the fire. She was enjoying its warmth on the back of her legs when the men appeared outside, silhouetted by the afternoon sun.

She listened as Tom led Ollie to the laundry sink and Ollie instructed Tom in how to remove sap from skin with the olive oil soap he had brought.

'We should have stacked it,' Ollie said.

'Really, mate. You've done more than enough. I can do that.'

Nora had to stop herself from laughing.

When they came inside, Tom went to the fridge and passed around beers. Ollie held one hand out towards the fire, wrapped his other around the long neck of Cascade Blue. 'Sometimes to have the thing you want, you must take something away,' he said.

Nora refilled her beer glass and started to drift – a combination of fire and alcohol. She drained her glass and recalled the afternoon like a short film playing on repeat. The simple movements of two men shaping trees, roaring noise marking the extremity of the act. And with it, the aroma of sap liberated from wood floating across the land.

The three of them sat by the fire late into the night, eating toasted ham and cheese sandwiches and drinking until there was no beer left and Ollie had to carry his chainsaw home in the dark.

Tom had to fly to Sydney for work, would be gone most of the week, probably back on Thursday. Friday at worst. He'd made a point of saying how unlikely it was that he'd need to stay longer, which Nora took to mean that he'd be gone for a week and a half at least. She was unsure if it was dishonesty or blind optimism that led him to say these things.

Nora got the girls off to the school bus, then called into the shop and picked up a few things. She scanned the noticeboard, trying to find something interesting, something that might divert her, but she kept remembering Ollie's silhouette. She was touching her lip, wondering if he was thinking about her, when Sally asked if she was coming to the school fete.

'When is it?'

Sally pointed at the flyer stuck to the noticeboard.

'Oh. Right. I don't know. I mean, should I?'

'It's usually a good day. You could help on the jam stall if you're interested.'

'I've never made jam,' Nora said.

'That's okay. No need. You could do a shift selling.'

'Okay.' Nora made her voice sound brighter, more enthusiastic than she was. They'd lived here for almost a year now, and though she and Sally had become close, she would have to make more of an effort.

Ollie opened the door, closed it behind her. He walked across to the ladder and climbed; he disappeared through the hole in the ceiling, and she stepped out of her shoes and climbed up after him.

As she slipped through the opening, he was moving out of his shirt, his back to her. She ran her fingertips over his shoulders, felt the muscles that covered his ribs, moved her hands until she had touched every part of his back.

He turned, watched her undress, and she stood before him. Naked. Animal skins on the walls. Sheepskins on the floor.

When they made love, she did not think of Tom.

After, Ollie put pillows behind his head so he was almost sitting. He looked at her, raised a hand to his nose. 'I smell of smoke.'

'Yes.' She smiled.

She dressed in time to pick the girls up from the school bus.

The next morning Nora drove straight to Ollie's after dropping the girls off. She parked behind the A-frame, beneath the limbs of the big gum. When she walked around the front, Ollie was waiting. They were naked almost before the door was closed. Made love quickly on the sheepskins in front of the fire. Then Ollie made coffee as she cleaned herself up in the bathroom.

'I didn't know if you would come,' he said, pouring her coffee at the table.

'Neither did I.'

They laughed together, a comfortable feeling of alignment spreading in the air between them.

From then on, it became a pattern. Nora would drop the girls at the bus stop then drive to Ollie's, park beneath the gum next to the smokehouse. Tom already at work or away interstate.

Within days, the soles of Nora's feet had remembered the rungs of Ollie's ladder. Twists and curves, branches stripped bare. Her fingertips knew the sinews and muscles of Ollie's torso; her mouth knew the full flavour of the coffee he made on the stovetop, the sweet fruitiness of his banana bread.

They did not speak of plans, made no attempt to explain this to one another. And Nora did not try to explain it to herself.

Sometimes she would stay until it was time to collect the girls;

lie on the sheepskins and read one of Ollie's novels. His shelves were lined with bilingual texts and she liked to refer across the pages. Even though she learnt French at school, she began to tell herself she could learn German if only she could finish all of his novels.

Other days, she would leave after coffee, go home and drive the tractor, feed the goats, make dinner. Wait for Tom to return. Wait for Tom to notice. But Tom had stopped noticing the things that she did. For a long time, he'd only noticed the things she did not do: if his shirts were not clean and ironed, if she hadn't made dinner, if her legs were unshaven.

She had begun to avoid Tom's advances. Went to bed after him. Pretended to have things to finish for the girls. She followed recipes, baked cakes and made slices to be sold in the school canteen. She went for long walks with Sally. Sometimes she went to bed early, told him she was tired, didn't know what was wrong with her. She did not apologise.

Summer seemed to hit full swing overnight. She and Ollie would spend the entire day naked, and she would have to rush into clothing, dust flying from behind her tyres as she raced down the gravel road to pick up the girls.

The shop was empty when she arrived, the school bus not yet in. She went inside to buy supplies.

Sally was crouched behind the counter moving boxes.

Nora selected milk, bread, cereal and approached the counter. 'You seem busy lately, Sally. How are you?'

Sally stood, picked up an empty box, placed it next to Nora's groceries. 'I'm not the only one who's busy.'

Nora raised her eyebrows.

'Oh, come on, Nora.'

'I'm not sure what you mean.' Her gut lurched.

'Look. It's your business. But people here notice, Nora. It's only a matter of time before someone mentions it to Tom.' She touched her chin. 'It wouldn't be the first time Ollie had …'

Nora pushed the lightweight front door open, heard it bang shut.

Outside she did not know what to do with herself. She wanted to leave, but the school bus had not arrived and her groceries were still on the counter. The door creaked behind her.

'I'm not judging.' Sally placed her hand on Nora's shoulder. 'It's just that I like Tom, and …'

Nora remained frozen. As the weight of Sally's hand lifted, she opened her mouth to defend herself. Closed it again.

'I suppose I thought you were smarter,' Sally added.

Nora stared at the bay. 'Then I don't suppose you know me at all.'

Tom rose early and dropped the girls at Marjorie's for the weekend then flew to Sydney for work. Nora had planned to stay at home. She'd let things get out of hand. But, as soon as Tom and the girls were gone, she threw clothes into a bag and headed to Ollie's. She needed to arrive early if they were going to catch the tides.

Ollie cut the motor and the prow of the dinghy dipped, rode, slapped against the rippling sea. Nora leant over the side, tried to see the place beneath the water where the anchor chain disappeared into ink. Seagulls punctuated the air with their beaky cries, and she tried not to imagine what it would be like if the girls were with them. She was carving her life into segments.

Ollie baited the lines, cast. His moustache curved, a glint of silver caught on the sunlight, strokes of an artist's brush. He reached for the icebox, grabbed a bottle of homemade ginger beer and handed it to her. She unscrewed the lid slowly and took a sip. The ginger was strong in the back of her throat, curled up her nose. Wind blew her hair into her face, wrapped strands around the bottle. In that moment she was the woman she might have become sooner if Tom had not been hanging off the edge of the pier, if she had not stopped to see what the noise was about.

Ollie was focusing on the line smarting in the water, held out his hand towards her. She passed him the bottle, tucked her hair into the back of her jacket. He took a long swig, leaving only the dregs. He turned and smiled at her, hairy ginger flecks caught in his moustache.

She felt small beside him, bird-like and petite. He could circle his hands about her waist. And yet she felt significant in a way she never had before. As though for the first time in her life she had substance.

The sky domed above them, clear blue against the darkness of the sea. A vast container for this life. This is, she thought, the extent of my world. She wondered how she'd got there.

The fish they caught were too small to keep. Ollie wound his line in. She did the same, replaced bait with cork, stowed her rod.

'Shall we go?' he said.

She nodded. Sniffed the salt-stained air.

Ollie didn't head back towards Kettering. Instead, he drove the boat on. Nora sat back, elbows on the icebox, face to the sky, and let the slapping of aluminium against sea reverberate through her body.

They headed into a bay, a long stretch of beach laid open in front of them. Ollie motored into the shallows and climbed over the side. She leapt into the clear, ice-cold water, and they dragged the boat onto the sand.

'Where are we?' she asked.

Ollie swept his arm out. 'This is the end of the road.'

Nora, unsure of his meaning, did not wait to find out. Instead, she walked up the beach. When she got to the place where water cut in a wide arc across the sand, she stripped, left her clothes in a pile on the damp sand and walked away from the sea into the lagoon. Ignoring the cold, she plunged beneath the water then floated on her back and stared up at the sky, felt the breeze snake across her face and breasts. She was free to do whatever she chose. Unlike Tom, Ollie would not direct her. He would not tell her it was time to go or suggest she might be cold. If he chose to swim with her, or if he didn't, it would not indicate anything more than whether he wished to swim. She smiled.

When she'd had enough, she walked out of the lagoon and shook herself like a dog then brushed her hands across her abdomen and limbs, flicking water away. She dressed, hugging her jacket tight around her damp skin. Found Ollie asleep on the soft sand near the dinghy, an arm across his eyes. She lay next to him, curled into his side for warmth, and dozed off listening to the shoosh of small waves licking the sand.

After Christmas, when the girls were up the coast with Marjorie and Tom was still in Sydney, she decided it was going to be the last time, she was going to end it.

Nora watched as the anchor disappeared, the clack of the heavy metal chain strumming against the dinghy. She placed her hand on the side of the boat to store the memory of it in her fingertips, an unbidden smile gathered at the edges of her mouth. All of these rhythms had set her at sea. She was thinking about how she should end it when Ollie leant across and kissed her. She smirked at him, knowing they were both calculating.

'Best to wait for the beach. I think the boat would tip.'

'Mmhmm.' Nora laughed.

Ollie brought them in closer to shore, and they rolled up their jeans, jumped into the shallows and hauled the boat onto the sand. He had her out of her life jacket, his hands on her breasts. She stepped back, pressed her hand against his chest. Used her other hand to drag her jeans down. He pushed her onto the sand and she pressed up to him, legs wrapped around his waist, feet hooked behind him. Licked the salt from his neck. They fucked like animals. After, they lay on their backs on the hard, wet sand. She could hear the anchor chain thrumming in her bottomless chest.

Ollie moved in next to the buoy and let the engine idle as he steered close to the craypot. He gestured for Nora to take the wheel and shuffled across to reel in the pot, revealing four scrambling spiny creatures.

'Meet your dinner.' Ollie smiled at Nora, dipping his hand into the pot and dropping three of the creatures into the icebox before snapping the lid closed. The fourth he held aloft. '*Ich drücke dir die Daumen!*' Let it drop into the undulating sea.

They worked together to guide the boat back onto the trailer, were drenched by a monster of a wave; they stripped, then climbed into the car. Ollie turned up the heating, and they laughed at each other, wrapped in bath towels, caked in sand. Ollie's towel draped about his shoulders, like a Superman cape he might have had as a boy, a handkerchief brought to cover the frame of Goliath. His bare arse on the seat, penis soft and small, nestled in the flush of hair between his legs.

Nora squirmed, grains of sand crunched against the vinyl. He switched on the radio and they listened to the host on Radio National talk to a poet who had written a collection about birds. Nora wondered whether the flight metaphor might be tired but she listened in case she was wrong, in case the poet had found another way of seeing it. Ollie reached across and held her hand.

Back at the house Ollie hosed down the boat while Nora carried the icebox up the front steps, then she stood while he hosed her too. She shrieked, the water like ice pins bouncing off her goose-bumped flesh. Her skin alive, she dried off; grabbed a blanket from the chest on the verandah and flicked it open in case of spiders, then wrapped it around herself. When she hosed Ollie, he stood like a starfish, rotated. He didn't cry out. She threw him the damp blanket and went inside.

By the time he came in, she had made coffee. The stockpot was full of water, lid rocking gently as it began to simmer. He stood behind her and moved close, binding them together with the blanket. Kissed the top of her head, and she was aware of him breathing her in.

While Ollie was dressing, Nora rinsed the crays. She looked each of them in the face before lifting the lid on the pot and dropping them in. She told herself that the shrill cry coming from the pot was only the sound of shifting air, the emancipation of gas from exoskeleton.

Ollie removed the crays from the pot with long-handled tongs and lowered them into the sink to run cold water over the vermilion shells. As he and Nora moved about the kitchen, they brushed against one another. She made more coffee while he moulded proofed dough into balls and placed a tray of rolls in the oven. The aroma of baking bread filled the room. Nora fed the potbelly stove, hovered her hands above it then rested her palms on her face for warmth.

They sat at the table, and Ollie removed the crays' flesh from their shells. She knew before seeing it that he would eat the bitter mustard that sat at the junction between body and head.

Nora watched the girls walk up from the bottom of their property, her stomach roiling, and it seemed important that she'd sent them fossicking on the other side of their land, far from the border with Ollie's. She brushed spider webs from window frames with the handmade broom she'd bought at the Huonville festival, tried to sweep away the nausea that came with the inevitability of where things were heading now.

'I'm sorry,' she said to the fat-bodied spider she dislodged from its home.

'Look, Mum, look.' Lara was running up the hill. She thrust her bucket into Nora's arms and bent over, panting. Trudie ran up behind her.

'Wow, you must be hungry.'

'Mu-u-u-m,' they chorused. Neither of them liked mushrooms but the deal was if you pick them, you eat them.

The girls yabbered about where the biggest crops were, agreed the absolute best place was under the pines down by the border with the new neighbours.

Nora examined the mushrooms. 'Nice work, girls.'

Trudie's bucket was filled with smaller specimens, cupped like toadstools, tight pink folds beneath; Lara's held the broader kind, flat with undersides of dark-brown pleats. Nora took the buckets inside and sorted through the two piles, tugged stalks away, put them in the bin for the chooks while the girls argued over whose turn it was to collect the eggs. She sent them both.

For dinner, she fried the field mushrooms with garlic and butter, the others with butter only. The girls ate their chicken, played with their mushrooms. She didn't complain. Sent them for a bath. When they were gone, she dished field mushrooms onto her side plate and ate them with her fingers, let the juices run down her chin and into her lap and tried not to think about the night to come. She wiped her face, smudged a buttery smear across the back of her hand. Was sniffing her skin when Tom came in.

Like any other night, Nora picked up a tea towel and took Tom's dinner from the oven.

'Thanks.' He sat down, burnt his finger on the edge of his plate. She saw him wince, pull his hand back, but his fingers were intact. His coat on the chair by the door.

'We need to talk,' she said.

'Are you fucking serious?'

As though it were the kind of thing she'd joke about.

She meant to say that she was sorry but was worn thin by the burden of their failure. 'Are you really surprised?'

Tom shook his head.

'Look.' Suddenly she wanted to explain, thought that she should.

'No, stop. I don't want to know.' He covered his face with his hands. 'You can leave in the morning.'

She watched as Tom fidgeted around the fireplace, moved the poker in and out of its holder. She filled the kettle and made coffee.

She took a second mug out for Tom before changing her mind and putting it away. No point making it harder.

Later, she lay in their bed wondering what she would do if he came in. Long after the sky had been shrouded in gloom, she fell asleep.

Nora woke early to the sound of the tractor, stood at the window as Tom wound up and down the front field, dragging furrows into the earth. At some point he stopped, and she could tell from the way he was hunched over the steering wheel, folded at the waist, that he was weeping. She observed him for a long time, until the windowsill left indentations in her elbows and the glass in front of her became misted. She tried to feel sad for the loss of the thing that was them but she couldn't find the grief, had let go of their early promise such a long time ago, and all that was left now was the disappointment of failure, the sorrow of causing pain.

The toilet flushed and nausea coiled in her stomach. She'd thought about it almost incessantly but still questioned how they would tell the girls. The fear of it crawled across her skin. She went back to bed, scratched furiously at her arms and legs. Knew it was simply something that must be done, inevitable as breath.

'Did you sleep in that?' Lara asked from the doorway, pillow creases pressed into the soft rose skin of her face, hair sticking out in all directions.

'Actually, I didn't sleep very much.' Nora, still wearing her clothes from the night before, beckoned Lara over to the bed and she spooned into the curve Nora made of her body.

'Some of us didn't sleep at all.' Tom stood in the doorway.

Nora was inside the shop as Tom's car pulled up out front. A sharp pain in her chest as the girls both leant across to kiss him, as they climbed out of the car and waved him goodbye, clambered up the verandah steps to meet their friends. Nora hid behind the shelves of sweet biscuits and pretended to consider a packet of Scotch Fingers, touched the plastic wrappers on the Swiss Crèmes.

Lara's hair was tied into two low pigtails, the kind that hid her ears, the kind she hated. Trudie stood close to Lara, close enough to be holding hands. Their uniforms appeared clean. Meanly, she scanned for signs of neglect, knowing they would not be there.

When she'd parked by the shop, she had thought it would seem like a coincidence, a chance meeting and a good way to smooth things out. But now that she was standing inside, peering out through gaps in the flyers that were plastered to the window, she wasn't sure.

She ran her fingers across the other biscuit choices. Remembered Malt 'O' Milk. The way the girls liked to dip them in milk until they softened, tried to catch them on a spoon just before they fell. She thought of the girls laughing, mouths full of soggy biscuits, and she felt a rupture as though the whole world might have been captured in one of those moments and she might never know it again.

Nora was still standing at the shelf when the school bus pulled up. Becky threw the shop door open, grabbed a banana from the basket by the till, shouted 'Bye, Mum', and, on her way out, almost collided with Nora.

A look of shock came over the girl's face and she went bright red. 'Hi,' she murmured and dashed back out as the last of the kids climbed onto the bus.

Nora took a packet of Malt 'O' Milk to the counter.

'That be all?' Sally was acting like she didn't know her. It had been that way since Nora moved to Ollie's. Judgement laid thick like jam.

'Yes.' Nora removed money from her wallet, deliberately didn't say 'please'. She accepted her change and stood at the counter methodically putting notes and coins into their right places, while Sally organised packets of lollies and chewing gum, wiped invisible crumbs from the counter.

When Nora opened the car, she didn't know what to do with the biscuits. Ollie would never eat them; there was barely anything packaged in his house. And though she was sure he wouldn't care what she brought into the house, she opened the boot and tucked the biscuits into the centre of the spare tyre.

Three weeks had gone by, and Nora still hadn't spoken to the girls. On the rare days that Tom picked up the phone at his office, he was curt, said they didn't want to see her; the girls were hurt, they all were. Nora thought constantly about how their faces had shifted when she'd told them.

When she'd planned it, she'd imagined they'd do it together, but Tom had refused.

'It's your mess, Nor. Just get it done and leave.' Then he'd gone to repair the rip in the wire of the chicken run that he'd insisted she shouldn't try to fix, the rip he'd been promising to mend for months.

Both of the girls bawled. At first, they didn't think she meant it.

'But when will you be back?' Trudie asked.

And she had to say it again.

'But you said you love us more than anything,' Trudie stuttered, hiccoughing through her tears. 'How can you want to leave us? You're meant to be our mother.'

And Lara, clinging to Nora, begging to go with her.

'Your mother has made her choice.' Tom, back from the chicken run, peeled their younger daughter's arms from Nora's legs, and held her tight to him.

Lara wailed, 'Mum-mmmee.'

She had reached for Lara, but Tom put his arm out to stop her.

'Just leave.' Tom closed the door behind her and locked it.

She told herself it was the trauma of shock; in time the girls would understand. She wasn't, after all, the only woman ever to leave her husband. But you only hear about the fathers who didn't take their children with them. No-one wanted to know about the mothers. It was like they didn't exist.

Then a letter from a lawyer was delivered to the shop, Sally reluctantly handing it over. Nora went back to the A-frame and screamed. That evening, before Ollie got home, she stood in the trees at the junction of the two properties, letter tucked into the belt of her dress. Tom wouldn't be home from work yet, but she could hear that the girls were out riding the mini bikes Tom had bought them the week after she left. She stretched the wires apart and climbed through the fence and onto Tom's land, her land. It was like stepping onto foreign soil. She wasn't sure if it was dense enough to hold her.

Nora wanted to run her hand along the top of the fence, to let it guide her up the side of the property, but the top wire was barbed. Instead, she stepped sideways, inched up towards the dam, her back to the fence, watching for the girls, checking they were safe.

The high-pitched whir of the mini bikes peaked as Trudie flew into view, rode the dip between the old potato paddock and the house. Lara rounded the corner. On the straight, her wrist bent forward and she roared up next to Trudie. They rode side by side to the dam and stopped the bikes on its bottom lip. Both of them used a forearm to shade their eyes as they looked down towards the A-frame. She could see their mouths moving, but the wind was too faint to carry their sounds.

Nora's heart stiffened. Her breath turned to stone. She was afraid they would see her and afraid they would not. Trudie climbed off her bike, flicked the stand down and moved to lean awkwardly over Lara, put her arms around her, and the form that was the two of them shook and heaved. A slight breeze delivered Lara's keening, and Nora covered her ears. Her feet set concrete in the ground.

She did not know how long they stood there. Long enough for someone to paint them into the scene, to preserve it as fact, or perhaps for moments only, an image too wide to be captured in one frame.

Trudie moved, held Lara's face before stepping aside to place her hands either side of her mouth like a megaphone. 'We hate you,' she shouted into the air.

Nora reached out to catch herself. She crouched, arse grazing the muddy earth, palms gripped to the wire.

Ollie found her dozing in his chair. The coals in the potbelly stove barely glowing. Her arms entwined between her legs, blood staining her dress.

'Nora.' His tone urgent.

She opened her eyes to his deeply lined forehead. It was, she thought, the first time she had seen him frown properly.

'What happened?' As he peeled open her palms she realised she did not dream it.

Ollie dabbed saline onto the wounds. It felt as though the barbs were still there.

Ollie had got up early and taken the ferry across to Bruny Island. He and his friend Harry were helping some bloke with a smokehouse. It was supposed to be one quick meeting, a few tips, but Ollie had warmed to the guy and it was now the fourth week he'd been helping to build the thing.

Like every other morning since she'd left Tom, Nora went to the shop and bought biscuits, timed it so she'd see the girls when Tom dropped them off. She loaded up with Malt 'O' Milk, the last from the shelves. She was standing at the back of the shop when she heard their voices.

She made her way to the counter, let packets of Malt 'O' Milk drop from her arms and went to the window. It was like the girls were in a film, like they were someone else's children or some kind of ghost children – there to see but utterly unreachable. Or maybe it was her. Maybe Nora was the ghost, the girls vaguely aware of her presence but not enough to make her solid and real.

'That be all?' Sally asked.

'Yes.'

'There'll be more in tomorrow.'

Nora turned to Sally, unsure of her meaning.

'The biscuit delivery.'

'Oh, right.'

As she climbed into the car, Nora wondered about Sally, couldn't decide if she wanted the disdain to abate, whether she wanted a friend who was capable of such judgement. But then she herself had become capable of things she'd never thought possible, of a selfish meanness that somehow felt justified and right, and she wondered what this said about her, what kind of a person it made her.

As she pulled into the driveway of the A-frame, it occurred to her that Sally's thaw might be contagious. Perhaps the girls would be next and then later, much later, maybe Tom would see that it had been the right thing for them, the only thing really.

Nora lowered herself into Ollie's sling chair and wondered what to do with the empty space inside her, that animalistic void that could only be filled by the girls. She longed for the smell of their skin in the way that she had craved tins of creamed rice and cucumbers when she was pregnant with Trudie, chillies when she was pregnant with Lara.

She went out to the car and took two packets of biscuits from the boot, one for each of the girls. Then she poured coffee and sat at the table, took first a biscuit from one packet then from the other and dipped them into her coffee until they began to sag, and then lifted them into her mouth, warm and soggy. She didn't stop until the biscuits were all gone, the wrappers empty on the tabletop.

It could not go on this way. She needed Tom to be reasonable. If she didn't get it sorted soon the whole boot would be filled with biscuits, or she would. Her chest tightened. Even now she was letting Tom get away with things, letting him take control the way he always had. But her thinking was wrong too. Who could blame him? She had let him believe that the life they had together was enough; she'd allowed him to think that they were okay. He'd probably thought she was happy. But she remembered the arguments. Tom's excuses, Nora wanting to timetable things, Tom telling her she was being controlling. Surely wanting the man to finish something, finish anything, wasn't controlling. Surely it wasn't unreasonable.

She got up early and looked out the window at the smokehouse. The scent of eucalyptus was thick in the air, the view up towards the boundary with her old place was all greys and greens and blues, a collage of trees and sky and scrub. She breathed deeply. The air in Hobart had never smelt of anything and she'd always taken that to be a good thing. She'd never caught the odour of pollution, the stench of sulphur that she recalled from trips to mainland cities. But in contrast to Kettering, clean and odourless had begun to seem blank and empty, as though the absence of the natural smells of the earth was a structured barrier against the way we fit into the world, a way of repressing or at least ignoring the fact of people as animals.

Nora opened the door to the smokehouse and stood with her face pressed in the gap between door edge and frame. She leant against the outer timber of the building, the fibres of her T-shirt catching on unfinished wood. With the tip of her left foot she made circles in the gravel, absently marking her presence. If she'd turned a little more she could have sidled through without opening the door any wider. But it was Ollie's space and, though she was certain he wouldn't mind, it did not feel right.

She scrutinised the interior as though she were looking into the cavern of Ollie's body, as though she'd stripped open his skin, unhinged his ribs and was inspecting the essence of him. Three rows of timber sat across the beams of the smokehouse; over them were loops of twine tied to hooks with hunks of meat attached.

Nora couldn't be sure what animal they came from. That was the thing about meat: once it was butchered, after it had been slipped from its skin, it all looked much the same. She pondered if the same were true of people. If from the inside Ollie and Tom might be indistinguishable, if she might.

On the thick slab of a bench that ran the length of the hut, whole salmon crusted with salt and herbs. Five in a row, ready to be flayed. Tight speckled skins. Nora observed them, first to last – a small school or a conga line. What would it have been like if on the day they'd met, Ollie had only brought a package of possum? What if she had never felt the sweet press of his salmon on her tongue?

She thought again of Tom; she could not help it. Up in the unfinished house. The end room, unlined still, tools strewn across the concrete floor. If he'd packed them into the toolbox at the end of each day, at the end of the week even, might that have been enough?

Nora looked back to the salmon, unable to swim away, and she moved her mind away from Tom.

Ollie would be back from Bruny soon. Tomorrow he would fire up the stove in the smokehouse, feed it with applewood and let the smoke billow in folds until there was no clear air left. Then he would latch the door from the outside. After, he might carry his chainsaw up to the top of the property. Then Nora would skirt the edges of the vegetable patch, follow the sound of the chainsaw, find him covered in the smell of freshly hewn timber, sap stuck to the hairs on his legs. Or, if he had enough wood cut already, she might find him in the house, reclining in his favourite chair, his bare skin against the sewn animal skins that were attached like a cradle to the simply made timber frame. If he were waiting for her, he would be looking at the door as she entered. He would beckon her with a slight movement of his head. Wait until she removed her underwear and straddled him. By the time they were done, they would both smell of woodsmoke.

The school bus had left, so Nora took coins from her wallet and walked around the corner to the phone box. She dialled the number to Tom's office and waited for him to pick up. It rang seven times before she hung up. After the next ring it would have gone to the answering machine. Nora rested against the glass side of the box and picked the dirt from under her fingernails.

Jenny Bridemont was available for a good time, any time. Stacey Light was a slut. Johnny and Tracey loved each other, forever. Nora wondered if Trudie's and Lara's names would be scratched into the aluminium wall of this phone box one day.

She dialled Tom's number again. This time she let it go to the answering service and left a vehement message saying that she must see the girls, she had a right. That she would come by tomorrow night at seven. When she hung up, her hands were shaking and she was anxious about what she had done.

Nora drove down to the terminal and took the ferry. For the twenty-minute trip between Kettering and Bruny Island she stayed inside the car, windows wound tight, and once the ferry docked she started her engine, cranked the heating up. When it was her turn to disembark, she nodded to the man in high-vis who directed her, and set off down the ramp onto the island.

She drove without knowing where she was going, without any plan at all other than a desire to shake loose her restlessness. She wanted to get out and walk, to let the brisk Bruny wind pummel her, but none of the placenames she passed sounded right; not one of them sounded like where she should be. Eventually, she stopped by the lightkeeper's cottage at the far end of the island, rested her head on the steering wheel and tried to cry until her stomach muscles ached. Then, leaning into the force of the wind, she walked up the hill to the lighthouse, touched its locked door, turned and went back to the car.

On the ferry home, she rubbed the back of her hand against her cheek, was aware of the wind's lingering chill, and tried to recall the noise of it filling her head. But instead Tom's accusation, 'You made your choice', looped in her ears.

The A-frame was dark. Nora pushed the door shut, put her bag on the table and looked around the room. What if she were wrong? What if she didn't know Ollie at all? She'd told herself she was leaving Tom for herself but what if that wasn't true? What if she was really exchanging one man's version of her life for another's?

She turned full circle, searching for clues, for something she might not have noticed, for a sign that she'd been wrong about him. She ran her palm over the sling chair, across the surface of the Huon pine dining table.

In the corner of the sideboard, tucked behind a sheep's skull, she found a photograph of Ollie. He had his arm around a squat woman, both of them grinning. Nora picked up the frame. She took it across to the table, turned it over and tilted the pins that held the thing together. Then she moved the heavy card away to reveal the back of the image. Ollie's slanted script: *1976 with Agnes – Cockle Creek.*

She gently removed the photo and examined it closely. The

woman was older and she had lost some of her teeth. Nora put the frame back together and returned it to its place on the sideboard.

She rifled through the bottom cupboard looking for photo albums. Found stacks of notebooks instead, all of them filled with sketches of plants and animals, trees. She flicked through the pages. Stopped at a drawing of a possum.

Mesmerised by the detail, she sat in Ollie's sling chair and traced her index finger over the lines of the drawing. It seemed to capture every hair, the essence of the thing. On the pages behind the possum, instructions in images. Notes on the edges: *Agnes's rules: sharpen knife, don't pierce the gut, peel skin off gently – like a silk jacket.*

When Ollie came home she met him at the door, circled her arms about him. He laughed softly then tugged her down onto the sheepskins in front of the fire.

Tom was closing the gate as Nora drove up. She watched him through the windscreen, expected him to open the gate to let her pass through. But he raised the chain for her to see a large padlock, waved a key in the air, then began to walk down towards the house.

Nora opened her door. 'Tom.'

He paused and raised his hand like a stop sign. 'They don't want to see you, Nora. None of us does.'

'You can't do this, Tom.'

'Really?'

His head had disappeared from her line of sight.

She lifted the chain, fingered the lock. She could climb over the gate, but what then? What if Tom tried to remove her? Would he do that? She didn't know anymore.

She sat on the bonnet of her car, the heels of her boots resting on the top of the registration plate. *NTL*: Nora, Tom, Trudie and

Lara. A birthday gift from Tom, the kind of thing he loved. The kind of thing the girls loved.

She looked down at their property and wished the house wasn't carved into the hillside, wished she could see the girls, but all she could see was the roof and the view down to Ollie's. The view of the bay.

She thought about the first day they'd brought the girls to the property. Digging in the crumbling earth on the side of the hill. Pockets full of fossils. So many that Nora had begun to think Tom had hidden them, used them as a ruse to lure the girls. But they hadn't needed luring. They had loved it all. Had gone home with bags of those stencils of long-dead animals. The car filled with the smell of dirt, excitement wound into air. All of them wrapped in possibility. They would live in a place where the sea had once been. When they got back to the house in Bellerive, the girls had lined up the fossils along their windowsills. And, when finally they moved, they'd hardly looked back on their old lives.

At dinner, Ollie was slicing cheese, laying it on the bread he made earlier.

'I tried to see the girls today.'

'What do you mean?' He continued to slice lengths of Jarlsberg. 'I thought you saw them every day.'

Nora bit the tip of her thumb. 'I haven't seen them since I left.'

Ollie put his knife down. 'You wouldn't tell me this?'

'Tom won't let me.' She was sure when those words came from her mouth that Ollie would think less of her, but he reached across and clasped her forearm. 'He said they don't want to see me.' She choked on the words, on the fear that it might be true, remembered Trudie shouting from the edge of the dam.

Ollie pushed his chair back. 'I can come with you.'

'Where? Now?' She remained seated. 'No. It will only make it worse.'

'Isn't it worse already?'

'I think I should see a lawyer.'

'If you want I can drive you in the morning.' He took his plate across to the sink. 'I was waiting for you to be ready to bring them here.' As he scrubbed the cheese from the dish, he turned to her. 'I wish you had told me.'

Ollie was up early. When Nora climbed down the ladder, he was sitting at the table drinking coffee, a bowl of dough already proving under a tea towel by the stove. She sat and poured herself a coffee. She picked the sleep from her eyes and yanked her hair back, secured it in a ponytail with the hair tie from her wrist then wrapped her cardigan tight around her, was aware of the damp between her legs from the night before.

'Do you want me to come with you?'

She knew then that she had made the right choice. That in Ollie's place Tom would have insisted on coming, commanded it. And Tom's words, though driven perhaps out of care, would have spoken of her presumed lack of capability.

She shook her head, smiled. 'No. Thanks.'

When Ollie went out to the smokehouse, she showered and dressed then drove to the shop, parked in the usual place. The biscuit shelf was full of Malt 'O' Milks. Sally was busy serving a tourist, giving directions to the ferry terminal.

Nora took two packets of biscuits, pushed them across the counter.

'I ordered extra for you. Becky thought you seemed sad,' Sally said.

'Thank you.' Nora couldn't decide whether to be grateful or furious and left before Sally could say more.

It was early, so she sat in the car and read, opened one of the packets and sucked at the sides of the thin wedges of biscuit, let them melt away in her mouth. She turned the engine back on and cranked up the heater to soften the sting of the morning air, held her hands in front of the top vents then adjusted the dial to blow hot air onto her feet. She checked the clock. Tom wouldn't drop the girls off for another half an hour.

She licked the edges of biscuits until Tom arrived, then watched as the girls climbed out of his car. Her fingers were wrapped around the door handle and she had started opening her door when Tom called out. Trudie ran back to his car, accepted the lunch boxes that he passed out the window, and Nora heard Trudie call, 'Love you too', and she let her door swing shut without getting out.

The girls disappeared into the throng of children on the verandah, and Nora sat staring, remembering the first caresses, their tiny heads cradled in the crook of her arm, at her elbow, tentative fingers gingerly reading their skin. Fresh from her body, they'd smelt of bacon. She was still deep in those moments when the school bus pulled away and a sudden sense of revulsion lurched up her throat. She flung the door open, rotated and bent over, head between her knees. Why hadn't she climbed out of the car? She'd managed to leave, why couldn't she manage this?

Nora switched on the engine and started her journey to Hobart. As she passed through Snug, Electrona and Margate, she wondered which way round it had gone. Whether Tom's paternalistic approach had been driven by her need for it, or if she'd come to require it because he had always behaved that way. Perhaps, she thought, it was not Tom's fault. Perhaps fate had put the wrong two people together. Again, she thought back to the day they'd met and imagined herself catching that bus, going straight home from the dentist.

She opened the car window, tried to shake loose these futile thoughts.

The lawyer's office was in an old sandstone building in South Hobart. Nora parked around the back then walked down a narrow path scented by a jasmine-shrouded wall. The heavy timber front door was difficult to open. She pressed her shoulder against the wood, forced it past the resistance of thick piled carpet. Vases of lilies, one on the corner of the reception desk and another in the middle of a large coffee table, almost masked the chemical aroma of recently laid carpet. Someone had cut the stamens from the centre of the blooms. Nora thought of her wedding dress, the faint yellow traces that the dry cleaner had been unable to remove. Nobody had told her the pollen would stain. She wondered if it was an omen, if the presence here of the castrated lilies lent credence to it.

She identified herself to the young woman at the reception desk and took a seat in the waiting area as instructed.

'He won't be long,' the woman assured her.

There was one other person in the waiting area: a young man, probably in his twenties. He was dressed in an ill-fitting light-grey suit and could not sit still on his chair, tilted up and down picking at the pile of magazines like a bowerbird. His suit pants too short for his long legs. He nodded at Nora as she sat, then continued to flick through one magazine after another with no indication of any intention to read.

A heavy man in a suit emerged from one of the offices, files tucked under his arm, jowls hanging over his collar. 'Ready, mate?'

'Yep. Me ma's meeting us there. She couldn't get off work.'

The lawyer held the door open. The young man walked through, then turned back. 'Good luck with your thing,' he said to Nora before leaving.

She should have been thinking about the girls, about what she would tell the lawyer, what she wanted from this, but her mind caught on the young man and his mother, mostly on his mother. What job did she do that she couldn't take the day off? Was this his first time? If not, did his mother take the day off the first time? Was she tired, worn down? Where was his father?

'Ms Gordon.' A man was standing in front of her, hand extended. Nora had forgotten that she'd made the appointment in her maiden name.

'Sorry, I'm … Nice to meet you.' She shook his hand and followed him into a modest office.

Nora sat with her seatbelt fastened and wondered how it had come to this. Character witnesses, custody dispute. This is the place where the end of it truly begins, she thought. The choices she would make now could not be undone. She tried to imagine herself going back to Tom. Even now she was sure he would take her back, and it was this more than anything that made it impossible.

At home, Ollie was waiting for her.

'I thought you might be hungry.' He was sitting at the table. The large oval platter with a slab of smoked salmon and on the Huon pine chopping board a loaf of freshly baked dark rye bread. 'And thirsty.' He picked up a bottle of wine and filled two glasses.

She felt the strain wash out of her in a wave.

Ollie sliced thick hunks of bread, passed the butter dish across the table. He had minced red onion, mixed it through the butter the way she liked it.

She reached across the table to clasp his face and kissed him firmly on the lips. 'Thank you.'

'*Dafür nicht.*'

They ate, Nora's small groans of pleasure the only sounds between them. She continued until her stomach ached, couldn't remember the last time she had eaten properly.

When eventually she stopped, Ollie was looking at her.

'What will you do?'

'Let's talk about it tomorrow. Let's go to bed now.'

He traced his fingers down the back of her calves as he followed her up the ladder. They undressed slowly, fabric transformed to skin. When both of them were naked, she stepped towards him and ran her hands from the front of his chest towards his spine. She was still surprised at the depth of him.

On the morning of the custody application, Ollie offered to drive, wore a suit Nora didn't know he had. He opened the car door, waited till she climbed inside then closed it.

'It will be okay,' he said, as he turned the key in the ignition.

On the way Ollie talked about the smokehouse he had built on Bruny Island. Described the project from beginning to end as though she had never seen the plans, had not heard him speak of it every day for weeks. As if she had never visited the place. And Nora made herself listen, ask questions; she played along and was grateful that Ollie could tell that she needed distraction.

At the courthouse the two solicitors nodded to one another. Then Nora's motioned her to a table and opened his file, shuffled papers, placed a pen on the top sheet and looked at her.

'Don't worry.' He patted Nora's hand as her guts churned.

It was over almost before it began, much less formal than she'd expected. Her solicitor was buoyant.

'The right result,' he said, outside the courtroom, a measure of self-satisfaction evident in his tone.

Tom walked past, faced away as Nora's gaze lifted towards him.

When Nora woke on Friday morning, she was restless.

'*Guten Morgen*.' Ollie rolled towards her, drew her in, spooned his body about hers; together they made a comma. Nora read it as a sign that something more was to come today and she relaxed into his flesh. Ollie kissed her hair, encased her in his arms.

After breakfast, he helped her set up the bed in the spare room, layered it with blankets, placed sheepskins on the floor. She was afraid to ask if it was okay.

He shook the duvets hard, forced air in between pockets of down. 'Don't want them to get cold.' He slipped a pillow inside a pillowcase. 'Maybe you should sleep with them.'

'No. I want it to be normal.'

'It's up to you.' He bent down to flick the power switch on the bedside light. 'But probably normal will take some time.'

Nora was not sure who he was talking about. She had never asked him about this, had been too afraid. 'Maybe I should take them somewhere.'

He moved to her then and held her forearms tightly. 'I chose you, Nora. Not for small parts, not for a slice of what is you. For all of you.'

~

In the afternoon, Nora went to the bus stop to collect the girls. She popped into the shop first to buy groceries – cereal, peanut butter, small measures of normal. Trudie and Lara got off the bus together, peeled away from their friends and walked slowly towards her. Nora kissed them both. Neither of them returned any warmth. She took their bags and put them in the boot with the biscuits. Both girls climbed into the back, and she knew they had decided not to make it easy for her.

She turned to look at them. 'I've missed you so much.'

They stared back at her, stony, and she slipped the key into the ignition before the girls could see the gloss of tears in her eyes. 'I thought we'd go get changed and I'll show you around the house. If you want we can go out after that.'

'Will he be there?' Trudie asked.

'Yes.' Nora checked the rear-view mirror. Lara was crying.

When they arrived at the A-frame, the girls were slow to climb out of the car, let Nora carry their bags. The house smelt sweet. Freshly baked banana bread sat on a rack on the table, steam still rising. Ollie must have been watching for them, must have left as they arrived. She imagined him sitting inside the smokehouse or resting in one of the seats that he liked to carve from felled trees and leave dotted about the property.

Nora showed the girls around, dropped their bags in the spare room. Though they pretended not to be interested, she could see their curiosity winning out.

'What's up the ladder?' Lara asked.

'My bedroom.'

'Does he sleep there too?' Trudie asked, hands on hips, challenging.

'His name is Ollie. And, yes, he does.' Nora poured water into a jug, took it to the table. 'You girls must be hungry. Want some banana bread?'

Lara started towards the table.

'No, we're not hungry actually. Are we, Lar?'

Lara stared at the banana bread longingly. 'Nope. Not hungry.'

'Right, well. Maybe later then. Shall we go out?'

She took them to the pier and ordered fish and chips, and the three of them sat on the jetty, legs dangling over the edge. Lara sat close to Nora then moved away when Trudie raised her eyebrows.

'I know this is difficult, girls. I want you to know that I'm sorry.'

'Does that mean you'll come home?' Lara asked.

'Fat chance,' Trudie said.

'It's not that simple. When you're older you'll understand. The important thing is that I love you both and nothing is going to change that.'

'Isn't that what you told Dad when you married him?' Trudie asked.

'It's not the same. You can never fall out of love with your kids.'

Back at the car, Lara opened the passenger door.

'Lara,' Trudie admonished.

But Lara climbed in and clipped her seatbelt. 'Thanks for the fish and chips, Mum. It was really nice.'

'You're welcome, darling.'

In the rear-view mirror Nora saw Trudie sitting crammed against the door, as far away from her as possible without getting out of the car. Her arms were crossed over her chest, her face pressed against the window.

Nora woke to sounds from the kitchen. Dawn was scarcely breaking, and it was still dark enough that Ollie had the lights on.

She climbed down the ladder and found Ollie and Lara sitting at the dining table playing cards and eating banana bread, woodfire blazing beside them.

Ollie looked up briefly. 'She is very good. I haven't won a hand.'

Lara stuffed more banana bread into her mouth. 'Do you guys always have cake for breakfast?'

'Only on special occasions,' Ollie said.

Lara smiled, teeth coated in mushed-up food.

The girls were standing in front of the shop and Tom was fussing over them, tucking a strand of Trudie's hair behind her ear, tugging Lara's windcheater down to cover the strip of bare skin between jeans and top.

Nora got out of her car and walked towards them. 'Hi, you,' she said, trying not to exclude Tom, trying not to exacerbate.

He did not look at her. 'Take care of each other.' He kissed each of them. 'I'll see you here at six o'clock on Sunday.'

'Why don't I walk them up?' Nora asked. 'Save you the trip.'

'You wanted the orders, Nora. Let's just follow them.'

She wanted to tell him he was being an arsehole, that there hadn't been a choice, but the girls were there, waiting. 'Fine.' She moved to the car and opened the back door. 'Come on.'

Lara climbed in but Trudie stood with Tom.

'Off you go, princess.'

Trudie hugged Tom tightly. 'Miss you already, Dad.'

'Miss you more. Both of you.'

Back at the house, Nora gave the girls the art paper she'd bought, set up a couple of easels outside and let them go mad with paints while she turned over the soil in the veggie patch ready for some planting.

By the time Ollie got home in the early evening, they were all inside: Trudie reading by the fire and Lara playing solitaire at the table while Nora made potato salad.

'Hello there,' Ollie said and went straight to the shower, came out ten minutes later in a flannel shirt and trackpants. 'Want to see the abalone?' he asked.

Trudie didn't look up from her book, but Lara was already on her feet. She and Nora followed Ollie outside, where he opened the nylon diving bag to a jumble of abalone shells.

'Grab one,' he said to Lara.

'Do they bite?'

'No teeth.' Ollie bared his gums and moved the bag closer to Lara and she tentatively reached inside and touched a shell. 'Okay, now grab one,' he said.

Lara put her hand across a shell and tried to lift it. 'It's stuck.'

'Yep, they like to stick together. Here.' He reached in and pulled at the abalone and six of them came out in a clump all suctioned up to one another's shells.

'Oh my God. They are so ugly.' Lara called towards the house. 'Trudie, Trudie. These things are so disgusting.'

Trudie stood in the doorway.

'You've got to see these. They are so, so, so disgusting.' Lara opened her mouth and put two fingers inside her mouth, pretending to make herself gag.

'Actually, they taste amazing,' Ollie said.

'Yeah?' Lara asked.

'What do they taste like? And don't say chicken.' Trudie had come closer, was on the edge of the verandah at the top of the steps.

'Crocodile. That's the closest. That, or abalone.' Ollie laughed softly.

Trudie came down to the yard and stood with them.

'If you help me clean and prepare them you can have the shells.'

Trudie went to leave, but Ollie took a clean abalone shell from the tackle box, held it up to the light so the mother-of pearl glinted in the afternoon sun.

'Are you for real?' Lara shouted.

They had an early dinner and the girls proclaimed it the best thing they'd ever eaten in their lives, the best thing in the world, no, the best thing in the universe. When Nora was drying the last of the pans, she heard Lara whisper, 'Thank you, Ollie', as she walked past his chair.

Their weeks took new shapes. From Monday to Friday, Nora and Ollie continued as usual: made love on the skins in front of the fire, on the dining table and, once, in the doorway of the smokehouse – Nora's skirt hoiked, bunched around her waist, one boot curled up behind Ollie's backside, the sound of his belt buckle banging against the timber frame. Wednesday to Friday, Nora, having taken a part-time job teaching art at Woodbridge, went to the shop car park and, after Tom dropped the girls off, drove her and Sally's girls to school, the five of them singing and chattering the whole way. On the weekends, Trudie and Lara stayed over. Ollie made banana bread and loaves of the darkest rye. He placed platters on the table: salami, smoked cheeses and salmon – his salmon.

'Dad buys us Coco Pops,' Trudie offered.

'That's nice,' Ollie said, stuffing salami slices into his mouth.

Slowly, as the weeks and months slipped by, their patterns shifted. They navigated school holidays, Lara moving from Brownies to Guides, Trudie starting her last term of primary school. Some mornings, when Nora woke last, she'd climb down the ladder to find Ollie and the girls at the table eating salami and cheese, chewing at the dense rye breads, playing cards or backgammon, or just sitting. He made pots of coffee and the girls learnt to drink it and, although Nora would prefer they didn't, she let it go, allowed things to develop as they ought. Sometimes, she listened from the mezzanine bedroom and it seemed as if she was in the wings of a stage, curtains obscuring her view, eavesdropping on a play. She listened to the chat, to the silences, and tried to place them, to glean if they might be comfortable, decided that they were. This was the thing about Ollie. He did not press himself on people. He let them lean into his life, to choose it for themselves, or not. And he did so without judgement. He did not expect.

In bed at night, after the girls were tucked up, Nora curled her body into Ollie's. Sometimes they made love, more quietly than usual. Ollie's usual grunts and moans held within his skin. And Nora wondered whether she imagined it or if, in those periods when the girls were back at Tom's, Ollie's noises were larger, magnified, as though held over from a time before.

Nora was in the kitchen when she heard it, the sound carving a hole in her gut. Her limbs went loose. Boneless.

She opened the back door. Ollie was already a blur between the trees. The world shifted, dropped away. Nora ran. Her thongs flapping on her feet, twigs digging into skin, rasping flesh as she flew across the land.

At the fence line between Ollie's property and Tom's she looked ahead and saw Trudie at the lip of Tom's dam, body folded. Keening. Hysterical. Nora felt as though she was running on the spot. When she reached the fence she climbed through then pumped her legs again, and still it seemed as if she was not getting closer.

Then she was over the lip, beside Trudie as Ollie emerged from the beige surface of the dam, water cascading down his frame, and Lara tiny, limp in his arms, a single gumboot hooked onto a foot.

Nora's knees buckled, rendered her an onlooker as Ollie worked at Lara's body. His hands spanned across Lara's chest, found breastbone, pressed, moved to pinch her nose as his mouth covered hers, blew air. Twice, three times. Lara coughed then spewed muddy water. And deftly, as though she were a calf just born, Ollie turned Lara on her side, slapped her back as she hacked out liquid, coughed, sucked at the air.

While Ollie worked and Lara tried to breathe, Nora was suspended in time, in the place between mother and not, knees sunk into the mud, the sound of Trudie wailing. And finally, when Lara lay quietly, staring into Ollie's face, Nora vomited at the edge of the dam and her body began to shake.

'It's alright. She's alright.' Ollie reached out to touch Nora's cheek. Raised his voice, 'Trudie. She's okay.' His hair was plastered across his face, wound about his neck.

Nora moved to sit beside them and placed Lara's head in her lap. 'It's okay. I'm here.' She bent and kissed Lara's forehead. Pressed her lips firmly against her daughter's cold, wet flesh, resting them there. Then she wrapped her body about Lara's to make her warm and closed her eyes, was vaguely aware of the sound of Ollie speaking.

When she looked up Ollie was standing, Trudie in his arms, sobbing, as he stroked her hair and whispered words in German that none of them understood.

'Mum.' Lara shifted. 'Can I sit up?'

Nora unravelled herself and Lara scrambled up, burrowed into Nora's embrace and began to cry, her breathing ragged. When the crying abated, she thought Lara had fallen asleep, and was surprised when her daughter lifted her head.

'I'm sorry. It was an accident. I slipped.'

'It's okay. You're fine.'

Trudie shifted from foot to foot, beat her fists against her thighs. 'She kept coming up. Then I couldn't see her. I jumped in but I couldn't see her. And I touched her but she was too heavy. I couldn't get her up. I tried, Mum. I really tried.'

Nora held her arm out and Trudie moved into the space. With the two girls tight against her chest, the smell of clay on their skin, she squeezed them hard.

'It's okay. You're both okay.' Nora saw Trudie's gumboots at the side of the dam. Filled with water. Crusted with mud. She beckoned Ollie with her head and he knelt behind her and she leant back into his embrace. Ollie's arms encompassing them all, Nora's heartbeat slowed, blood returned to her limbs.

The wheels of Tom's car crackled on the gravel driveway, and they all turned to the house as Tom parked, climbed out, closed the door. He began to move towards them slowly then dropped his bag, broke into a run.

Tom leapt across the corner of the dam, mud spraying up his suit trousers. 'What happened. Jesus. Shit. Nora?'

None of them responded immediately.

'It's alright, Dad. I'm okay,' Lara said.

Nora closed her eyes, exhausted.

'Ollie saved her,' Trudie said. 'Ollie saved her.' And she sniffed, hiccoughed a sob.

Tom dropped to his knees, hugged Lara to him. 'I'm so sorry, honey. I'm so sorry.'

'It's not your fault, Dad,' Lara said. She looked down, speaking quietly. 'I was wearing my gumboots.'

Tom squeezed Lara, kissed her matted hair. 'It doesn't matter,' he said, and he drew Trudie to him too. 'You're both okay. Nothing else matters.'

They sat there for what seemed to Nora like hours.

When Tom released the girls, he held his hand out to Ollie. 'Thank you,' he said. Then he let go and wound his wiry arms as far around Ollie's frame as they would reach.

Nora put on yesterday's dress and climbed down the ladder. Ollie had let the fire go out. She poked her head into the girls' room. Covers dragged back, bodies gone.

She threw on the cardigan she'd left on the sofa and slid her boots on at the back door. Walked first to the smokehouse, then the woodpile, then up to the place where Ollie had cut down a tree, left it for the girls to make a cubby house. She didn't call out in case it made her sound afraid.

Back in the house, she checked their bedroom again then saw a note on the sideboard: *Pulling in the pots.* She imagined the girls out there: Trudie following Ollie's instructions, rotating the wheel this way then that, letting the throttle idle gently, being careful not to run the motor over the rope that connected buoy to craypot. The boat bobbing, Lara's head poking from the top of a life jacket like a turtle. Trudie's hair whipping about in the wind, concentration on her brow, and the singing inside her for this man who would allow her to do things on her own.

Nora ate breakfast on the front step in the sun. Ollie would probably teach them to use the chainsaw next and, though Nora wouldn't remind the girls to keep it from their father, neither of them would tell Tom.

She was still sitting in the sun when they returned. Trudie and Lara both squashed into the front seat, a single seatbelt bound tight about them, smiles as wide as the bay.

'Mum, Mum, did you see me? Did you see me changing gears?' Lara said as she scrambled across Trudie, flew from the car, hands in the air, salt on her skin.

'Is that what you were doing?'

'Yeah, well, I drove the boat.'

'You only steered it,' Lara countered.

'Did not.' Trudie turned to Ollie. 'I drove, didn't I, Ollie?'

'You did.' He lifted the icebox out of the boat. 'You know, Nora, it's true, there was hardly any work for me. Next time I think I'll take a book, maybe a pillow.'

'When can we go again?' Trudie asked.

'Yeah, Ollie, when?'

'Next weekend probably. But you know there won't always be crays. Sometimes you do the work and nothing is there.'

'Who cares? We don't mind, do we, Trudes?'

'Nup.' And, in a small voice, Trudie added, 'Thanks, Ollie.'

Ollie dragged the hose towards the boat. 'Now, girls, I want to say thanks for your help but you know the job is not quite finished.'

They looked up at him expectantly.

'Now we must clean the dirty things.' And he turned the hose, first on the boat, and then on the girls, and they snorted, shrieked, ran away and came back for more.

Nora could have cried with happiness.

~

Later, they ate crayfish for lunch with homemade bread and pickled radishes. Ollie showed the girls where to crack the legs to extract the meat.

'This is the best.' Trudie sucked the flesh from snapped spindly legs.

Lara used her sleeve to wipe juices from her chin. 'Better than Kentucky Fried Chicken.'

The four of them cracked and scooped, mopped juices with deeply sour bread. Ollie ate the mustard and laughed when the girls turned up their noses. In the middle of the table, a growing tower of crustacea.

That afternoon, once they had cleared the detritus from lunch into newspaper, placed it in plastic bags and stowed it in the freezer to dull the smell, Ollie let the girls light the fire. They lounged around, Ollie with his face in the newspaper, half reading, half dozing, Trudie devouring *Jonathan Livingston Seagull*, and Lara and Nora on the floor doing dot-to-dots and colouring.

They all fell asleep, then woke for bread and cheese.

Later, Nora tucked them into bed. 'Love you, girls.' She kissed them goodnight.

Ollie was propped in bed reading. He had let his hair out and it was fanned against the pillow.

Nora watched his eyes scan across text, lifting occasionally in her direction as she undressed. 'Thank you.'

'It was a good day.' Ollie took his glasses off and put the book aside.

She climbed onto the bed, rested her head on his chest then moved up his body to kiss his neck. She lifted his hair, let it canopy about her head as she burrowed her face deeper against him, towards the place behind his ear. He ran his fingers lightly up and down her back, traced his knuckles against her ribs – bone to bone – brushed against the spaces between, the places where anything could penetrate, with the mildest of pressure.

'Got time for a walk?' Sally untied her apron.

'Now?'

'Yep. That okay?'

Nora wasn't sure how to answer. Part of her wanted to punish Sally, but she'd been making an effort lately and it seemed childish not to forgive her. 'How much time have you got?'

'Darren's here all day. Long as I want.'

'Bruny?'

'Haven't been in ages. Why not?' Sally shoved biscuits and bottles of water into a crocheted bag.

As the ferry moved away from the dock, Sally and Nora climbed out of the car, stood at the rail and watched as Kettering diminished.

'How are you?' Sally's hair blew across her face. She pulled the hood of her windcheater up, tucked her hair inside.

'Fine. You?'

'Same as ever. And the girls?'

'Apparently peace can be bought with a couple of crays and a lesson in boating.'

Sally laughed. 'He's a hard man not to like.'

'Yeah, he is.'

'I know this is kind of presumptuous but I was wondering if you'd help me make jam for the school Christmas fete next week.'

'I can do that.'

~

Nora had thought she'd be back before dinner, but there was more fruit than she'd expected, and the stirring and bottling was running into the evening.

She phoned Ollie. 'We're still going. Do you mind if I stay another hour?' She hadn't left Ollie alone in the evening with the girls before; they hadn't discussed it.

'We're fine. I'm cooking sausages.'

Nora thought she heard Trudie begin to complain in the background. 'Thanks.' She hung up and commenced ladling again, placing filled jars on the scant empty places on the table.

Sally rotated a spoon in her hand, blew on it and licked off the remnants of red stickiness. 'So you're all settled with the new arrangements?'

'I don't know. I think so. The girls seem to be getting used to it. And, well, you know Ollie.'

'What about Tom?'

'I think he might be seeing someone.' Nora couldn't believe how little she felt in the saying of it.

'Really?' Sally twirled her spoon in the air. 'I find that hard to believe.'

'Why?'

'Well, it's just he still seems so upset. Sorry.'

Nora ran her hands under the tap. 'I'm pretty sure he was seeing someone before.'

'When?'

'Before we split. Before Ollie.'

'Really? Are you sure? Nah.'

Nora turned to her. 'I don't know where everyone got this idea of Tom and me. Like we were the epitome of a perfect couple. I can't remember when we were last that. Probably never.'

Sally refilled their wineglasses. 'Still, an affair? I can't even imagine it.' She paused. 'I had no idea.'

Nora shrugged. 'I could be wrong. Either way, we weren't happy.'

Sally took the jam pan across to the sink and filled it with water. 'I'll leave it to soak.' She lifted her wineglass.

Nora clinked her glass against Sally's. 'Cheers.' She sipped. 'God, that's good.'

'It isn't that I'm unhappy with Darren,' Sally said. 'He wants to send the girls to boarding school in Hobart. Who does that when they don't have to? Who would do that to a kid like Ava? She'd never cope and Darren doesn't seem to understand.' Sally drank, sighed. 'Some days I really do wonder if this is all there is. You know?'

'Yeah. Yeah, I do.'

They chuckled, clinked their glasses again and drank.

It was dark when Nora returned. The lights in the house were off, only flickers of illumination in the windows, tigers' eyes thrown by the wood heater. Nora opened the door quietly. Ollie's head was tilted forward, his novel fanned on the sofa beside him, hand pressed down on its back, and Lara on his other side, her upper body and head curled like a seahorse, asleep on his lap. Trudie slept on the floor, her hand resting against Ollie's sock-clad foot. And Nora knew they had managed it.

Boy

Harry sat in the ute, window down, and watched from across the road. Kids running wild – wound up and let loose. The bell, petering sounds, then quiet. He read the newspaper and waited. Drank coffee from a thermos and ate mandarins, used torn-up peel to make a collage on the passenger seat and rubbed the stickiness from his fingers onto the sheepskin steering-wheel cover.

At recess, kids rushed into the playground like a freak wave. A pack played dinosaur games, shrieked around the prefab wooden fort by the fence. The boy ran to the top, tyrannosaurus elbows tucked tight to his body. He opened his mouth and roared.

Harry had taken the early ferry, got off at Kettering and driven north. He'd parked outside the kindergarten in North Hobart and watched Caitlin leave. Seen the curve of her mouth as she waved goodbye to the boy. He'd been watching the boy for weeks, trying to work up the courage, but every time he moved his hand towards the door handle his heart flipped in his chest and he lost his nerve.

Back on Bruny Island, Harry looked across the haze of stubbled grass that tumbled down to the casuarina-fringed coast and tried to picture the boy in the grey wooden shed he'd turned into a home: limbs folded in the awkward angles of children, nestled into the couch that was still covered in the saris Caitlin had bought in India.

When he'd met Caitlin she'd been the only other person in the tiny, shabby cinema at McLeod Ganj. She was wearing Thai fisherman's pants and her hair was in dreadlocks. The smell of her patchouli almost masked the stench of body odour trapped in the grimy cinema seats. The movie had been a Bollywood offering, and a number of times they'd caught themselves laughing and groaning at the same places. The film was less than halfway through when Caitlin tapped him on the shoulder and asked if he wanted to get out of there.

The rooftop terrace cafe of the Ladies' Hotel was perched between the road and the steep tilt into what was almost a ravine. Harry and Caitlin sat opposite one another on bench chairs. She ordered them banana pancakes and chai.

When she got up to go to the toilet, he watched her walk away then turned to look down the valley. The land dipped and flattened into a clearing where the concrete Tsuglagkhang compound of the Dalai Lama sat.

Caitlin returned and sat next to him, followed his gaze and told him she'd been waiting for six months for the Dalai Lama to be in residence.

'I think you're a sign,' she said, and she squeezed Harry's knee beneath the table.

Harry went inside and sat on his bed, pulled out his battered tin and rested the lid on the windowsill and rolled himself a joint – filled and tucked, licked and tightened. He should fix the gap in the window frame; the evening wind had begun to whistle through as it flew up from the coast. It reminded him of the annoying noise Caitlin made when she slept.

He wanted to light the joint, but images of the boy and the

sound of his voice filled Harry's mind. He tried to roll a box of matches around in his palm the way he used to roll the Chinese chime balls Caitlin had given him while they were still in India. He wondered where those balls had gone, whether she'd taken them with her when she took all of the things she'd wanted, when she took the boy. He felt the newly familiar flare of anger in his throat, tried to swallow it.

Outside, Harry stuck the thin, papered cylinder of the joint between his lips. Against his skin it felt like the right kind of substantial, seemed to connect him to the earth, and he imagined the papers as trees before they changed shape and became something else.

He shook his head. Caitlin was right; he was always too far up his own arse. He wouldn't have made any kind of father. A memory snagged then – Caitlin sneering across the kitchen table, laughing at his feeble attempts to philosophise – and he felt the anger reignite, felt bile rise in his throat.

He lit the joint, savoured the taste. He'd never liked the smell of it much, only the flavour. Caitlin said that was dumb, said the two things were almost the same, so entwined as to be only the one thing, really. Caitlin was like that. She thought she had the measure of everything, of everyone, and for a time after she'd left, without her as yardstick, Harry hadn't been sure of his margins. But he'd seen the boy now.

When Caitlin left, the boy had only been a tiny bump, and she had given every sign of being furious, repulsed. She'd refused to discuss what they should do, so Harry had been sure she hadn't wanted the child. Could remember nothing to suggest she had. He began to suspect he was meant to have begged her, to prove that it mattered, that they mattered.

The letter about the boy had come from some government department. Harry's name was on the birth certificate, and they wanted to know about money. But he didn't have any. He'd had to send copies of bank statements. They never sent him any proof the boy was his, though he figured it must be right. He'd taken a beer from the fridge and sat at the table outside with the letter in his hand, and rubbed his forehead until it stung. He'd imagined Caitlin – her round, taut stomach rippling from the movement beneath. He'd thought of their last days together – how he'd somehow got used to the sharpness of her judgement and it had seemed accurate and fair. He hadn't amounted to much; he didn't finish anything. She'd told him that until he believed it. Then, not long before she left, she'd said, 'You're not the sign I'm looking for.'

Harry got stoned a lot, cleared some of the larger eucalypts from the property so that he could see the coast. It took months before he began to breathe more easily, trust himself to make the simple decisions that Caitlin had taken control of.

When the shock of the letter dissipated, Harry was washed in anger. He looked up Caitlin in the phone book, circled the local kindergartens with deep-blue pen marks in the street directory. Remembered her last words: 'You are a stranger to me now.' He realised she had always wiped the slate clean. She never talked of her past and he had never met her family or friends. He'd assumed that she had wanted him for herself, but now he could see that she only moved forward. He considered what this might mean for the boy, whether it was healthy.

The first time he saw the boy – hand invisible inside Caitlin's, an orange Winnie-the-Pooh backpack slung over his shoulder – his small face was turned up towards hers. Harry smiled, felt a visceral pull towards this unknown creature, an unbidden searing rage towards Caitlin.

The boy's features were neat, unlike his or Caitlin's, as though the boy had conjured the idea of the perfect child and drawn himself. Harry wondered briefly whether it galled Caitlin that the boy didn't look like her. But Caitlin wasn't like that; she didn't believe in regret, was surely incapable of it.

The day before the custody application, Harry got out of the car, walked past the kindergarten fence, stopped when the boy ran over to retrieve a ball. He was about to speak when a teacher called the children inside.

Before recess, a police car parked behind his ute.

'He's my son.' The words felt like stones tumbling out of his mouth. Even he didn't believe them.

'Is that right?' The officer took his hat off.

Harry started the engine. 'It's alright. I won't come again.' He turned the handle and wound his window closed.

The officer looked at him, raised his hand to knock on the glass, then withdrew and slowly walked back to the footpath. The officer was still visible in his rear-view mirror as Harry rounded the corner and headed back to the ferry.

Tomorrow, he'd take the early ferry again. The lawyer would meet him at the courthouse. He wouldn't be able to smoke a joint to calm his nerves. He didn't like the thought of it, but the lawyer had said if he wanted visitation rights he'd need to be squeaky-clean – as though Caitlin was squeaky-clean, as though she'd ever been. The boy had probably been stoned on second-hand smoke every day of his life.

Harry stopped at Kingston, bought cereal and tinned food from the supermarket, lingered in the toy aisle, ran his hands over packets of bright plastic things and tried to imagine how any of it could be necessary. He felt a compulsion to fill his trolley with the kinds of disposable junk he hated.

At the department store he bought a mattress and doona, chose sheets with trains over the ones with bears, and loaded the mattress into the back of the ute.

In the corner of the storage shed that was his workshop, he rubbed sandpaper over the turned legs one more time and wiped them down before pouring oil on a soft, blue cloth and running it the length of each leg and then all along the frames. He let it dry for a few hours then carried the small bed into the house and set it down by the wood heater.

Caitlin didn't turn up. Her lawyer asked for an adjournment and the judge let him have it.

Back at the office in South Hobart, Harry's lawyer took him out to the terrace of the old sandstone building, said Caitlin not showing up didn't mean anything, then went on about the beehives that lined the rear fence of the property, as if Harry, being from the island and all, ought to give a shit.

'I'm not going to lie to you, Harry. It's not going to be easy.'

Harry nodded, an image of the boy in his head. 'The boy's got my brother's ears. You could pick him up and swing him around by them.'

The lawyer cleared his throat, scraped his shoe against the pavers.

'Not that I would. Obviously.'

~

Next time, they waited in a corridor lit by fluorescent tubes. Harry felt self-conscious, his new jeans dark and stiff. Shirt with creases from the packet. Beard trimmed neatly, hair pulled into a ponytail at the base of his neck. Caitlin could arrive at any time. She might be in the car park or drinking coffee in a cafe down at Salamanca.

'Don't worry, mate. Just smile, be polite. That's all you need to do.'

Harry tried to relax his brow, let his face fall slack, but the nerves were roiling, making his face tight, his limbs twitchy and alien.

He told the lawyer he needed the toilet. Walked straight out the main doors. Caitlin was walking up the courthouse steps as Harry turned the key in the ignition.

He drove onto the ferry, yanked on the handbrake and got out to lean over the rail. Curved peaks of water plinked at the steel sides of the ferry. He yanked free his ponytail and let the wind wrap his hair around his face. Watched through strands as the Kettering cove disappeared and Bruny Island became larger.

At his outdoor table, he drank beer from a long neck and smoked a joint, completed the dot-to-dot of his property, eucalypt by eucalypt, finished up at the line of casuarinas. He left his jeans on the table and fell asleep on the train-covered sheets, feet resting against a turned blackwood leg. Woke in the night to the sound of the wind, the roar of a tyrannosaurus.

Leaven

At first, his mother made bread as if the dough were air and to stop would deny her breath. Ollie worried that her hands, unbusied, might find a way to dig into her chest and pull out her heart. He sat at the table and ripped open steaming hot loaves of dark rye with his small hands, buried his nose in the sour yeasty aroma. Observed his mother's shoulders shift and roll, as she pummelled at another batch of dough.

Before and after school, he chewed and waited, watched her back as though the answers he needed might play across her wide expanse like a movie at the small theatre his father had taken him to in Frieberg. But he only ever saw ripples of fabric, creasing then stretching and straining over her terrain.

He was ten when he asked if his father was dead. Felt the sting of her palm, fat red slug marks across his face for hours. His mother wept and squeezed her hands, as though she could turn her flesh into a love-knot roll.

She maintained that his father would be home soon; they need only be patient. She would say it standing by the sink, facing away from him. Always facing away.

The children at school said his father had run off with Sebastien's mother, said Sebastien had gone to stay with them on the coast of Spain in the holidays. But Ollie knew it was a lie. If there was one place his father wouldn't live it was Spain. He hated paella, couldn't bear the way the Spanish let their children stay up till midnight, despised the lazy siestas.

When Sebastien returned to school, face marked with chickenpox scars, Ollie knew with certainty that his father was dead. That he was probably in a cemetery on the edges of the Black Forest and that his mother had been weaving her loaves because she couldn't work out how to tell him that Papa had been cleaved in two by a chainsaw; swung an axe through his own leg and been taken by wolves; been crushed by a fallen tree, his arms out to either side, pressed into the earth.

His mother's brother, Herman, moved back to Germany. Made signs with his hands about Ollie's size the last time he saw him, the size of him now. Slowly, Ollie warmed to the stranger, felt an easiness enter the room on the man's arrival, the crust of unfamiliarity sloughed with each visit until Ollie began to look forward to them, to the reprieve they offered from the stifling presence of his mother.

Herman called on them most days, came for dinner and cooked the meat. He bought a cottage two streets away, and Ollie started to spend time there; at first under the guise of helping with chores like chopping wood, as if Herman with his one stiff leg could not manage the task himself. Within months Ollie was staying there most nights.

'You mustn't abandon her,' his uncle said, as though it were up to Ollie to atone for whatever sins his father had committed.

But Ollie and his mother were estranged in their house, each of them refusing to bend to the will of the other, and so the air when he stayed there was stained, bitter with his mother's lies and denial and Ollie's contempt for what he saw as dishonesty or weakness, perhaps both. In the end they arrived at a truce: dinner on Tuesdays and Thursdays, and lunch on Sundays; Ollie going there straight from school during the week to peel the potatoes.

On those afternoons his mother's house was all yeast and Ollie had to throw open the windows to be able to breathe. He wondered if one day he'd arrive to find his mother suffocated, shrouded in the thick of swollen dough that would ooze out the door when he opened it.

When it became clear that Ollie was living with Herman permanently, his uncle called a meeting. Poured them a stein each and pulled out a blank piece of paper.

'These are the rules,' he said, and pushed the sheet of paper across the table. Herman cleared his throat and motioned for Ollie to pick up the pen. 'First you do your homework. I will help you with the arithmetic. The rest you will have to work out for yourself.' Herman pulled his chair closer to the table. 'Second, no beer until homework is done.'

Ollie wrote the rules down.

'Actually, change that.' He laughed. 'No beer for Ollie until homework is done.'

Ollie waited, pen poised, and Herman reached across the table and laid his hands on Ollie's forearms. Then he crushed the piece of paper into a ball and threw it in the fire.

'Let's just be good to each other, alright?' He lifted his stein. '*Prost.*'

They drank to it.

One day when his uncle finished work at the bank they walked around to Ollie's mother's house. Having filled her bread orders for the local shops, she'd replaced her baking apron with her dinner apron and was preparing the evening meal. Ollie went out to her backyard to split logs.

His mother's clipped tone leaked out the kitchen door. 'It's good of you to help him, but he needs to come home.'

'A boy needs a father, Gerte,' Herman said.

Ollie rested the axe on the chopping block and listened as his mother stormed out of the front door, slamming it behind her.

He and Herman finished cooking the cabbage, sat and waited a while then ate plates of cold pork and vegetables before washing the dishes and covering his mother's plate, putting it in the oven to warm.

They walked home in silence and, with each step, Ollie felt himself splitting from his mother, as if stepping into a new skin. At the entrance to Herman's house, his uncle stopped and enveloped him in a hug. 'She'll come round,' Herman said.

And she did. Perhaps not because she wanted to but because Ollie refused to buckle, and Herman would not try to make him.

Their routine continued over the years. Gerte stopped complaining about Ollie's absence, kept her words about his father to herself. But Ollie knew by the reek of yeast that permeated every fibre of her house that his mother could not let go. It was comfort and pain. The thing that bound her to the life they'd had before.

Some nights when the three of them ate at his mother's house, they chewed on her grief in silence. Swallowing like an act of hiding, a way to distil the life that was lost.

Life was good with Herman. Warm, amiable. Ollie had school, and Herman went to work, had friends over on Friday night for poker. He taught Ollie how to use his smokehouse. To prepare the salmon, fill sausage skins so they didn't burst. Herman taught Ollie the things that a father should teach his son, and every evening before bed the two of them sat together and read, played backgammon. They joked, accommodated one another, and when Ollie needed to behave badly Herman let him. As long as there was an apology at the end, they were okay. When he was at Herman's, Ollie tried not to think of his mother, barely thought of Papa at all.

Ollie had finished school, was working as a labourer for one of Herman's friends, when his mother had a stroke. He and Herman had dinner with her on the Sunday, and the next time he saw her was in a hospital bed, the left side of her face slack and useless, her eyes blank. He took over her baking obligations, supplied the local shops with their regular orders and thought about moving back into her house to care for her when she returned home, but her recovery was scant, her body half limp, and she could no longer swallow food or speak. The doctors said it would take time, that they should not lose hope, but she would need extensive rehabilitation and, although she was in her forties, the best place would be the aged care facility in the next village.

To start with, Ollie visited every day. Then days strung together and he couldn't make himself do it. His mother diminished; the robust scope of her gave way to reveal a woman who was slight and frail, stooped. Her eyes were perpetually blank. She showed no sign of recognition and so his visits comprised him moving her pillows around then sitting on her bed and talking about the way the dough had risen, how well the loaves had turned out. He wondered then if he'd been too hard on his mother, if this might be some kind of sign that it was time for kindness, for deeper understanding. Sitting there, wiping drool from her chin, he yearned for the days when she would tell him he was a keen watcher, an even better listener. Back then, he'd only wanted her to say that he was good, strong and smart. He ought to have understood that, for her, the virtues she saw in him were the very best of things.

The day before he left Germany, Ollie got up early, baked a loaf of his mother's darkest rye. If it brought her back he would stay. He put the bread to her nose and waited for her to breathe in the aroma but nothing happened, and so he kissed her on each cheek and took the loaf with him, drew the yeasty smell into his nostrils then dropped it in the bin. The following morning, Herman saw him off at the train station and, as the train pulled away from the platform, he stuck his head out the window and yelled, '*Danke, Papa.*'

One of Herman's poker friends had talked about the beaches of southern Portugal, and Ollie thought it would be as good a destination as any. He would take his time but that was where he would go and once he got there, well, then he would see.

First he took a train to France, moved from one village to another. He hiked in the mountains, stopped here and there, and slowly, without plan, weeks bled into months and became years. Relationships worked then didn't. He picked grapes, milked brebis sheep in the French Pyrenees, fell into short- and long-term arrangements, lived with families, and slept draped over his pack in the corners of train stations.

He corresponded with Herman through it all. Once a month, he sent a postcard and, when it was possible, he collected letters in return through poste restante. In his letters, Herman asked if Ollie was well, gave brief news of Gerte, questioned when Ollie might be coming home. *Soon*, Ollie replied, *soon*.

Ollie spent a year making German breads in a small hotel on the northern coast of Spain, where more than once he thought he spotted his father walking ahead of him, turning a corner. Eventually, he gave up tapping startled strangers on the shoulder, decided to head to Portugal. By the time he arrived in the Algarve, it was three years since he'd left Germany.

He had been in Portugal for four months and had just arrived at Faro when Herman made contact to say Gerte had died. There was no point coming back. The funeral was over, his mother already in the ground.

'*Das tut mir leid*,' Herman whispered down the phone line.

'*Danke, Papa. Danke.*'

That night, Ollie drank too much beer. Had sex on the beach with a girl from Australia. Crawled away when they'd finished and vomited in the sand.

'Thanks for the endorsement,' she said and laughed.

'My mother just died.'

'Christ.' The girl stroked his face, tucked his hair behind his ear and he fell asleep.

When he woke the beach was strewn with people, and the girl had gone. A note was carved into the sand beside him: the word 'thanks' framed by a love heart.

The Australian girl had spoken of golden beaches, itinerant farm work. Ollie thought he should go home, but Herman said perhaps he'd retire at the end of the year, visit Ollie instead, wherever he might be. And so Ollie took a job on a cargo boat. Wound up off the coast of Darwin on a prawn trawler for six months, until he was salt-crusted and could no longer discern the scent of yeast on his skin.

By the time he made it to Tasmania, Ollie had been in Australia for two years, done stints picking watermelons, carving out paths in rainforested national parks, building timber-framed edging and stone steps. Somewhere along the way he picked up the local habit of adding 'eh' to the end of his sentences as though everything were a question. But he still struggled to understand the accent, the words running together and cut short.

After the north Australian tropics, the wildness of Tasmania's rugged hiking tracks was a revelation. Ollie walked deep in the bush, rolled out his swag wherever he could find a clearing. The smell of eucalypt on his skin, under his nails. He was fascinated by unfamiliar creatures: spiny echidnas swinging their hinds from side to side; rock wallabies, heads lifted, staring at him.

Determined to make it from one end to the other, he drove through Geeveston, took the corrugated gravel road into Cockle Creek and crossed the single-lane bridge. He camped in a sheltered clearing by the sea and spent three days resting, swimming, watching the sea wash inland to join the tannin-stained lagoon, separate then return again.

He went for a walk.

'You right there, love?' A white-haired woman in a sundress was stacking wood at the front of a shack.

Ollie was startled. Had thought he was there alone. Was grateful he'd pulled on underpants after his swim. 'I am going for a hike.'

'The Cape?'

Ollie nodded.

'Right, then. Take it easy.'

Ollie packed his gear and began the walk out to South Cape Bay. Undulating trails through lightly wooded forest, exposed roots underfoot, then the headlands, wind throwing itself hard and unrelenting across the terrain, and button-grass heads leaning away from the coast. He waded through mud and took in a watery-eyed view of the Great Southern Ocean. Stopped at the top of the vertiginous trail to Lion Rock. Used a stick to scrape the mud off his boots and made his way down the hill and along the stony beach towards the campsite.

When he arrived, he dropped his pack and walked onto the slabs of stone that faced Lion Rock. He was bending to run his fingers along the outline of a crop of mussels when he lost his footing – legs out from under him, pain piercing his side. He rolled onto his back, took sharp, shallow breaths and felt down his torso, his fingertips finding a rough stick. He held his breath, pulled hard. Put pressure on the wound. Warm soak of blood.

He lay there for a long time, tried to gauge how bad it might be. It felt as though he may have punctured a lung. He told himself he was being dramatic. Surely it was a small hole, a minor thing. World spinning, he managed to half sit.

It was hard to say how long it took him to get back to the campsite. He'd done it mostly on his hands and knees. Stops to breathe, to concentrate on staying conscious. It was impossible to escape the assault of the cold, unrelenting wind, and so Ollie resigned himself to walking back. Knee-deep in water, he dragged his legs through the button grass.

It was late, dark. The bush was alive with activity, the shining eyes of wallabies and owls; Ollie felt less alone. He couldn't stop shivering. He unfurled the swag and did his best to climb inside but the penetrating cold was like a fire in his bones.

He slept in snatches. Spikes of pain radiating down his side. He heard the swoosh of the waves or his own pulse, throbbing through his body, pushing blood from his wound.

By daybreak Ollie was hot and shivering. Shock or hypothermia; he wasn't sure, couldn't think straight. His uncle's voice speaking German; a remembered dream or delirium? He made himself stand, had to hold on to a tree to stay upright.

When he tried to roll up his swag, a fresh wash of blood oozed through the bandages he'd applied and he felt as though he might pass out, conceded that his swag would have to be left behind. Step by step he made his way back towards Cockle Creek.

As he approached the old woman's shack, his legs were all bends and soft joints, his head barely lifted from his chest.

'Christ. Look at you,' she said.

His beard was matted with muck; his arms felt nailed to his torso, his right side sticky and swollen.

'Lean on me.' She slipped in beside him, wound her arm around his back and directed him into the house.

Ollie sank to the floor.

It was dark outside when he woke. He was covered in a blanket, his clothes thrown over a drying rack by the fire.

'Take these.' The woman held two pills in her hand, put a glass of water to his lips. 'The wound was filthy. I've washed it best I could but you're going to need these.'

Ollie swallowed the tablets, disappeared into oblivion.

The next time he woke it was morning. A dog was snoring alongside him.

'Hungry?' the woman asked.

The dog looked up.

'I know you are, you mangy mutt. You're always bloody hungry.' She leant down and scratched the dog behind the ears.

She brought in steaming bowls of stew. Waited for Ollie to manoeuvre himself into a sitting position and gave him a bowl and spoon.

'*Danke.*' He almost swallowed the word together with the knot of emotion in his throat. 'I'm Ollie.'

'Agnes, and this fat mutt is Dog.'

Ollie wasn't sure if he could eat, but once the first spoonful hit his tongue he continued, the dog standing expectantly next to him.

'I'd have moved you to the spare bedroom, but you're a bit bloody heavy for me.' She chuckled. 'Thirsty?'

He nodded and Agnes left the room, returned with a long neck of Mercury cider and poured them a glass each.

'Medicinal.' She smiled and handed him a glass. 'Want some more?'

Suddenly, his eyelids were heavy and Agnes was helping him lie flat. Checking his bandages, pulling a blanket back over him.

The next two days continued much the same. Agnes kept the fire going, checked and dressed Ollie's wound, fed him antibiotics, stew and homemade bread. She brought him a bucket to piss in, emptied the thing without comment. Organised for the ranger to pick up Ollie's swag.

By the third day, the heat was gone from Ollie's wound and he was able to get up. Found Agnes outside, wallaby strung up, knife poised. He stood in the doorway and watched the grace with which she deftly separated body and skin as though she were undressing the thing.

'My girls always hated seeing this.'

When he drove off later that day, he took with him a feeling that seemed deeper than gratitude, made a promise to return to Cockle Creek. He would bring packets of Tim Tams and Agnes would teach him to skin.

Ollie took the short ferry ride from Kettering to Bruny Island and drove straight to Adventure Bay. He bought supplies and a postcard with a picture of a whale on it, sent it to Herman with the words *Alles ist gut*. He camped a night or two at different places with just his swag, some bread and a knob of salami. Fell into sleep to the sound of thin-lipped waves washing up the beach.

One night he camped at Periwinkle Bay, dreamt of waves lapping at his legs, woke to a king tide pushing its way towards the treeline like an advancing army. Dragged his swag up into the native grasses and tried to find a place between clumps that was long and flat enough, but the spaces between were narrow, winding tracks fashioned by wildlife. In the end, he slept in the back of his truck, feet wrapped in a towel and, for the first time, he dreamt in English.

In the morning, the sun was squinting between clouds. He stretched his swag out the length of the truck's tray and weighted it down at each end to let the sun do its work. He was driving along the isthmus of the island when the steering wheel spun from his hands and his truck pulled suddenly to the left. Ollie had to fight the wheel as the tyres slid in the gravel at the edge of the narrow road.

Car jack wound up to full height, he was twisting the tyre iron and removing nuts when a guy around his age pulled over and climbed out of his ute, introduced himself as Harry. Rubbing the tip of his chest-length beard, Harry ran commentary, slow broken-off words and morphed consonants, as if he were speaking a language altogether different from English, like his was the quintessential Australian accent, if there were one.

Ollie stayed at Harry's for months. Swag under the stars next to Harry's greyed timber outdoor table. He traced the outline of the stars each night, arm fully extended. Went to sleep when his arm muscles started to shake and he could no longer feel his fingers. Couldn't imagine why anyone would want to leave this place.

One night, after more weed than either of them had needed, he thought he saw the Southern Lights, but Harry, laid out flat on the table, said it was just the weed, that no-one ever saw the Southern Lights.

'Gotta have a special lens,' Harry said.

Ollie wondered if the Southern Lights might be something made up, an attempt at balance in celestial displays by this place at the bottom of the earth. He wanted to talk about it, but Harry got started on India. Ran his mouth about the heat and noise, blaring music and putrid smells from makeshift dumps and trainside shitting grounds.

'It's like an attack, you know. Assault on the senses.'

Ollie let himself imagine the aurora as Harry mellowed and started speaking in a way that seemed almost a hum. He floated on Harry's memories of the Himalayas.

'Like waking up on top of the bloody world. Fair dinkum, mate, it's like you're a god.'

Harry had more words than seemed reasonable that night and Ollie let them run over him, until finally the meaning of every word pulsed through him in a way that could be understood, and Ollie thought he knew what Harry meant about being a god.

'It's a pain in the arse,' Harry said, when Ollie admitted he was thinking about living on the island. 'Gotta wait for the ferry. Don't even get priority. Not so bad in winter but when the tourists come across in summer it's a bloody nightmare.'

'I could buy a boat.'

They were passing a joint between them and Ollie took a drag.

'Yeah, a tinny'd be great for fishing and all of that. But what are you gonna do when you get to the other side? Walk to Hobart?' Harry laughed, spluttered on smoke and collapsed into a coughing fit.

Eventually, Ollie settled on a plot of land in Kettering. Used most of what was left from his inheritance and bought the kite-shaped block more for its view than the thing itself.

It seemed important that the house was made of timber, that it was tucked into the trees, facing out to the Channel. If he wasn't going to live on Bruny, Ollie was going to look at it, wake up to the view across the bay. He'd get a boat and have the best of both worlds. And when the place was finished, he'd convince Herman to visit, convince him to stay.

Harry helped Ollie peg out the boundary, borrowed a star dropper and they thrust posts deep into the earth, set them in place with concrete, and marked out distances for star pickets, bound the lot of it together with wire.

By the time the A-frame was built, Herman was unwell; lungs thick with disease, he was too sick to travel. Ollie said he'd go back to Germany, but Herman said no. Ollie imagined Herman alone in his house. Some nights, he thought he could feel Herman there beside him, felt his own lungs swell as though the acrid yeast of his mother's stubborn unwillingness to move on had contaminated both of them.

In the end, Ollie had to build the smokehouse on his own. Carefully followed the plans his uncle had drawn, putting his hands in the places where his uncle's might have been.

When Ollie fired up the smokehouse for the first time, Harry came over and they sat under the old gum on logs that Ollie had fashioned into stools. It felt just like it had with his uncle – sitting there, talking or not, drinking beer.

Harry had just found out he had a son and, when Ollie asked him what he was going to do about it, Harry took a sip of his beer then got up and pressed mortar into a fissure where a wisp of smoke was curling into the air.

The day the first of the smoked salmon was ready, Ollie rose early and made dough. Lit the woodstove and opened all of the doors and windows, waited for the dough to leaven. Then he tore it into pieces and fashioned and baked love-knot rolls. Thought about the way his mother had tried to live her life by the one recipe.

Midmorning, he sat down to a feast of smoked salmon and fresh love-knot rolls, butter flecked with minced onion the way Herman liked it. Ollie looked across the Channel to Bruny Island and, as he swallowed the first mouthful, he closed his eyes and remembered the pulse of his uncle's fingers resting on his forearm. The gentle, deep tones of Herman's voice: 'Let's just be good to each other.'

When the news came, Ollie flew to Germany, couldn't fathom why he hadn't done so earlier. He found his uncle's house exactly as it had been when he left, as though Ollie had walked down to the shops for supplies only hours before.

He sat at the kitchen table and set up the backgammon board, filled a stein with beer. Poured another then another. That night, he slept in the single bed in his old room, his mother's crocheted shawl pulled up under his chin.

It took three weeks to pack Herman's belongings, arrange to sell the house furnished, arrange his own mind. Memories clicked together, lapped over one another, and some nights Ollie woke in a frenzy not knowing whether he'd dreamt of his father or his uncle, his mother or Agnes; a blend of German and English that he felt unable to translate.

The ceremony was on the outskirts of the village. The poker men, hunched and wiry, strained under the weight of the coffin while Ollie stood by the trench in the earth. They buried Herman on the edge of the Black Forest in a place where the light was filtered and kind, and the yeasty air smelt of life itself.

Stone

WALDE CLIMBED OUT OF THE rivulet, stumbled and dug his heels into claggy earth, mewling kid tucked tight under his arm. Its tiny hooves drummed the air, damp body warm against him.

He was at the ridge when Liesl knocked him sideways. He caught the ground with one hand, placed the kid down with the other and sat in the mud laughing, as the kid scooted under Liesl and began to suckle. Walde lay back and let the damp soak his flannel shirt to his skin, like the first layer of papier-mâché to a balloon. He listened to the sucks and groans of the kid and watched the sky move from ash to the palest blue. It reminded him of duck eggs, the colour of their whites, which were really always blue. Like snow, if you looked at it properly.

He picked his path across the property, grass licking at his ankles, brushing against the muck that coated his woollen socks. He turned back to look at the track he'd made, tall blades of grass flattened by his mud-laden boots.

Near the house, his girls wove around his feet, a cacophony of appeals. Walde shook his head, reached into his pockets and threw chicken pellets in an arc, watched the girls dash as if their lives depended on it, as if he hadn't thrown pellets only half an hour before.

There was a harmony in his tribe, but at the centre Walde felt a kernel of loneliness that refused to abate, as if there were some place reserved for human connection. It had begun, he thought, after his father had left, his mother pouring hope down her throat one bottle at a time. Walde pressed himself into the corner of the room, watched her – wanting to be near her, not wanting to be with her. Now the space inside him felt as natural as a limestone cavern – hard, empty, but almost beautiful. It had been a long while since there'd been someone to fill the space.

'You're never going to love me, Walde,' Phoebe had said before she left, her face puffy and red from crying. Although Walde had wanted to reassure her, wanted to ask her to stay, he was afraid to allow the space in him to be permanently filled. He'd begun to feel crowded out, claustrophobic.

He'd watched through the window as she walked down the drive with the last of her boxes and climbed into her mother's car. When he could no longer see or hear the car carrying her away, he went outside and sat on the step, drew one of the girls onto his lap and ran his hands down her feathers.

'You understand, don't you?' he said, bending to kiss the chicken's wobbly red comb.

When Phoebe moved in it had felt like a miracle. Walde would wake expecting her to be gone, incredulous that this living, breathing human seemed to want him. For a time they were happy, fell into an easy routine of morning sex, coffee, omelettes: the kind of life that belonged to other people. Walde felt the whisper of memory: his parents holding hands when they were in Poland, or perhaps in the early days in Tasmania, before the promise of their new life had given way and all that was left between them was cheap vodka, accusations and vitriol.

Walde remembered his mother, ruddy-faced, pointing her finger. 'Do not expect, Walde. Do not expect.' He'd only been eight, maybe nine, and he hadn't yet known what she meant. But he remembered the places where her dress had worn thin, the way the other mothers stood aside when she dropped him at school, and he recalled that bag of someone else's clothes left at their doorstep; his mother's fury. Her standing in the shared laundry, hands over her ears, screaming.

Walde had met Phoebe at a site in Salamanca. He'd been asked to do some restoration work on Kelly's Steps. A lecturer from the university was overseeing the abutting archaeological dig and asked Walde if he could bring his students over. Would Walde show them what he did, have a chat? He didn't much like talking to people, but the bloke had asked nicely, and Walde found it impossible to say no.

The day the students visited was grey; there were supposed to be eight but only four turned up, and Walde was relieved.

The lecturer introduced him to the students, and Walde, embarrassed, smiled then turned back to the stone. He worked and, as he did, he talked to them. He was surprised that his spiel came instinctively, like a chef on one of those cooking shows his mother used to watch on daytime television. Walde smiled as he remembered his mother sprawled on the sofa eating toast with melted cheddar, writing out recipes she'd never cook.

'How do you decide what to fix?' Phoebe had asked.

It was the first insightful question he'd been asked in a long time and Walde turned to her. The students were all crowded around him, and he was talking and demonstrating like it was perfectly natural.

At the end of that morning, Phoebe and one of the other students asked if they could come back the next day. When Walde arrived, Phoebe was already there. By the end of the week, she was in his bed – thin legs covered in fine blonde hairs, breasts like fried eggs. He began to feel as though it might be himself he was restoring.

The early weeks were laden with new routines. They walked, looked after the girls, Phoebe went to university, and he went to work building walls and fireplaces and cottages of stone. Then, at the end of the year, Phoebe finished her course and got a job with the museum down near the docks in Hobart. Clear summer nights stretched long and light, and Phoebe begged him to come up and join her for drinks after work, but that would mean other people, and Walde wasn't good with crowds, had never known what to say. He always felt under scrutiny.

He didn't mind the driving, offered to pick Phoebe up. They arrived at a kind of stand-off: she asked him to join her, he offered to collect her. Neither acquiesced and some nights Phoebe didn't come home, stayed with a friend in Hobart, hitched a ride back down to the rivulet sometime the following day so they could make one another suffer for a while until they found themselves making love again in the mornings and things returned to normal.

One morning in bed Phoebe rolled over, ran her fingers through the tangles of his beard. 'I looked it up and I don't think you can be claustrophobic *and* agoraphobic at the same time. I mean, I think you have to choose, Walde.'

He kept his mouth closed, aware of his morning breath, then shifted onto his back. 'Oh.' It came out like the rippled waves you sometimes see set in the roofs of caves.

Inside his house, Walde warmed his fingers in the glow of the electric hotplate and imagined it was a fire. He made instant coffee, topped it with goats' milk and sat at the small laminate table, let his mug make a fresh coffee stain on the latest bill from the electricity company. After this job, he'd have enough money for the solar panels.

He sipped his coffee and mapped out his day. He'd have another cup then give the girls the scraps and leave them to it. On the drive over to the job, he'd rev the Holden hard whenever he had to stop, try to ease the gritty shift between first and second gears and hope the thing would get him there, get him home again. When he got back, he'd milk Heidi then drag open the gate to the laying boxes and collect the eggs. For dinner he'd cook up a pot of dhal and sit on the back step and talk to his girls, listen to them *tok* and *kwak* as he scraped a spoon across his plate. If the dhal was good, he'd lick the plate clean, drag long lines with his tongue until he'd covered the entire surface. Then he'd rinse the plate in the sink and lie down and wait for sleep to take him.

On the way to the job he felt the old darkness grow in his chest, and he wondered why he hadn't been able to make it work with Phoebe, why he'd been so afraid when she'd begun to fill the space so completely.

He should have brought one of the girls with him, sat her on his lap to try to soak away the black, but the girls always shat everywhere and there was nowhere to put them once he arrived at a job. He pulled a lamb's wool jumper from his bag and lifted it to his nose to breathe in the smell of lanolin, then he bunched it in his lap and pretended that a heart beat within it. He tried to concentrate on the aroma, the imagined pulse, but memories pushed through. Reaching up to touch his fingers to the underside of his father's coffin, his mother's crumpled form in the corner of their bedsit and the stench of her vomit-crusted hair. And earlier, way before: inside a suitcase, legs numb, the hot dampness of breath and urine, and the overwhelming need for space as some stranger carried him, folded and tucked, across the border. He remembered the sharp return of feeling to his limbs, searing light, and then the relief on his parents' faces in the place that was not Poland.

The relief hadn't lasted. If only he could have captured that feeling, held on to it. If only they all could have.

The claustrophobia from the border crossing burgeoned, was compounded by night terrors and panicked impulses that made it impossible for him to go to school, impossible for him to go anywhere, impossible for him to be soothed by anything other than the cold, hard curves of the stone walls of their miner's cottage.

Then his father won Ida in a bet at the pub. Ida was supposed to be killed and plucked, she was supposed to be roasted, but Walde's mother was busy tending to his younger sister and pushed the chicken towards Walde. Ida was still on Walde's lap when his father, having finished his cigarette, came back in from the street and his mother returned from the bedroom carrying his sister.

'Will you look at that,' his father said, and his mother jiggled Kylie on her hip and chanced touching Walde's hair. They ate roast vegetables and boiled peas with gravy for dinner.

Walde thought of all the other pets they'd had in those years that he now marked as the happy years. But, as always, it ended in the same place – brought him to his father's accident, his mother's breakdown. And there he was again, pressed into the corner, pressed inside that suitcase.

Walde went to turn on the radio. Remembered it hadn't worked in ages, remembered he'd stopped trying to fix it a while ago. Thought he remembered the soothing music of his grandmother's gramophone back in Poland, but he'd been so small and it didn't seem likely. For a long time, while he drove, he'd been making his way through the songs from *The Sound of Music*. In the beginning he'd sung, but he could never recall the words, so he'd moved to whistling. It was slow progress, his range limited to a couple of unreliable octaves, but it passed the time and it felt like company.

The job was in Kettering. They were the kind of people who made a lot of noise about it. Wanted to get involved, as though observing could teach them the skills and eye he'd spent twenty years acquiring. He preferred to work for the registered builders. Not that he had any time for paperwork or rules, but those blokes left you alone, didn't need to check every stone laid. They just wanted the job done.

Walde liked it best when he was alone with the stone. He made a point of leaving something of himself behind – a sliver of hangnail, a whisker, sometimes a piece of rolled-up snot. It wasn't for the people; mostly he didn't think about them after he'd finished a job. It was for the works themselves. It was some kind of continuity, a way of being a part of them as much as they were a part of him.

Fireplaces were his favourite; there was something about heating a thing so solid and heavy. He imagined himself in the flames, imagined himself in the smoke that would lift from the chimney or cling in soot to its walls. It was his way of flying, another way to remain.

'You should come for dinner,' Rob said, as he stood too close.

Walde didn't know how to respond. He dipped his trowel into the mortar bucket and spread the thick, grey slurry on the side of a stone then pressed the next stone into place, tapping and scraping until he was satisfied.

'How 'bout Thursday?' Rob continued.

He looked up, couldn't think of an excuse. 'Okay.'

Walde washed his hair, found the nailbrush in the laundry trough and scrubbed his nails until the ends of his fingers felt raw. Dressed in a clean flannelette shirt and the least dirty pair of overalls he could find. He took some eggs and a pint of goats' milk from the fridge.

'Glad you could come.' Rob opened the door wider and invited him in, handed him half a glass of beer.

'Lynn'll be back soon. She's picking Hannah up from gymnastics.'

Walde took a sip, wiped the froth from his beard and nodded.

'Bloody nice work you're doing here. Really nice.' Rob gestured towards the half-formed fireplace.

Walde felt the skin on his face prickle, like every hair in his beard was being pulled. He looked down, dragged his socks against the seagrass matting. 'Thanks.'

Light swept across the room, the sound of car doors slamming, the high-pitched voice of a child. Walde felt relieved for the distraction from scrutiny.

'Ah, you're here already.' Lynn's smile traversed the landscape of her face in a wide arc. The effect was strange, almost a caricature, but her extended hand was small, smooth and firm, like the best kind of stone. He resisted the temptation to rub his finger across the top of it, trace its contours, search its textures through touch. Behind his ribs, emptiness evanesced.

'You're making our fire?' A wiry girl ducked under Rob's arm, looked up at Walde.

'I am.'

'Will you ever be finished?'

'Don't be rude, Hannah,' Lynn said.

'I wasn't.'

'It's hard to tell. Sometimes you have to wait for the fireplace to tell you it's done,' Walde said.

'That's weird,' Hannah said.

'Knock knock,' Walde said.

'Who's there?' Hannah asked.

'Goat.'

'Goat who?'

'Got to be a bit weird if you want to have fun.'

Hannah grinned. 'You must be lots of fun then.'

'I think all the best people are weird,' Lynn said, running her hands across the stones Walde had laid earlier that day.

He felt the seagrass matting shift like a wave beneath his feet.

'Hope you like curry. Rob's made vindaloo; it's his specialty.'

Rob pulled on oven gloves and carried a casserole dish to the table.

'Please, Walde, take a seat,' Lynn said, placing cutlery and serving spoons around the crockery. 'Can I get you another drink? We have wine or beer.'

'Yes. Thanks.' He scratched his fingers through his beard.

Lynn laughed, a soft laugh like a sigh, came back with a long neck of beer and three fresh glasses. 'For curry, beer is the best.' She flicked off the bottle top and poured their drinks.

He noticed the easy way she'd made the head on each beer the exact same depth. He ate his curry and they talked about country life, but mostly they talked about the fireplaces he'd made over the years. He rode the buzz of the beer, and for a while it felt like he was important in the world.

The road on the way home was smooth and curvy, like a

slowed-down roller-coaster. Walde cranked up the heating and pulled the lamb's wool jumper across his legs while he waited for the air to warm. Through the windshield, skinny trees silhouetted against the charcoal undulations of the land, like the paper-cut models his grandmother made for him when he was tiny, before they left Poland.

Dense fog hovered just ahead like an ever-retreating shroud. It hid the road, obscured its edges and filled the crevasse of the creek. When the moon snuck behind cloud, Walde almost missed his turn. The neighbours complained about the mist, reckoned it was dangerous, hated the frost that came with it. But he loved the way it snaked into the creases of the land, like a puff of smoke from a dragon's throat.

Once home, he checked on the girls then made himself a mug of tea, sat on the back step and replayed the night in his head. Hannah saying, 'You're weird', and the small gauge of Lynn's wrists, the way she tilted his glass. The perfect symmetry of the beers. He imagined rubbing his fingers across the stones where her pressure had been, checked his chest for signs of the empty place and imagined stalagmites growing in the cavern there, reaching for human connection.

Chainsaw

It rained all night, like stones against the corrugated iron roof. Lynn tucked the quilt under her chin and stared at the timber ceiling, at the knot she used to watch some nights when Rob had drunk too much and it felt as if he might press on for hours, way after she had lost interest.

She ran her hand across the sheet where Rob used to lie, checked for the impressions of his body, but the mattress felt flat. Outside, the pre-dawn calls of wattlebirds counted out her heartbeats, like the notes of an ancient song.

It had taken months for Lynn to get used to the quiet, to stop putting her hands on Rob's favourite foods at the supermarket. And still it felt impossible to accept that he was gone. Unbidden thoughts, the trace of her fingers on his skin, the hairs that had grown on his back as he'd got older, the wide grin that made her chest leap when she'd first seen him standing in the doorway of a hut on the Overland Track. He'd been holding a mug with two hands, wisps of steam dancing in front of his face.

Lynn ate breakfast at the outdoor table, her back to the view of the Channel, and stared into the place below the lip of the hill where a wire fence carved a track through the land and divided their place from the Eddingtons'. She remembered Rob laughing. They'd just moved in, and Rob had pointed at the fence and told her it was stupid the way we divide up the world as if the divisions themselves gave meaning. She said she thought it was important to know where your limits were. Rob agreed that she might be right. It was in the early days, back when they still discussed important things, smiled at each other and meant it. She found him funny; he was still trying to figure her out. They didn't have Hannah yet.

From the beginning, Rob had loved their girl with a ferocity that surprised Lynn. He'd taught Hannah to fish and kayak, to whittle dolls and small animals from driftwood. She'd been Daddy's girl from the time she could walk. But when Hannah hit high school she morphed, moved further and further away until it felt as though she could hardly stand to breathe the same air as her parents.

Hannah stayed awake all night making mix tapes and playing them back to herself, refused to help out around the house, and informed them that she didn't believe in homework, or housework, or any kind of work. Not unless someone was paying and, as far as she could tell, nobody was. Infuriated, Rob refused to bend.

'She's getting older. We need to give her some leeway,' Lynn reasoned, but Rob shook his head.

'No, Lynn. She needs to know who's the boss.'

By the end of year eight, Hannah was a shape shifter and they never knew which girl they would get. Compliant, almost serene, then bare-toothed, spittled shrieking. The vitriol when it came was incomprehensible and, at the height of those episodes, Rob would threaten to kick Hannah out as Lynn pleaded with both of them to stop.

And always, the morning after every fresh Armageddon, Hannah would behave as though none of it had happened. Go to school.

Come home on time. Set the table. Do the dishes. Sometimes the aura of calm stretched into weeks, but the more caustic episodes they endured, the longer it took for Rob to soften. Sometimes it was days before he could look at Hannah. Lynn, on the other hand, could barely look away from either of them. She feared she might be some kind of talisman that stopped everything from disintegrating.

Over the course of that first terrible year after Hannah changed, Rob and Lynn fell into fresh habits. Rob closed himself off from Hannah; Lynn leant in, tried to read the coming weather.

She began to sense when things were escalating. Hannah would get twitchy, overly sensitive, and Lynn would say to Rob, 'It's normal, this boundary pushing. She has to move away to come back.'

And it would all rise up again. Then, after, in those strange swathes of calm that followed, Lynn would say to Rob, 'See how she's coming back. More and more. Soon the other stuff will stop. We just need to wait.' Lynn was never sure who she was comforting.

The morning after Rob left, Lynn woke on the floor in front of faintly flickering coals, her mouth coated with booze and bile. Blue icing under her fingernails.

She didn't eat for three days. Felt so ill that she couldn't imagine the act of placing food into her mouth.

She didn't know where to put herself, felt the margins between herself and the world become porous. She went to the doctor for sleeping pills. In the waiting room she was agitated, paranoid, had to force herself to sit. She opened a magazine at an article on flooding.

That night, she dreamt Rob was swept away by rains, stranded on the only patch of dry land in kilometres. Somehow she found a boat but the oars had been washed away. She propelled the thing with her hands until her arms felt as though they no longer belonged to her. By the time she could get to him, all that was left were bones and scraps of mostly decomposed flesh and, though it made her sick to do it, she took his femurs and used them to row herself to safety.

The days rolled forward and Lynn languished, mind addled, limbs shaky and weak. It felt like penance with no clear notion of a focal point, without any reason to atone.

Lynn popped pills and rode waves of sedation. She moved chess pieces around the chessboard, tried not to think of those last days with Rob, tried to shift her grief to fury. She slept when she could, which was mostly in daylight. Woke at odd times with her head on the dining table, sun illuminating the room like fluorescent light, her hair plastered to her forehead with sweat.

One night she rotated the chessboard for hours, making moves for Hannah, then moves for Rob. She tried to keep score, but her brain couldn't hold the numbers, and she was too tired to look for pen and paper.

It's always the mother's fault. She'd read it, heard it more times than she could recall. She remembered Rob's accusation: 'You were always trying to fix things, always trying to make things into your version of right. If you'd just left her.'

'I don't know how to do this anymore' was the last thing he said before leaving. As though, despite all that had come earlier, the failing might, after all, be his.

Hannah was only in grade nine when she began to disappear, at first overnight then sometimes for days. Rob and Lynn had to swallow a new reality, accommodate something worse into their already fractured normality. Their lives were pocked with phone calls followed by long drives and, even when they found her, more often than not Hannah refused to come with them. Once, Rob tried to lift Hannah up, but let her drop to the ground when she tore tracks down his face with her fingernails.

Another time they drove until dawn, climbed in and out of the car, checked parks, public toilets, alleyways, recessed stone doorways down at Salamanca, behind dumpsters out the back of restaurants.

'She's made her choice, Lynn,' Rob said, on the drive back home.

'She's sixteen. Christ, Rob, she's still in high school.'

'Really? When was the last time she went?'

Lynn didn't have the energy for more so they passed the rest of the trip in silence; Rob flicking the high beams on and off in deference to the occasional oncoming car, Lynn with her face pressed to the cold window.

It was five in the morning when they got home, the sun a scant wavering line in the distance. Lynn put the kettle on.

'Sandwich?' Rob's peace offering.

'Thanks.' She kissed him on the cheek.

He took cheese and pickled onions from the fridge and carved thick slices of bread. They ate at the table, leaning on their elbows, and she tried to work out when and how this had become normal, wondered if they'd ever feel the shameless ripples of simple joy in their lives again.

After that, Rob hadn't gone with her to look for Hannah. The first time she had been sure he would change his mind. She sat in the car, engine idling for five minutes, before giving up and going alone. She didn't bother with the local streets, the beaches around Kingston and Blackmans Bay; she went straight to Hobart and shone her headlights into dim alleys, checked the Emergency Department at the Royal Hobart Hospital. When she arrived home, Rob got out of bed and turned on the kettle. Held her tight while she cried, as she purged the sizzling fury and fear. It was like a kind of madness, this need to know if Hannah was alive. But Rob was still and solid as he kissed her hair, cradled the back of her head in his hands, washed peace through her body.

Days later, when Hannah came home gaunt and apologetic, Rob went outside, didn't come back in until Hannah was in her room.

'You can't trust her, Lynn.'

Lynn smiled, tight-lipped.

He gestured towards the bedroom where Hannah was passed out. 'That's not our girl.'

Her hand shot out and Rob caught it before she could slap him. He folded her into his arms.

When Hannah next disappeared, Lynn battled the contagion of Rob's heavy cloak of pointlessness. She had trouble getting in the car, let alone leaving the property. Night after night she walked in her nightie and boots to the ridge of the hill and shrieked, 'Fuck!', holding the sound for as long as she could, expecting an echo, then remembering that nothing was certain anymore.

Beyond hope there was nothing she could do.

Rob's absence first hit her when she was lying in bed, her leg stretched across the space where he should be. He'd been gone for days, or it might have been weeks. Lynn felt hollowed out, loose limbed. She curled into herself and pressed Rob's pillow hard against her face, tried to imagine herself slipping away. Then Rob's voice or maybe Hannah's, somehow Hannah's, called to her. She felt the warm rush of hope, then it dropped away as she realised there was someone at the door. She pulled the pillow back onto her head, hoped whoever it was would go away.

When she woke next, it was morning again, and her stomach was growling. The living room felt unfamiliar, and she tried to remember when she'd last moved beyond the bedroom and bathroom. She must have eaten but she couldn't think when.

She looked at the wall calendar; three weeks had passed since Rob left and she wasn't sure how. She tried to think how many pills she had taken. Had a vague recollection of phoning work but couldn't recall the way it had gone, not exactly. She was eating toast when she saw the note: *milk and supplies in fridge, one of us will call in tonight, Sal and Gurj*. Then it dawned on her – the remnants of cake were gone, the dishes washed and stacked away. She remembered a conversation with Rob. She couldn't think when.

'You're always trying to peel things back, Lynn, like you think you could fix it if you could just get to the mechanics of it. But it doesn't work like that.'

'At least I'm trying. At least I'm not pretending it isn't happening.'

It was in the thick of the dark days. Hannah was sixteen and they'd just found out about the hard drugs. They'd thought it was as bad as it could be. But it had only been the beginning. Later, Hannah would turn wraith, become disconnected as she slipped deep into the slick drugged escape that would ultimately claim her life, all of their lives really.

Lynn finished her toast and put the kettle on for peppermint tea, slid two more slices of bread into the toaster and scraped butter across them when they were done. Her arms shook as she poured boiling water into a mug. She sat at the kitchen table, sunlight streaming across her face, down her arms. She kept making toast, kept eating until all that was left of the loaf were crusts. She thought how, if he were there, Rob would eat the crusts. Thought again of the day Rob left, every day after that he hadn't returned. It was like a film reel played in reverse, as though there were something more to reveal, some hidden meaning, the answer to where divergence had become an un-bridgeable chasm. Why Rob had noticed and Lynn had not.

The first night Rob didn't come home, Lynn knew she should be worried, but the place in her that was supposed to carry emotion felt dead and she didn't know if she had the capacity to make herself care. She felt sure he would return, was too tired to wait up and worry anymore. Sat instead on Hannah's bed and touched the things on her bedside table. The tiny butterfly set in resin, hair scrunchies and a half-used chapstick. The next day she woke buoyant, like someone had tapped a new bore and there it was: a stream of hope. Lynn was halfway out of bed when the fact of Hannah's death seized her anew. Then Rob's absence, like an anvil on her chest.

'We've got this. You and me, babe, you and me.'

She couldn't quite remember which of them had said it but she was sure that one of them had, or maybe she'd dreamt it. No, Rob had said it, definitely. It was early on when they still thought they could control things, rein Hannah back in. Well before they'd lost sight of the idea of things being fixed or restored.

Lynn thought about the last time Hannah and Rob were together. They were going to make a throne chair. Hannah had been clean for five weeks; she and Rob had begun to play chess in the evenings, and Lynn had said nothing, too afraid to break the possibility.

Rob and Hannah had sat by the fire and planned the chair until blackness leaked in through the windows and the flames from the woodfire threw shadows on the walls. Together they made calculations, discussed proportions, agreed on height and width. The following morning, Lynn watched from the house as the two of them felled the straightest, thickest gum tree on their property, and Lynn sensed the chance of trust. Later it would seem like a premonition, and Lynn wished she could have willed away the moment when rain had sleeted down and Rob and Hannah had run into the house laughing and drenched. If only she could have willed them back out into the storm to finish the task, the making of that tree into a throne might have rescued them all.

Lynn woke late, wished it were the weekend, that she could stoke the woodstove, drink a cup of peppermint tea and go back to bed with a book, let her eyes run across lines and pages until her arm sagged and her head nodded. Let herself do all of the things that she'd done to console herself since Rob left. But it was Tuesday and she had to go to work.

She turned on the heat lamps and waited for the water to get hot then dropped her robe and stood under the pelting showerhead, let the sensation wash away thoughts of a time when Rob would climb in behind her, hold her to him so that the water pooled between his chest and her shoulderblades. She hugged her arms about herself and felt the scant inadequacy of her ribs beneath her skin.

When she got to work, a huge ute had taken her parking space again. She felt a flicker of annoyance, let it fizzle. She parked in a space near the back of the car park, turned off the ignition and, eyes closed, inflated and deflated her chest until the hardness in her stomach began to dissipate and she slipped into that liminal space between wakefulness and sleep.

It was a typical day on the dementia ward with patients who were no longer themselves. Lynn avoided the advances of men in their nineties, cleaned up incontinence, fed, bathed.

Agnes was Lynn's last patient for the day. It was late in the afternoon and the old woman was agitated, pulling at her nightgown, words spilling out of her mouth, run together in an unintelligible stream. Lynn wasn't sure the woman was speaking English, wondered if it might be Gaelic. She wheeled her back to her room, tried to get her settled while the woman rocked and soothed the doll that she carried like a child.

When she finally got Agnes into bed, although she couldn't really be bothered, Lynn made a show of changing the doll's nappy. Agnes smiled, pawed at her nightgown.

'Oh.' Lynn closed the door to the room then reached across and undid the top two buttons of the elderly woman's nightgown, handed her the doll.

Cradling the doll in one arm, Agnes deftly dragged a pendulous empty breast free and put the doll's head to it then sat back serenely, eyes closed. Lynn sat at the end of the bed and waited for her to snore before gently slipping the doll from her arms, tucking her breast away and resting the doll next to the old woman's wasted body.

Lynn drove the road home on autopilot, tried to think of what she might eat for dinner but she hadn't been shopping for days. She parked outside the local shop.

'You look tired.' Sally was behind the counter.

'Thanks.'

Sally grabbed a chocolate bar from beside the register, tore the wrapper and offered it to her.

She broke off a square of chocolate and put it on her tongue to melt.

'How is everything?'

'Okay.' The word was flat and shapeless. 'It is what it is. I'll get there.' Lynn felt like a fraud; she'd always hated platitudes. Her stomach growled. She went to the fridge of homemade dinners, chose a tub of soup and took it to the counter.

'Shit. I almost forgot. This came for you.' Sally handed her a large yellow envelope, A4-sized, thick with papers.

Back at the house, Lynn stuck the soup in the microwave and got the fire going, wished she'd set it in the morning the way Rob used to. When the soup was hot, she sat down to eat. The fire was giving off that early, bright flame, more light than warmth.

She was halfway through her food when she remembered the envelope, took it from her bag and ripped the top off. Inside, a stack of papers. On the top, a document titled *Application for Divorce*. She dropped her spoon, a threshing sensation in her body. She'd felt it before, on the day of Hannah's funeral, in the weeks after, then again last year when Rob left.

The soup shifted in her stomach and she thought of the heat on the day they got married, Rob's grin when he picked her up and spun her around. Her shoe had fallen off and he'd joked that if the slipper fit she must surely be his Cinderella. At the time it had seemed so out of character, and she remembered the feeling that came after it, a momentary fear that now they were married things would change. They would, he would, she would. But it had only been that moment. It had taken Hannah to shift things.

Lynn started reading the legal papers. She cradled her head in her arms and wondered why she wasn't crying. She thought of the week after Rob left. Day after day, Lynn had curled like a foetus on the ugly carpet that he had bought at a garage sale on the way through Snug one Saturday morning, her face close enough to the fibres to breathe in their dust-ridden stench of age, the smell of Rob's feet.

There had been no logic to anything in her last frenzied week with Rob. It had begun with her trawling through photographs. It was almost Hannah's birthday, almost two years since her death. Rob was fixing the water pump in his car. Lynn finished the breakfast dishes, unfurled the Sunday newspaper and pretended to read, but the articles were insubstantial. Tokenistic coverage of important events, the only article of any depth was a one-page exposé on the massacre at Port Arthur and, following it, pages upon pages of local sport.

Lynn put the paper in the kindling box and took the photo albums from the bookshelf. She was sitting at the dining table, flicking through one of the early albums, working through memories. Hannah in her high chair, the three of them with chocolate-smeared grins. Rob and Hannah dressed as Peter Pan, Lynn as Wendy. She flicked through the years, looked at the three of them, arms around each other. Every year they'd given Hannah a special book: *The Very Hungry Caterpillar*, *The Velveteen Rabbit*, *Where the Wild Things Are*, *Adventures of the Wishing-Chair*. It was hard to tell where things had gone wrong.

Lynn picked up another album and opened it to Hannah's eighteenth. Hannah with a copy of *Metamorphosis* and a bottle of scotch, Lynn and Rob flanking her. Only two of them smiling.

Rob wasn't in any of the photos from Hannah's twenty-first. Only a few people Lynn hardly knew, and one shot of Hannah and her. Lynn's face tight. Before that, it had started well before that.

Lynn returned to the first album and, when Rob came in for coffee, she told him she wanted to recreate the ballerina cake she'd made for Hannah's fifth birthday. Rob shook his head and said it was a stupid idea, and they argued, raw and vicious, until he backed down and told her to make the fucking cake, make all of the fucking cakes. While Lynn was mixing batters in the kitchen, Rob, heavy footed, went in and out of the house.

Lynn took the week off, and five days later the fridge was filled with copies of each of Hannah's childhood birthday cakes. Lynn lined them along the bench by year, got stuck on the frog and Spiderman, had to consult the photo album to see which had been for Hannah's sixth birthday, which for her seventh.

'What do you think?' Lynn asked when Rob came in from work on the Friday.

He looked at her, made himself coffee, then sat at the kitchen table and stared at the cakes for longer than Lynn could bear. He got up and closed the door to Hannah's room.

'What are you doing?' Lynn started towards him.

'It's time, Lynn.'

'No.'

He stood in front of Hannah's bedroom door. 'Come on, Lynn. It's time.'

She looked at the cakes then back at Rob. 'Open the fucking door.'

In the morning, she woke to Rob dividing. She pushed the door to Hannah's room wide open and stood in the kitchen drinking coffee while he moved back and forth.

She watched as he made up boxes, packed half of the cups, half the plates. She watched him count out teaspoons.

'Really?' she asked each time he took a box out to the ute.

When he moved to Hannah's room, Lynn felt herself buckle. 'You've made your point,' she said, without knowing what it was.

Rob gathered things he'd given Hannah: a poster of Bob Marley, fossils, a box full of fishing floats that Hannah had thought looked like fairies.

'Why are you doing this?'

He kept his back to her.

'For fuck's sake, Rob. Put them back. Please.'

'It's only a few things.'

She stood in the doorway to Hannah's bedroom and watched, numb. A familiar mantra: *this cannot be happening, this cannot be happening*.

'It's for the best,' Rob said, as he pushed past her and took another box out to the ute.

When he came back in, she thought he might have changed his mind, but he went to the bookcase and started pulling out Hannah's books.

'Leave them.' Her voice was guttural.

'I just want *Where the Wild Things Are*. You can keep the rest.'

'No.' Lynn tried to get between Rob and the bookcase.

He pushed in front of her. 'Come on, Lynn, don't make this harder.'

'I don't know what you're doing. How did this happen? How the fuck did this happen?'

Rob stopped. 'I thought you'd move past it, Lynn. I thought we could move past it together but you're stuck. I think maybe you want to be stuck and I just can't do it anymore. I'm sorry. Really, I am.'

She listened to the sound of the ute's tyres on gravel until her ears hurt with the strain of trying. Sprawled on the carpet, she ate cake by the handful.

True beauty, Lynn had thought, lies in symmetry, but in the months after Rob left she began to feel the idea loosen in her. She became transfixed by incompleteness, the beauty of what had been left. She drew pictures in her mind, hooks for her memories. There was the cup she used for raspberry leaf tea that week she was overdue and thought she might be pregnant forever; the red-wine glasses filled with shiraz, futile attempts to soothe fractured nerves; and plates piled with food from friends, the ones who'd stuck around, were still there when finally Hannah died.

At her worst, Hannah had been a liar and a thief. At her best, she'd been infectious energy, with easy open smiles, the wire that bound them. For Lynn, she'd come to be everything, even after she was incapable of truth, after she'd spat in their faces, after she'd sold Lynn's engagement ring and Rob's grandfather's watch.

One night, when Hannah was nineteen, in one of those spells when they didn't know where she was, long after they'd stopped looking every time, Rob had said it was Lynn's fault. And he rubbed at his arms as though it was his skin shadowed with tracks.

Lynn went outside, walked the perimeter of the property, hand trailing along the barbed-wire fence. When she got back, Rob was sitting in front of the fire. Cold through, she rested her head on the mantelpiece and let blood drip down her hand.

'Fuck, Lynn, you'll stain the sheepskin.'

She went to the bathroom and sat on the edge of the bath,

watched her blood, thinned with water, wash down the drain. Rinsed herself away.

She bandaged her hand and dressed in the long nightie that she'd bought for Hannah one of the times she was in hospital, when they were still trying to fix her. The nightie was the old-fashioned kind that might look sweet or country on a woman with smaller breasts, but it made Lynn look huge and ridiculous.

She had lain in bed, knees pulled up, and imagined Hannah sleeping rough, or worse. She tucked her feet into the bottom of the nightie, like the sleeping sack her mother had made for Hannah when she was a baby.

When Rob came to bed, his breath smelt of beer and sardines, and she both hated him and wanted him near. She kept her eyes closed while he undressed, her breath soft and even, stayed very still, too still.

'I'm sorry, Lynn.' He pressed against her and wrapped his arm across her body then trailed his fingers up and down her forearm. 'I don't know why I said that.'

She wanted to keep her body taut but she felt her traitorous torso relaxing into him, like a caterpillar in its cocoon.

'Say something, Lynn. Tell me I'm a prick. Call me a cunt.'

Lynn thought of the time right after Hannah's death. She had known by his slumped posture that Rob was broken, but it hadn't occurred to her, until that week before he left, that they might not make it. She tried to remember if there had been signs of a permanent cleft but when she thought to pin it down she found, since Hannah died, she couldn't recall a single day, a single thing they'd done, a single thing they'd said. It was as though time had been woven so tightly that they'd been caught in one continuous thread — a space filled both with nothing and everything — and she honestly couldn't remember any of it, not properly.

She knew that they'd hunkered down after the funeral. Friends and colleagues dropped off meals and flowers, invited them for drinks, for dinner, but they couldn't bring themselves to go. They politely declined the offers that kept on coming. Small talk: it would be like swallowing nails.

Neither of them had gone to work. They barely ate. Hannah dead in the ground, and a fridge full of donated food gone to blue and green bloom. When they finally went back to their jobs, days were nipped at either end; no energy for anything unnecessary. Breathe in, breathe out.

Rob started going to work early, coming home late and drinking too much. He became the kind of cliché he'd always hated. Lynn could tell, by the way he jumped at the smallest of noises, that he was holding himself in, emotions roiling beneath a thin veneer. She must have tried something, though she couldn't remember what. Could only remember him telling her to stop.

The months bled into one another and before any time had passed at all it was Hannah's birthday again, almost a year since Rob had left. A letter arrived for Hannah: a new Medicare card with instructions for use, its expiry date in ten years. Lynn slipped the card into the back pocket of her jeans and, when she wasn't sure what to do with herself, she took the card out and ran her finger over the raised print of Hannah's name. Wondered again how she had missed the exact moment when everything began to go badly with Hannah.

On the way home from work the next day, Lynn flicked the radio to AM. A council on the mainland had made it possible to write letters to marked trees, to receive responses. Lynn thought of the throne tree. She'd always loved those log chairs, the idea of being cradled and held by the heft of a trunk that had grown from the ground, been anchored by long tendrilled roots.

The next morning, as soon as the sun splashed across the ground, Lynn dressed and walked down to the throne trunk. She tried to put her arms about its moss-covered girth then strode back to the house. She would lop the thing with the chainsaw and carve it into rounds to complement the chairs that Rob had left behind. Moulded steel chairs upholstered in orange vinyl together with carved chunks of tree. Hannah would have loved it.

YouTube videos made it look easy. Lynn watched them over and over. It was her legs she was afraid for. It would be so easy to slip, to remove a limb of her own. She practised holding the chainsaw to get used to the weight of it, then she took it into town and had it serviced.

'Dropping it off for the old man, eh, love?'

She wanted to tell the bloke where to shove it, asked instead when the chainsaw would be ready.

When she went in the next day a woman was serving, already had the chainsaw out before Lynn made it to the counter.

'All set to go?' The woman made it sound like a question.

'You tell me,' Lynn replied.

The woman shook her head, took Lynn's money and smoothed the notes neatly into the cash drawer.

Rob had barely used the chainsaw. The last time he'd bought railway sleepers to make raised garden beds when Hannah was fourteen and decided to become vegetarian. They'd planted all sorts of things while Lynn watched from the kitchen window, waiting for one of them to tire of it. They'd only just started to harvest when Hannah fell prey to fish fingers, suddenly couldn't help herself at a sausage sizzle, and the plans for more raised beds dissolved. The chainsaw, stowed in the shed, was forgotten.

The day was dry and clear, the sky a washed light blue. Lynn stood in front of the bedroom window and stretched towards the ceiling, fingertips almost grazing the top of the window frame. She bent her body to the left, then the right, and did some of the breathing exercises that she'd done with Hannah when she'd come back from one or another of her rehab sessions.

Lynn wanted to be naked when she carved the tree, to feel the warm envelope of air on her skin the way Hannah never could again, but she remembered the safety spiel on the videos and pulled on pants, a long-sleeved top and boots. She tried to find the protective goggles that Rob had bought, but they weren't in the shed.

She measured and marked the trunk, put on her sunglasses, fired up the chainsaw, and carved the trunk into sections, severed its limbs. She tried to carve a back but she didn't have the skill and so the first two chairs became stools.

It was late the next day that she rolled the final log into the house. Rudely made with chunky, ill-formed lines, the chair fitted perfectly into the space at the end of the table. She put a cushion on its seat then she lit the fire, poured herself a glass of shiraz and settled down to listen to the news on the radio, but her thoughts turned to Rob and Hannah.

As she sifted through the divorce papers, it occurred to her that she had been mourning a phantom. Since Rob left, she had lamented a thing long gone, a feeling that had disappeared way before they'd lost Hannah, and suddenly why it had happened didn't matter anymore. She simply knew that it had.

She was tired, so very tired. She sat back in her throne chair and wondered how her life might go now that she no longer expected joy, no longer felt a right to its return. She ran her fingers over the pearls of sap on the side of her chair. Tears like congealed blood, markers of the deviations from the path she'd thought her life would take.

The letter requesting acknowledgement of service was handwritten in Rob's looping scrawl. She read it twice. Words suffused with warmth and something that might be nostalgia, and there on the page she recognised the man she had met at the hut, the man she married, the man who taught Hannah to whittle. Lynn felt an unfamiliar lightness in her limbs as she signed the acknowledgement and slid it inside the stamped envelope provided.

Faal

GURJ STOPPED AT THE EDGE of the road, wound down his window and tried to read the grooves on the weatherworn letterbox. Looked down the hill to the enormous willow tree that obscured the house, its long sweeping branches that could be hiding everything or nothing at all.

They'd only been there once, on the way to the Woodbridge District School fete. Graham had just been appointed principal at Kingston High and he'd been keen to check out local feeder schools.

Gurj turned Graham's old Mercedes into the driveway, drove through the curtain of the vast willow, its leaves softly brushing the car like Graham's memories painting themselves across his mind. It was like being in one of those giant car washes, only this was all supple dancing limbs caressing the earth in time with the wind. This was all Graham, Graham, Graham.

Beyond the willow, a squat weatherboard with a deep verandah the length of two sides; their retirement fixer-upper looked smaller than Gurj remembered, but then everything looked different these days.

The verandah squeaked under his feet, sent soundwaves into the space beneath the floorboards where Graham used to hide as a boy when his father came to collect him. Not because he hadn't liked his father, Graham had said, but because he'd loved his great-aunt more.

Gurj went into the house, sat on one of the vinyl-covered kitchen chairs where, decades earlier, Graham's great-aunt had made tea, where Graham had sat doing homework, been rewarded with extra biscuits if he got everything right.

Gurj had met Graham on a blind date. For the entirety of a five-hour shift at the bookshop, Tara and Alex had worked on him. They were adamant he needed a distraction and there was a new man working in the education department with Tara's father.

'He's very good-looking. Unmissable actually,' Tara said.

'Not interested.' Gurj ran a Stanley knife down the tape on a box and started to unpack the books onto the bench.

'Yeah, and he's just moved back from overseas.'

'So?'

'He's here to stay.'

'You haven't even met him. Have you even met him, Alex?'

Alex laughed. 'I don't need to. I trust Tara's impeccable taste.'

'Did you meet Scott?' Gurj asked. 'Tara introduced me to Scott.'

'Oh, fuck off,' Alex said.

After that, Tara told Gurj that he might ruin his life if he didn't take the opportunities thrown at him, and that he would also ruin her life because if he was going to give up on love then she might as well too.

He leant on the new-release bookshelf and knocked several books onto the floor.

'I'll pick them up if you agree to meet him,' Tara said.

'Fine.'

Tara and Alex held hands and jumped up and down like teenagers.

'Is this really what you're like?' Gurj loaded the pricing gun with fresh tape, priced the new books and began to worry about what he'd agreed to.

Tara and Alex were notorious for stretching the meaning of adjectives, so the idea that this new man was 'unmissable' was wildly unlikely. More likely he was eminently missable. But Gurj didn't have the energy to argue, let the refusal sit behind his teeth and get stuck there.

Toby had left two months before, and Gurj was still in that can't-see-how-I'll-get-over-it phase. There could be no life without Toby. It was simply a matter of time. Toby would realise that they were made for one another. Toby would be back. But, in the meantime, Gurj was lonely, and so, with the thought of sex and the desire to silence Tara and Alex, he agreed to meet this new man.

Gurj arrived at Vanna's carrying the heavy weight of low expectations. The place was packed and, when he opened the door, the air was thick with loud conversation, Bollywood music and the aroma of spices. He spoke with the waitress, and she pointed to the back corner of the room.

Graham had chosen the restaurant. Gurj would have preferred a bar, some place that would lend itself to easier egress. He hadn't been to Vanna's before, but felt wearied by the prospect of a man who would assume his tastes wouldn't extend beyond his heritage.

Graham was sitting at a tiny table for two. He was broad bodied, and was wearing glasses and a plain blue shirt that looked as though it might be chambray. His head rested on the wall and he was reading a book, the cover of which had been covered in a deep-red paper – wrapped the way Gurj's mother used to do with his school books.

Weaving between tables, Gurj noticed the way Graham didn't take his eyes off his book when he sipped his wine. His stomach flipped. If the book was right, he might fall in love with this man. Then he thought about Toby and how soon they'd be together again, how stupid it was to fall in love.

'Good story?'

'Sorry, I didn't see you come in. Yes, yes, I think so.' Graham put the book down and clasped both of his hands around Gurj's. 'It's Gurj, right? I'm Graham. Graham Adams. So nice to meet you.'

'Ditto,' Gurj said then felt stupid. They'd talk about that later. About the way it summed them up: Graham always with so many words, Gurj usually the opposite.

'I hope you don't mind me choosing this place. I've been wanting to come for the longest time and, well, it hasn't been very convenient.'

'Until now.'

'Yes, until now.' Graham smiled. His teeth were large, the front two slightly less white than the others.

When the waitress brought their menus, Gurj kept looking over the top of his. He noticed the way that Graham's hair curved, sheltering one ear and revealing the other. The way his nostrils were identical, perfect teardrops. It reminded Gurj of a lion cub, which in turn reminded him of his mother, who had always called him her *pashushaavak*.

'Ready?' the waitress asked.

'Do you like hot food?' Graham asked.

'I'll have the butter chicken, thanks,' Gurj said.

'Right, and you?' The waitress nodded at Graham.

'Can you make a faal?' Graham asked.

'We can make beef vindaloo – I'll bring you extra chillies.'

Graham handed the menu to the waitress. 'Rice, naan and raita, thanks.' Then he poured wine for Gurj and refilled his own glass.

'My parents are horribly embarrassed that I don't like spicy food. My mother acts as though it's a deep failing, a hole in her obligation to raise me properly.'

Graham laughed, and Gurj began to relax.

'The thing is, it gives me hives and I sweat, but the worst of it is that I can't hear properly. For an hour or so after it's like listening underwater.'

'Well, we're all different. It's not like there's any obligation to be a particular way or to like a particular thing.'

The pappadams arrived and the two of them heaped mango chutney onto the crispy wafers.

'So what made you decide to come back to Australia?' Gurj settled into his chair.

'I got tired of short, grey days. I wanted to feel the sun on my skin.'

'And so you moved back to Tasmania?'

They both laughed.

'Yeah, Queensland might have made more sense. But the short-sleeved business shirts.' Graham shivered. 'I just don't think I could.'

'Cheers to that,' Gurj said.

They raised their glasses and clinked them together.

The rest of the food arrived and, while Graham was eating his vindaloo, heaping it with freshly chopped birdseye chillies, Gurj scooped spoonfuls of butter chicken sauce into his mouth and they talked about their experiences of boarding school in Tasmania, the places they had travelled, the things they liked most and least about travelling. And they talked about coming home and debated what it meant.

Halfway through the meal, as Graham was putting his spoon in the vindaloo dish, he said, 'Shit, you're not Hindu are you? I mean fuck, it's not like it would bother me but I ordered the beef, and …'

Gurj laughed. 'No, it's fine. My grandfather succumbed to the Christian missionaries well before I was born. My mother always says it was a neat way of avoiding the bum hand he'd been dealt in the caste stakes. She's quite pious though, my mum. It's probably some kind of penance.'

'Well, thank God for that. It would have been a travesty not to eat this. It's bloody delicious.' He poured the rest of the vindaloo onto his plate.

An easy feeling settled between them as they ate and talked, hardly noticing the waitress sashaying around tables, reaching across to refill their water jug or deliver another dish of pappadams.

When Graham had almost finished his meal, beads of sweat formed on his face. Gurj thought of the one time he'd made Toby go out for Indian, how Toby had whinged, asked the waitress a hundred questions then ordered the steak and chips. Gurj had pretended it was cute – him being so utterly unadventurous, even more so than Gurj – but the truth was there was a kernel, as early as that, of knowing that Toby was really just banal. A bland and unimaginative person held together by the perfect form of muscle and prettiness.

Graham passed the pappadams, and Gurj tried not to think what staying with Toby all of that time said about his own vanity or lack of depth. But he wasn't being fair. There had been good times and Toby hadn't been all that bad. It was just that, in the end, Toby had been far more invested in pleasing himself than pleasing Gurj.

'You okay?' Graham squeezed Gurj's shoulder.

'Sorry. Shit, sorry.'

'Don't apologise. It's good to let your mind wander sometimes. As long as you want to come back.' And with that Graham half stood, and kissed Gurj full on the lips.

When Graham sat back down, Gurj was trembling, couldn't work out how or where to place himself, couldn't work out whether the surge through his veins was thrill or horror.

'I hope that was okay.' Graham poured more wine for each of them. 'It's just I'd been wanting to do it since you arrived and I couldn't think straight till I did.'

Gurj didn't know what to say.

Graham put his hands to his face. 'Oh shit, that was creepy, wasn't it? I'm so sorry. Can we pretend I didn't do that?'

Beneath the table, their knees pressed against one another's, blood pulsing through Gurj's limbs like a quickening.

Later, Gurj admitted that he'd never kissed a man in public before. Not unless you counted nightclubs, car parks or alleys – all the darkened spaces. That and those air kisses at cafes and Salamanca Market. Times are changing, Graham said, and he tucked Gurj's hair behind his ear. Said it was up to them to make sure of it.

Gurj thought about trips home to India. In India he could hold his cousin's hand, put his arm about another man's shoulder. In India men were free to do that, as long as nobody thought there was more to it.

They'd been living together for six months when Gurj's mother, Amrita, came to visit. Gurj introduced Graham as his flatmate.

'Of course, he's joking.' Graham reached over and kissed Gurj on the cheek.

His mother looked between the two of them, burst out laughing. 'Oh, this one is funny,' she'd said.

Later that night, after Graham had washed up, he came into the lounge room and said that he had a big week ahead. He wished Gurj and Amrita goodnight. Slept in the spare room for the entirety of Amrita's visit.

By the next time Amrita visited, Gurj was working as the school librarian at Woodbridge and Graham, trying to alleviate the stress of his role as principal, had become obsessed with Mexican food.

While Gurj was racing to the airport to collect Amrita, Graham made guacamole, quesadillas and crème caramel.

At the end of the meal, Amrita told Graham to sit. 'I will wash up.'

'No, Amrita. You are our guest.'

She sat back and rubbed her stomach. 'By God, Graham, if I weren't married already I would marry you.' She turned then to Gurj. 'But, of course, my son has beat me to it.'

Then later, as Amrita went to bed, she said, 'Please sleep in your own bed tonight, Graham.'

That day outside the hardware store had been two days shy of their eleventh anniversary. It was the longest Gurj had been with anyone, the longest either of them had. And there in the car park, a garden fork almost in the boot, Graham had grabbed at his chest, fallen to his knees, and Gurj had burst out laughing as if the whole thing had been an act, as if Graham wasn't dying before his eyes, heart done before he hit the asphalt.

The sausage sizzle that day was for St John Ambulance, and four of the volunteers had run over and set to work. Graham's shirt pulled open. Graham's chest thumped, someone else's breath in Graham's lungs. The sausages all burnt before anyone remembered to turn the barbeque off. Gurj saw a couple of kids pilfer soft drinks and he was appalled, not so much that they were doing it but that he could be noticing it, that anything other than the blowing into and pressing on Graham's body could matter enough to be noticed.

The paramedics were there within eleven minutes. That's what someone said after. But that had to be wrong. There was no way it could be right. Surely it had been longer.

Graham's will had been very specific. Typical of Graham, really. But then he'd known his family a lot longer than Gurj had, so he'd known what to expect. There were also notes for Gurj, little sayings like affirmations:

Don't let the cunts get you down.
You're the pants for my ants.
Marry me.

He'd chosen music too: Bob Marley, Tracy Chapman, Hunters & Collectors, and a couple of tracks from *Dirty Dancing*.

It seemed such a grown-up thing to have done, all of that arranging when he wasn't even sick, when he wasn't even that old. Gurj wasn't sure whether it was Graham being ironic, looking for an opportunity to have the last word with his family, or if it was all designed to unburden Gurj. Either way it didn't matter. Graham was gone.

Gurj filled the kettle then remembered there was no power. Poured cold water into a teacup he found in one of the cupboards then set two places at the table, placed three serving bowls in the centre, one for beef vindaloo, another for butter chicken, the last for steamed rice. He sat on one of the vinyl-covered chairs. The bright green hills through the window like the undulations of Graham's body in repose.

Graham's ring on Gurj's left hand, his own ring on the right. And, in between the plates, indentations in timber.

He ran his finger across Graham's loopy handwriting. Shadows of a life. Grammar rules pressed into soft pine. Dreams of the life they were meant to be having. Through the tips of his fingers, Gurj traced himself back into the grooves of Graham's life.

Bruny

THE HOUSE HAD BEEN MARKED for demolition. Stakes driven into the ground at intervals with orange fluorescent tape between them, a pathetic bunting skirting the perimeter.

Arlene ducked under the tape, pulled back the swollen door to the kitchen. Soot-stained cabinets, blooms of smoke like vague murals across walls, over ceilings. She felt unsteady on the spongy waterlogged floor.

The air inside was oppressive, tasted ashy and thick. Arlene lifted her T-shirt to cover her mouth and nose. She should be wearing a mask; she shouldn't be there, but in a day's time it would all be gone.

Rachel had been delivered on the porch, her scrawny body in Tiny's arms just as the ambulance arrived. She'd taken her first steps in the lounge room and, for the fifteen years that followed, the three of them had carved out a life on the island. Rachel with a tight group of friends, inseparable from Abby since they'd met at playgroup as three-year-olds; and Tiny, with his unfathomable capacity to recall people's names, the stories they told, knew everyone.

The house had been Arlene's haven, the one place on the island where she felt seamless. Now, standing in its ruins, she felt stretched to the limit, her skin taut and sensitive as though the smoke from their burning home had wound its way inside her, brought with it all of the memories that had been bound to the place.

In the early days after they'd moved to Bruny Island, she hadn't known what to say to people; with her sleep-addled mind she'd talked too much about the mainland. Tiny said she should just be herself, but Arlene couldn't tell him that she didn't know who that was anymore. It had been that way since Rachel's birth, the demands of a child so much greater than she'd imagined. It was okay for Tiny. He got up and went to work, he got off the island, but she was alone with a baby.

On the weekends, when Tiny did the night feeds, she lay in bed trying to sleep, listening to the sounds of the bush and, as Tiny sang lullabies, there seemed to be some kind of inverted formula in which his happiness was exchanged for her loneliness.

Tiny had been sensible. He'd thought to shut the door to the hall, replace the door snake with a sodden towel, so the rooms at the far end of the house were mostly unscathed. But the living area looked like a set for a post-apocalyptic movie. Furniture burnt or water-damaged, or both. All of their appliances destroyed. Sections of ceiling hanging and torn.

Arlene scraped a finger down the kitchen wall and sniffed the black scum under her nail, wondered about structural integrity. Thought about the charred remains of the old schoolhouse that was just inside the entrance of their property: hinges from the original desks, and the knobs and handles that were the only remains of an antique sideboard and dresser. Just like that, Arlene's dream of a bed and breakfast had been extinguished.

She walked down to the beach, sat in the sand throwing shells into the frothy swash of waves, and considered whether all of this might be a sign that it was time to move on. But the leaving words had tumbled in her head before, sat in the lower lobes of her lungs, and she knew she wouldn't be able to cough them out because somehow Tiny belonged on the island as though he'd always been there, and Rachel had never lived anywhere else.

Rachel had been the first to wake. She'd smelt the smoke coming from the schoolhouse, roused her parents. While Tiny did his best with the garden hose and the pissy pressure from the water tank, Arlene and Rachel threw things into the back of the station wagon. Items that had seemed like essentials at the time but which later, when they were unpacking, were baffling. Clothes and bedding made sense, the obligatory photo albums and official documents, but Arlene's wedding dress, the ugly set of Edinburgh Tattoo commemorative teaspoons Tiny had brought back from his one trip overseas, Rachel's threadbare bunny?

In the minutes it took for the Country Fire Authority to arrive, the fire had shot across the property and begun on their house. Flames climbing the outer walls, licking out from under the eaves. The fire crew reeled out the hose from the back of the truck and doused the house and grounds, what was left of the schoolhouse, until the entire place was a sizzling, steaming mess.

To begin with they stayed with Abby's parents, Georgia and Gary, at Alonnah. Rachel holed up in Abby's room, and Arlene and Tiny on a mattress on the floor, in the sewing room. Georgia let Abby have a week off school, and the two girls shut the door to Abby's room and threw themselves into full-blown melodrama. Sobbing followed by loud and off-key singing; bursts of shrieking laughter spilt into the lounge.

'You know you can cry,' Georgia told Arlene as she passed her a cup of tea across the bench.

Arlene managed a tight-lipped smile. 'Thanks.'

~

The first Friday evening after the fire, Tiny was sitting in Gary's recliner, lying back drinking tinnies like they were Cokes, and telling everyone that everything was okay, that everything would be fine. He was like a pianola or some kind of wind-up toy, and Arlene, who mostly felt as though she might shatter in those first days, was affected by it, couldn't decide if she wanted to punch him in the face or kiss him.

'Right, come on. Time to get out of here.' Georgia flipped the handle on the recliner so that Tiny shot upright and almost fell out of the chair. She picked up her keys. 'I'll drive us all there. We'll stumble back.'

Arlene didn't want to go to the pub, didn't want to talk to or look at anyone. Felt too bone-tired for pity. But Georgia insisted, said it would lift her spirits, and Tiny put his arm around Arlene's shoulders and gave her a squeeze.

Walking into the pub was like walking onto a stage naked. She ducked her head under the weight of scrutiny, looked up to smiling faces, sympathetic tear-filled eyes. So many pats on the back, offers of help. Rachel asked for raspberry lemonades for her and Abby, and Arlene dug into her purse.

'No need to worry about that, love. We've got you covered tonight,' Bruce shouted from behind the bar.

Several times throughout the night, Tiny caught her eye and winked, and she couldn't help but feel they were trapped in a performance, that she was the only one who knew they were acting. The truth was not much happened on the island and, though they'd never admit it, people were glad for the excitement, for something noteworthy to have occurred. Grateful that it hadn't been their property.

It was almost closing time when Bruce announced that the

proceeds from the night's meat raffles were for their family, to help them rebuild. Arlene felt embarrassed, and Tiny, unusually drunk, stifled a sob, pretended to cough and took another slug of beer.

'Well, that was a good night,' Tiny slurred as the six of them walked home, four adults strung across the road, Rachel and Abby walking behind.

Arlene sensed the leaving words snaking up from her lungs, filling her throat. Felt as if she might die if she didn't expel them.

In the morning, their neighbour Harry dropped by, thanked them for putting the fire out so quickly, said he was sorry for them.

'Friend of a friend's moving to Sydney. Wants to rent his place in Kettering. It's not on the island but I reckon it could work for you,' Harry said. He handed Arlene a piece of paper with a phone number.

The rental was mudbrick, and Arlene kept putting her hands to the walls, couldn't believe it wouldn't wash away in the rain.

'At least it's fireproof,' Rachel said. She unpacked her bag into the small bedroom at the other end of the house then closed the door.

Near the top of Wiggins Road, the rental was only a two-minute drive to the shop where Rachel caught the school bus up to Kingston, and Arlene, without the ferry trip to worry about at either end of the day, had extra time in her days. She'd thought it would be a relief to get off the island for a while, bleed into anonymity, but Kettering wasn't nearly far enough away for that.

She tried to put the fire out of her mind, tried to focus on the construction of the new house. But sometimes, on the weekend, when Tiny would take Rachel to netball, Arlene lay in bed late and watched grey plumes twist into the air from the smokehouse on the property below. She worried that the smoke was leading to her, somehow pointing her out.

Arlene had only ever bought ciggies when she was in Hobart. Hidden the packets in the lining of her handbag. Run her index finger across receipts in the Argyle Street car park, a single line: *Benson & Hedges Menthol*. Somewhere near the scout camp off the Southern Outlet, she'd throw the latest receipt out the window. The 'Clean Up Australia' jingle from the radio playing in her mind as she told herself it was only a tiny slip of paper, was surely biodegradable, either that or a scout would pick it up and bin it, use the receipt as fodder towards a new activity badge like environmental care or recycling.

The smoking had begun when she was feeling homesick for Melbourne, when the fresh, clean air on Bruny Island slipped so easily in and out of her lungs that she wondered if she were real. She'd wait until Tiny and Rachel were deep in sleep and walk down to the beach, sit on the damp sand and light a cigarette. Hold it up and pretend to herself that its burning tip was another point of light against a night sky that seemed to hold millions. Then, bringing the ciggie between her lips, she'd close her eyes, drag long and deep, and imagine traffic fumes, the blare then shake of a freight train trundling past their old house in Spotswood in the middle of the night.

Arlene had heard people argue that you were more real when you lived somewhere small but it wasn't true. She'd been living on the island for fifteen years and still she was a faint outline, a shadow. Back in Melbourne she'd had substance, known who she was, where she fit. Jammed up against strangers on peak-hour trains she could let her limits blur, and she'd felt like she was part of something. Something anonymous and safe, a place where her history was unknown and she could show as much or as little of herself as she chose. She could be whoever she wanted and no-one knew enough to contradict.

The move to Bruny Island had been a whim. They'd holidayed there once before they were married; talked their way onto a cargo ship to Tassie when school finished and hitchhiked all the way to the tiny island. Tucked in their tent at Adventure Bay for two idyllic weeks, they'd discussed how they might live there one day. Then they'd taken the ferry back to Kettering and returned to Melbourne and that had been that.

Arlene was in the late stages of pregnancy, could barely breathe for the pressure the baby was putting on her diaphragm. Pelvic instability so bad that some days she had to crawl around the house, her distended belly rubbing against the floor. She told Tiny that she just needed some clean air. Air that wasn't pumped full of car fumes, of industrial smog, of the stench of so many people's breath.

Tiny had always said he'd never leave Melbourne, but, since the collapse of the Westgate Bridge mid-build, his conviction had wavered to the point where he now took stairs instead of lifts and said, 'You never know. Just like those blokes on the bridge. You never know.'

The ad for the place on Bruny Island was on the back page of one of those real-estate lift-outs in the paper that showcase obscure remote properties. They didn't even go down to look at it. They took the estate agent's word and packed up their house in Spotswood.

'Better to raise kids where life's simpler. Somewhere you can trust what's what,' Tiny said. Neither of them mentioned the accident that had brought down the mid-section of the Tasman Bridge in Hobart only two years earlier.

The week after the preliminary report blamed the fire on a cigarette butt, Arlene found a packet of matches when she emptied Rachel's schoolbag; the following week, a crushed and tattered cigarette packet, Benson & Hedges of all brands. After that, a box of half-used fire starters.

Rachel cried, said she didn't know where they'd come from, that she had no idea who had put them in her bag. 'It's like someone's accusing me, but I didn't do it. You believe me, don't you, Mum?'

'Course, love, don't be silly.' Arlene kissed her forehead.

They'd just got into bed when she began to tell Tiny about the things she'd found in Rachel's schoolbag.

'Bloody hell.' Tiny rolled onto his side to look at her.

She put her palm against his chest to stop herself from falling into the dip in the middle of the borrowed bed. 'I don't think she did it,' she said. She wound her fingers through his chest hair and slowly marched them down his abdomen until neither of them was thinking about Rachel or the fire or anything much.

As she was drifting off after, too tired to move out of the wet patch, she heard Tiny's faint words. 'No wonder she was so upset.' Then, 'I can't believe she'd do it, Arls.'

She let out a sigh that spoke of sleep, faked a slight muscle twitch, and eventually she felt Tiny roll away from her, begin to snore.

By the time they moved into their new house on Bruny, the accusations had stopped showing up in Rachel's schoolbag, and Tiny seemed to have made peace with what he suspected were his daughter's lies. By then the rumour mill had settled on a backpacker wandering the island, looking for somewhere out of the way, somewhere free to pitch their tent. Plenty of tourists from Europe at that time of year, and they all seemed to smoke.

The full report was shorter than Arlene had expected; clean, neat text that ruled out other causes, then the short punchy sentence about the cigarette butt like a filthy aberration. A single stub of guilty pleasure. She felt the leaving words thicken in her throat once more as she walked into the house.

A copy of *The Mercury* was on the table. Arlene pulled it towards her, read the small article on the front page about the proposal for a bridge between Bruny Island and the Tasmanian mainland, smiled at the picture of Tiny, hands on hips, posing on the Alonnah pontoon. The caption: *Local Trevor Whittle says salvaged section of Hobart's old Floating Bridge 'all the bridge we need'*.

Later that night, when Tiny was asleep, Arlene watched him for a while, smirked at the funny purring sound that travelled from his deep barrelled chest and out through daintily pursed lips. Then she pulled on trackpants and a windcheater and quietly left through the glass sliding door that led to the verandah.

Down at the beach, she sat in the sand and traced patterns with sticks as the breeze shifted her hair. She waited for the old feeling. Opened her mouth wide, but the leaving words had gone and there was nothing left to dispel. Eventually, she got up and went back to bed, tucked her body around the contours of Tiny's and drifted.

Nao

WHEN SOPHIE DIED LAST MONTH, the grief was overwhelming, a wild tumble of loss. Nao hadn't thought about her old life in Japan for years. But Sophie's death unhinged her.

Nao hid beneath the covers while Jay showered. With crusted eyes, she'd dragged herself out of bed long after he'd gone to work. Slept and woke wrapped tight in the dragonfly-print dressing-gown that Sophie had given her. Shuffled between rooms in ugg boots, heating on high. Nao made tea that she didn't drink, howled. Lay on the sofa in front of vacuous daytime television, her mind a soup of unbidden images: the coroner cutting Sophie open; Sophie separated from her organs; Sophie sewn back together like a rag doll, the mystery of her death revealed; then suddenly, as though they came from beneath the earth's crust, Nao's little sister, Yume, in her school uniform with Nao's first mother, Haha, in her best kimono.

Eventually, Nao rose with sea legs. Wobbly, she pulled on jeans and a jacket and went for fresh air, found herself at the bottle shop. Bought sake to get rid of the taste of salt water.

That night Jay cupped her face in his hands, said it was probably a breakdown. But it felt more like a loosening – a current back to who she used to be. She liked that about it, painful as it was.

She went to the funeral home with Rod and her siblings. A woman dressed in a conservative black suit showed them into a neat room. In a voice designed to soothe, the woman explained the items on the table: a box of tissues; a pot of tea and cups; and a pile of folders with lists of music, hymns, service run sheets, a selection of caskets and urns.

'Let me know if you need anything.' The woman closed the door behind her.

Tess poured tea while Pete handed out folders and Matt picked his teeth. Nao flicked through images of caskets. Pale, dark, glossy, silver handles, gold handles, satin lined, velvet lined. She wondered how it would be possible to decide. Her eyes were half closed when she heard the rush of the sea, imagined Haha running up the hill behind their house, fleeing from the deluge, screaming for Yume. Bile rose thick in her throat and she reached for a cup of sake to wash it down, took a sip of tea instead. Closed the folder.

Tess pushed a list of hymns towards her. 'What do you think, Nao?'

The words floated on the page. 'I don't know.'

'What do you think, Dad? Cremation or burial?' Tess asked.

Rod sat mute, hands clasped in his lap.

'We have to decide,' Tess said.

'Cremation.' Nao said it quietly, the way an outsider might make an offering on a matter when they ought not.

'No.' Matt was loud. 'We can't burn her.' He pulled the sleeves of his jumper down over his hands.

Matt had been nine when Nao arrived on exchange. At first he'd been friendly, but after the tsunami Nao had taken too much space, robbed him of precious time with his mother.

Rod shook his head from side to side, looked at the floor. Shoulders hunched, he seemed smaller than usual, unanchored in the middle of them. Nao felt bad for him but, mostly, she felt the dark drowning weight of the last few weeks push the air from her lungs. She tried to read the list of hymns, but the letters swam between the lines, shifted into Japanese characters, and she wondered if she might be losing her mind.

'She doesn't like the cold. I don't want her in a box. Not on her own.' Rod's shoulders shook, and Nao's mind flicked through images of Haha and her first family, all of them wet, cold, alone.

Tess phoned later in the day; she'd allocated tasks, and Nao felt herself sinking further, leaving Tess – the real daughter – to hold them all together. As she put the phone down, Nao caught hold of a memory: a tightness at her waist as she'd bowed, long and deep, when she said goodbye to the funeral director. Had no idea when she'd last bowed to anyone. The bottle shop; she may have bowed to the guy behind the counter when she was buying the sake.

'How did it go?' Jay was walking in from work.

'Can you take off your shoes?'

'What?'

'I think we shouldn't wear them in the house. It's not clean. It doesn't feel right.'

'Okay.' Jay left his shoes by the end of the kitchen bench.

'I'm doing the food. The boys are choosing the casket and Tess is sorting the flowers and notices, everything else.'

'How's Rod?'

'I don't know. Not good. I'm thinking about setting up a shrine at his place. I think it might help.'

'Really?' Jay took a beer out of the fridge and flipped the top off, then pulled her to him and kissed the crown of her head. 'What kind of shrine?'

'I don't know. I just think it might be the right thing to do.'

He took a long swig of beer. 'Maybe you should ask him.'

She picked up Jay's shoes and moved them next to the front door. 'I'm doing nigiri and maki,' she called.

'Great. I'm starving. Thanks.'

'Not tonight. After the funeral.' Nao walked back into the kitchen.

'Right. Sorry.' Jay sat at the bench. 'It sounds like a lot of work. Why don't we get a caterer?'

'No.' She threw burgers into a pan and felt time slip into itself. The weight of Jay's gaze; the interminable shift of the second hand on the clock as it moved a single stroke; the sound of Jay swallowing beer; the shift of the washing machine from one cycle to the next and the swish of the water as it swirled over and around, tumbling their clothes together.

A wave of nausea gathered in her gut, and she had to put the knife down and press her hands against the bench to try to steady herself. When she closed her eyes, a list of hymns that might be sutras swam in her mind and her thoughts rolled back through the days right after the tsunami. What had happened? Who had looked after the bodies of her family? Who had cleaned their skin, wiped the dirt from their eyes and mouths? Who had brought the dry ice? Had anyone remembered to moisten their lips, to give the last water? Or had someone, a stranger, decided there had been enough water already?

Why had she not asked these things before? Had she *really* not asked these things before? She didn't even know if anyone had read the sutras, and yet earlier in the day she'd sat in a small warm room pretending to make choices for Sophie when there were others who were better equipped to do so, who had more right. When Sophie's real daughter was there.

Who had kissed Yume's head? Had they put her with their parents or had Yume been left with the other children, as estranged from their parents as Nao had been, stranded on another continent? Her legs faltered.

'It's going to be alright.' Jay scooped her into his large arms and carried her to their bedroom like a child. 'I'm here, Nao.'

It was the last thing she heard before slipping into sleep.

Nao wasn't used to the mornings, the way the days in Tasmania began in darkness. So she slept, floated around in stupid dreams while her family was washed out of their home, while all of their village was washed away and some idiot in a helicopter filmed their dog Kaito riding the wave, Kaito's head just above the swell of water that filled the space between rooftops before he was finally sucked under. They used that video on the news, as if it was somehow emblematic of the tragic inevitability of it all, as if to show that survival was never a real possibility. Then, days later, another dog barking on a rooftop, surrounded by debris-thickened seas, scooped up and winched into a helicopter.

It was the week after her sixteenth birthday when Nao arrived in Tasmania. That first night, Rod made a barbequed dinner and Sophie said Nao could call her Mum if she wanted. But it felt foolish when Nao tried to make the word come out of her mouth, and every time she opened her lips the name Sophie emerged. In the weeks after the tsunami, Nao was angry with herself for even trying to call Sophie Mum, as if the mere attempt might have shifted the tectonic plates. After Sophie's death, she told everyone how Sophie always said 'I'll never be your Haha', but had then done everything to show she was.

Nao had been with Rod and Sophie for only three weeks when the wave came. The day before was a Sunday and they'd had nigiri and maki rolls for dinner, and everyone had behaved as if it was normal. Nao hadn't been sure whether the meal was their usual Sunday ritual or something concocted for her.

She couldn't remember Sophie telling her what happened. Couldn't remember the actual day or the months that came after, not properly. There were only shards and impressions. The muffled sounds of Sophie and Rod talking into the night. Tess and the boys quiet, not fighting. Nao sitting on the edge of her bed in the room they had given her, willing them to keep her. She had nowhere else to go, barely had the strength to walk down the hall. Later, someone told her that the Japanese newspapers said she should go home, but her exchange family had asked what she wanted and they fought for her. They didn't know each other then but they still fought for her.

In the fog of those days, sleep was a blank space where nothing could be lost. A void. The sharp agony of waking, the experience of loss all over again. Her chest a cavern; she wanted the space around her left empty, wanted to rest inside her shell. In the evenings, Sophie would come into her room, wrap an arm around her shoulders, and some nights when she did that Nao let herself cry. But mostly she sat there and waited until Sophie had finished. Until Sophie felt like she had done something, and Nao could close the door and lie on the bed until the dark morning came.

When the night was too heavy for sleep, she would sit on the floor in her room and draw. She drew herself like a manga character but she had to be careful not to draw her eyes too large because they always held pools of water. If she made them too big she might fall into herself and drown.

~

It was months before Tess and the boys blamed Nao for anything, before they pushed her out of their way or complained about anything she said or did. None of them treated her the way Yume used to, the way Matt would come to later. They were all pretending, and that singularity made her feel more alone than anything.

At school she was like a magnet – she both repelled and attracted. People said she was lucky that the government let her stay, that she was lucky to have her new family. They said things like: 'What kind people' and 'How nice they wanted to keep you'. But she didn't feel the luck on her side.

Teachers said she should dream of a new life. Dream a new way to be. Dream how to be part of the new family. What they meant was that she should dream how not to be Japanese; how not to be Yume's sister; how not to be her mother's daughter, her father's brightest light. And Nao tried, but you can't control your dreams.

In her dreams, Nao's father chopped wood for a fire they never had. Haha made pickled daikon for Yume, enough for when Nao would come home from exchange. In Nao's dreams, if Haha had not made so many jars of pickles, Haha and Yume would have been visiting Baba when the wave came. In Nao's dreams, if it weren't for her obsession with pickles, her mother and Yume would be alive. Her grandmother's village was washed away too. Dreams are stupid.

Nao was never meant to have a sibling. Her parents had only planned to have one child, but her little sister was a gift. Baba said Yume floated down the river inside a giant peach. Jiji said they found her inside a pole of bamboo. When the water came,

Yume was wearing her uniform from nursery school. The bus was washed away further down the valley. A lot of kids were still in it. They didn't even make it home.

It's Yume who calls to her most often, her dream voice thin, channelled down the tiny aperture of a bamboo sapling.

'Nao,' she calls. 'Nao, Nao, Nao.'

Some nights it is a pleading: 'Nao, Now, Now' and Nao searches a dense bamboo forest. Knows from her voice that Yume is in there, that she is slight like a needle. Nao takes her father's axe from beside the house and hacks pole after pole. She cleaves the forest until she is surrounded by empty cylinders and, with every pole she cuts, Yume's voice becomes smaller, thinner, until it is small enough to slip into the curve of a blade of grass. It disappears, hides away until the forest has re-formed in Nao's next dream.

For a time after the tsunami, Nao dreamt when awake, imagined her skin tattooed with articles and images from the newspaper. Saw them in the almost-light that crept into her room well after the sun rose. She scratched herself, not sure if she was trying to score the images away or get a clearer view, remove the layer of skin that obscured what had really happened. As she ran her nails down her arms, the words of her native language scrolled in Nao's mind and she heard the loudspeakers, Emperor Akihito, the Japanese prime minister, the press conferences and the wailing relatives. She even heard Kaito barking in Japanese. All of this she translated, wrote in a notebook so that later, if the pictures faded, she would be able to make copies of the words and she could paper herself like a wall to ensure that no-one forgot, to make sure that she didn't forget. It was tiring to think of everything twice. Sometimes it felt like her whole life would be a translation.

Two years after the tsunami, a Japanese dignitary came to Tasmania. The Japanese government was allowing exchange programs to resume and Principal Adams called to ask Nao what she thought about it.

Nao shrugged. 'This is not for me to say.' Then she went to the toilet and vomited up the vegemite toast she'd eaten for breakfast. When she flushed, she swore she could see Kaito and Yume swirling around the bowl, Yume's arms outstretched as she was sucked away. A sob leapt up Nao's throat, and she vomited again. She had thought that part was over.

That weekend there was a picnic at Waterworks Reserve with a bunch of kids from Nao and Tess's year level. Nao didn't want to go, but Tess begged her.

'It's not that big,' Tess assured her. 'And anyway, it's a dam. It's perfectly safe.' Tess threw towels and food into a bag.

When they got there, Nao was relieved to see the 'no swimming' signs, but most of the kids stripped down to their bathers and jumped into the dam right away. She spread her towel and lay on the grass by the edge of the bush, tried to imagine that she was in a forest in Japan.

She was nearly asleep when she heard Tess's friend Lara say she'd nearly drowned in a dam when she was nine. Sea snakes writhed in Nao's chest, and she cast her eyes up Mount Wellington, searched for Yume in the whispers of cloud that floated and obscured the peak, but Yume wasn't there – none of Nao's family was.

On the way home, Nao noticed her knees were burnt, looked like the sun on the Japanese flag. She wondered if it was a sign from her Japanese family, a reminder not to forget who she was.

That afternoon Sophie had already set the table, laid out cutlery instead of chopsticks for Sunday dinner. Nao picked up a fork.

'Thought we might have a change,' Sophie said.

Sophie opened the oven door and lifted a roasting pan onto the bench. The kitchen was filled with the smell of roast chicken. For a moment Sophie was hidden in the steam, and Nao was swept into her old house, her old life and her old family, and she imagined Haha fanning sushi rice, shrouded in mist.

Last week marked a decade since the tsunami. Nao was struck by how much it sounded like 'decayed'. As if it was telling her something more than the passage of time. She wondered what it would have told her if she'd moved back to Japan. In Japanese, those words are as different as she might have been.

The day before Sophie's funeral, Nao didn't know where to put herself. She'd told Rod and the others that she didn't want to see Sophie again, that she'd prefer to remember Sophie the way she'd been last time she and Jay went round for dinner. But as Nao remade the sushi rice for the third time, she thought about her Japanese family – how she hadn't been there to moisten their lips, to hear the sutras, how she wasn't even sure where they were now – and she had a deep yearning to return, to find them. Felt a strange sense of serendipity that Rod had decided on cremation, as though this were Nao's chance to atone for past omissions, to be the kind of daughter she should always have been, to attend to the rituals that were demanded of her.

Nao tried to cut the salmon fillets – thin slices to be draped across rice – but a feeling of urgency was building in her, thick and vibrating like the roll of a wave, the tearing power of a rip.

By late afternoon, she had destroyed most of the salmon and the uruchimai was mush. She could hardly still her limbs. Jay was taking his shoes off at the door.

'I need to see her,' Nao said.

Jay called the funeral home to make an appointment, and Nao placed the things she would need into a box. On the way, he steered the car with one hand, held Nao's hand with the other. He told her about the wind phone in Japan. He'd been listening to the radio on his way to work, heard a story about a man who'd lost his cousin in the tsunami. The man had put a phone box in his garden and people were coming from everywhere for a chance to stand in the box, pick up the wind phone and speak to the people they had lost, to try to make sense of it all.

'You sure you don't want me to come in?' Jay's hand was on the seatbelt clasp.

She shook her head and heaved the ritual box out of the car. The wind wrapped her scarf across her face so that, for a moment, she couldn't see where she was. Let herself briefly imagine she was in Japan and that she was preparing the rituals for her first family.

Jay leant across and talked out the passenger window. 'Call me when you're ready. Take as long as you need.'

Alone in the room with Sophie, she was halted by a moment of indecision, unsure whether there was anything authentic about what she was about to do, about the person she was. Maybe these rituals didn't belong to her. Maybe they would dishonour Sophie, dishonour her first family by offering them to Sophie. Then she remembered the night Sophie had sat on her bed and said it was up to her to decide who she wanted to be, that it didn't mean choosing between her old life and the new because, no matter what, both would be part of her.

Nao took the pot of ink from her bag and unscrewed the cap, unwrapped the small calligraphy brush from the set Haha had bought as a present for her exchange mother and that Sophie had returned to Nao on her first birthday in Tasmania. She made careful strokes, formed neat kanji marks on a piece of rice paper. Gently blew across its surface until the ink was dry.

On the morning of the funeral, Jay drove to the shops while Nao ironed her new kimono, then they stood together in the kitchen scooping and squeezing and shaping until there was more maki and nigiri than could possibly be eaten. When they arrived at the funeral parlour, Rod, Tess and her brothers hugged them, and they all went in to look at Sophie one last time.

Sophie was lying in the casket the boys had chosen and was dressed in her favourite nightie. There were flowers from Rod and a card from Tess, and the six coins and piece of rice paper on which Nao had written in careful kanji the death name she had chosen for Sophie.

At the end of the service, as the casket rolled into the incinerator, she felt a wave of cold and she pulled her kimono tight across her body and closed her eyes. In the pulsing coloured lights behind her eyes, she could just make them out – Sophie, Haha, Papa, Yume, her grandparents, Jiji and Baba – as they were sucked into the flames together.

When Nao opened her eyes, she knew that she would not give her family the chopsticks she had bought; she would not ask them to sit with her to pick Sophie's bones. Instead, she and Jay would fly to Japan. They would find the wind phone and Jay would wait patiently in the grass while she stood inside the box and spilt her words to her Japanese family until they were the softest whispered memories, small enough to slip through hollowed bamboo saplings, to come to rest cradled in the curve of a blade of grass.

Smokehouse

PART TWO

W︎HEN NORA GOT BACK FROM the market, Ollie was hunched at the table. The components of his Uncle Herman's cuckoo clock spread before him.

'You said you wouldn't be long.'

'I wasn't.'

Ollie raised his eyebrows. 'Is that right?'

She balanced the box of groceries against the wall and pushed the door shut with her foot. 'Is something wrong?'

'You tell me, Nora.' He was sifting through cogs and weights.

'I have no idea what you're talking about.'

'So you're not going to explain what you did to the clock?'

She lifted the groceries onto the kitchen bench. 'Seriously, Ollie, I don't have a clue what you're talking about.' She put the pecorino, basil and gnocchi into the fridge. 'It's probably the year 2000 bug that everyone's so worried about. Maybe the virus has gone rogue,' she joked.

Ollie exhaled loudly. 'I've taken it apart. We both know I'm going to work out what you did, so you might as well be honest with me.'

'Have you and Harry been doing mushrooms again?'

'I haven't seen Harry in years.'

Nora frowned. Harry had been over the week before, spent the day with Ollie preparing and smoking wallaby from the last cull on the island. 'What's going on, Ol?'

'I'm not the one who fucked with the clock, Nora.' He took the cuckoo from his pocket. The bird was riven in two.

'What the hell happened?'

He picked up a hammer and waved it in the air. 'I told you – it's not working properly and I'm trying to get to the bottom of it.'

Nora woke to the sound of Ollie snoring loudly. Out the window a sharpened black sky. Press-studs of light in the dark like pins in a map.

Her back to his, she curved the arch of her foot around his calf muscle, and tried to push worry about Ollie's deterioration over the last year from her mind. She dozed for a few minutes then quietly climbed down the ladder, clothes tucked under her arm. She fed the fire and stood in front of it to dress, the woodfire door left open for extra warmth. Coals glinted in the half-light.

The smoked salmon was almost all gone and, though she'd asked Ollie several times to teach her to use the smokehouse, Nora still didn't know how to do the smoking. There was always an excuse, as though showing her would be some kind of admission that it was no longer the thing that he did.

She decided to save the salmon to eat with Ollie; poured malt vinegar over sliced onion and made sandwiches with soft, white store-bought bread, tinned sardines and the pickled onion.

When she went upstairs to wake Ollie, she was hopeful.

'*Ja.*' He sat, scratched his head and began speaking in German. Though she didn't understand a word, she nodded, smiled. It had alarmed her at first, but she'd come to realise that he was calmer on the days he woke in his first language, as though it were a lullaby lifting him from sleep and placing him in a state of mind that was familiar and safe.

Nora gave him time. Put fresh clothes on the bed. The car was packed already, boat trailer on tow ball, chain fastened, brakelights connected. Ollie nodded approvingly when she clipped his seatbelt then sat upright, staring ahead.

She switched the radio on and drove towards Trial Bay. Following familiar roads, she flicked her eyes at the rear-view mirror every now and again to check the boat. Tried not to be obvious when she looked at Ollie.

Midweek, the boat ramp was empty.

'Okay, let's do this.' Nora drove into the gravel clearing. She checked the side mirrors and slowly backed down towards the ramp. She ran the counterintuitive script in her head: left for right, right for left. Not too hard a lock, then ease it out, straighten up. Ollie did not so much as glance her way. Trust or absence, Nora couldn't be sure, but she'd done a good job of it, directly down the centre-line at the top of the ramp. At least there was that.

Ollie got out of the car. She wound the windows down, opened the glove box. She located the key to the boat among scraps of paper, removed something that used to be fruit and threw it out the window. She searched about for something to wipe her hands on, settled for her pants.

'Ready? She looked around in her seat. 'Ollie, where are you?' She climbed out, scanned the water's edge, the car park. 'Fuck.'

She should have been watching. 'Come on, Ollie. This isn't funny.' As though this were the kind of joke Ollie would make. As though he'd ever been that kind of man.

He appeared at the end of the boat, arms loaded with wet rope. He grinned.

Nora wavered. What if they were well offshore and he wanted to get out of the boat? What if he forgot who she was? Who he was? When might those shifts happen? She felt the weight slip out of her plans before they had gained form. But she was being defeatist, pre-empting the losses that would come before they'd occurred. She let the negative thoughts go.

'Okay.' She climbed back into the car, reversed incrementally. She followed Ollie's hand signals, pulled on the handbrake. But what if he needed to pace? What would she do? What could she do? Her confidence was eroding. It was hard to tell who she was now.

From the day she'd begun their affair, Nora had remade herself. She'd learnt to trust her instincts; reconnected with her creativity, made art from driftwood and gumnuts, from sheep's wool snagged on a barbed-wire fence; and eventually she'd told the museum that she wouldn't be returning after her leave, took a job teaching art at Woodbridge school. Gradually she'd become what felt like her natural self, as though she'd been dormant until the right time had come, the right partner – or, perhaps, not the wrong partner.

But now she had to put Ollie first: his wellbeing, his safety. If he fell out of the boat there was no way she could save him. She got out of the car. 'I'm sorry, Ollie, but I don't feel well.' She put her hand to her stomach to lend credence. 'Can we do this another day?'

'For sure.' He tapped the bonnet of the car. 'Should I drive?'

She thought of the last time. He'd ignored two stop signs and almost sideswiped a parked car. 'Thanks, but I need something to concentrate on.'

Ollie clipped his seatbelt and knocked on the dashboard. 'Let's roll, baby.'

On the drive home, he ran his hand up her thigh and, though her body responded, she didn't know how to feel about it. She put her hand over his and laced their fingers together.

'Too rough today?' He said it like a question.

'Mmhmm.' Nora thought about the first time he took her in the boat down to Cockle Creek: Ollie walking in her footprints, both of them following a trail made by someone else.

The afternoon started uneventfully. Ollie walked the side fence from top corner to bottom corner and back again. Exhausted from lack of sleep, she sat on the outdoor chair that she'd positioned behind the smokehouse, equidistant between the upper and lower points of the fence. She half watched him while she sorted dried leaves and gumnuts into boxes by size and colour. At some point he'd tire, stumble, but still he wouldn't stop. Eventually, when his gait shifted to a shuffle, she'd be able to take his arm, and he'd allow her to lead him into the house.

Months ago, when Ollie first began his fence laps, she had walked beside him, reminiscing out loud about all the things they'd done together: fishing trips, hiking on Bruny Island and up the east coast, snorkelling off Malaysia, the African safari. And she'd talked about his smoked salmon, reminded him that they would run out soon. But Ollie was always more interested in counting the posts, got annoyed when she interrupted him.

Every time she asked him to teach her how to do the smokehouse, he'd tell her he needed to check the fences. He'd brush past her, march back up the property. Counting out loud, first in English and then, as the day wore on and he tired, in German.

Today he walked for hours. He shouted at the fence, pulled his hair. Late in the afternoon on a pass down from the top of the property, she noticed his right forearm was ripped and dripping blood. Her patience evaporated; her heart rate accelerated.

'For fuck's sake, Ollie, stop!'

He barely glanced at her, continued to count the posts.

She strode across to the fence line. 'Come on, Ollie. You've cut yourself.' She reached out to try to bring him back towards the house, and he pushed her in the chest, hard, so that she fell to the ground. He turned away, continued his counting and pacing.

She curled onto her side. Gumnuts pressing into her hip and cheek as she lay in the dirt and cried for ten minutes. Then got up and went back inside, tried to swallow the stones of their changed life.

She filled the coffee pot, and rationalised that the behaviour wasn't him. She told herself it was his disease, and she took the last of his smoked salmon from the fridge and pushed it into her mouth until there was scarcely room to chew.

When they'd first received the diagnosis, she and Ollie agreed it would be different for them. Ollie would keep his mind challenged. They'd work hard to block the advance of the disease. Privately, Nora decided to ride the peaks, keep herself afloat for the lows and concentrate on every swell that washed them back to normality. But it wasn't as easy as that. She hadn't accounted for her lack of patience, her frustration, and the depth of bitterness she'd feel at the loss of Ollie, of their life. The erosion of herself.

She returned to the yard and rested against the smokehouse. Though she was desperate for him to stop, to come inside and be himself again, she resisted the desire to call him in, or draw his attention to the abnormality of his behaviour. The smokehouse wall was cold and hard against her back.

When Ollie finally ventured inside, she closed the door behind them and locked it.

'Can I see your arm?'

Ollie ran his finger over the congealed blood. Stopped midway between his wrist and elbow. 'I don't know what happened. I never know what's happening anymore.'

They sat at the table, and she cleaned and bandaged the wound. 'It's going to be okay,' she said.

Ollie wept. She stroked his hair, trying to soothe them both. But it wouldn't be okay; there would be no upside. He would lose his mind, and it would destroy them both.

She recalled their earlier conversation.

'We need to talk, Nora. We need to make plans,' Ollie had said.

She had objected. Asked him to stop.

'You need to leave,' Ollie had said.

She'd cried then.

'I want you to leave me,' he'd insisted.

She'd told him that it wasn't his choice to make, then she'd sat on his lap and rested her head against his and made him promise not to ask again.

Later in the evening, it was as though Nora had imagined the events of the afternoon. Ollie in the sling chair reading Kafka, Nora at the table twining driftwood and threading leaves into shapes that might become something. She wondered whether sometimes the retention of certain memories might be more painful than their loss.

She watched Ollie running his finger across the pages of parallel text. For weeks, he'd been working his way back through the Kafkas, and Nora couldn't begin to reconcile the man who walked the fences with the man who read these books, the man who could tell her to leave. It was like he was two different people. One she knew, the other a stranger. And, though it was the thing she thought she cherished least about their lives, Nora wished more fervently than anything for some semblance of predictability. Was exhausted by the impossibility of understanding the shifts from one moment to the next.

The sky was turning navy when Ollie snapped his book closed and announced he was finished. He stretched his broad muscular limbs, and Nora wished she could still want him in the ways she used to, that they could make love again without the tentative worry of the shifting currents of Ollie's presence.

He opened the door to the woodfire and tossed the book inside. She half stood but the pages were already burning and so she sat back down.

'Time for something new.' He climbed the ladder to fetch another book.

Minutes later, she heard the familiar drone of his snore. She relaxed. When he was asleep, he always seemed himself.

Nora sat alone by the fire. She needed to get out of the house but it was hard to know anymore whether it was okay to leave Ollie, how long it was okay to leave him for. It was like having a young child, only Ollie was becoming less independent rather than more.

She wasn't hungry but she ate cheese and bread for something to do, and tried not to think. Eventually, though the house was still illuminated by the long summer light of daylight saving, she headed up to bed. These days she never knew how much sleep a night would hold.

At the top of the ladder Nora watched the slow rise and fall of Ollie's chest. As usual, the rhythm was punctuated every fourth or fifth breath by a space between that seemed longer than reasonable. And, as ever, just when it seemed a fresh inhale was not to come, he tugged at the air sharply and the cycle continued.

She undressed and peeled back the covers next to him, felt the shifting cadence of his breath as his body registered her presence. Out the window she watched the changing sky wash rose through grey, like a giant galah.

She closed her eyes and tried to sleep but she couldn't still her limbs, couldn't shift the feeling that she was trapped; the world outside as unreachable as Ollie and the life they had together was becoming. Memories and fears swirled through her brain, and she pressed herself closer to Ollie, tried again not to think of the way he'd pushed her to the ground and walked away. Finally, moulded to the shape of his back, she slipped into sleep.

Gurj was standing in his yard, his tiny paunch hanging over a hefty pair of boxer shorts. Nora stopped walking and watched from the gravel road as her old friend pegged brightly coloured waves of fabric across the clothesline. Watched him wind the Hills hoist and stand back as the thing spun, a kaleidoscope against the bright green hills.

Nora was desperate for company, wanted to call to him, welcome him back, but there was something private about his manner. The way he stepped forward to touch the vibrant fabrics, let them brush across his skin as the wind carried them around and around like children's scarves winging out from a carousel.

Nora walked on to the place where the road ended and a trail wound into the bush, then snaked up and away from the last of the houses, meandering towards the summit of the hill. She retied her laces, drank some water. This was her favourite part, the first step from bitumen onto earth. She concentrated on the aroma of eucalyptus and kept walking. Twigs crackled underfoot, grasses leant in and brushed her ankles, like the trace of fingers on skin; she felt her anxiety dissipate. Ollie had been up for much of the night, would sleep for hours yet.

She stopped to press her palms against textured trunks, wrap her arms about the girth of a massive tree. Cheek on bark, she thought about Ollie. The smell of his skin and the vast landscape of his muscular frame. Fast-breathed, desperate sex upon the bench of the smokehouse, against tree trunks and on beaches. Languorous, slow sex in the sling chair. The taste of her scent on his lips.

Honeyeaters skirted between the scrappy branches of smaller trees, disappeared into thicker foliage and drilled holes in the white noise of the bush. Nora plucked leaves from a peppermint gum, crushed one in her hands, put another in her mouth to chew, and walked until sweat trickled down her spine and the sound of blood in her ears drowned out all other noise.

Well before the summit, the world began to tilt. She sat on a fallen trunk and breathed deeply, had a sip of water and picked at the curled edges of bark. This was usually where the tears came and so she rested and waited for the pressure in her chest to erupt. But the weight remained constant.

On her way back, Gurj was at the beehives. Nora walked down his driveway, waited for him to notice her arrival, but he was pulling a rack out of a hive, and speaking in a voice that sounded like singing. She called his name.

He slid the rack back into the hive, moved towards her. 'Nora,' barely a whisper carried on the breeze.

When she got to him, Gurj was bent double, sobbing, his face still bound in the keeper's headgear. He let her help him up, guide him into the house.

In the kitchen, carer again, she made tea and tried not to dwell on herself.

Gurj removed his headgear and wiped the snot from his face. Sniffing and puffy-eyed, he sat with a turquoise sari wrapped tight about his shoulders, threw his tea back in a single swallow.

'She kept opening her mouth. And she was small, like some other woman. My father wouldn't stop wringing his hands, watching me as though there was something I could do. But what could I do?' Gurj picked up his empty teacup, put it back down.

'I'm so sorry.'

'This was her favourite sari. I took it when my father wasn't looking.' He lifted the fabric to his nose.

Nora poured more tea.

'For three days I waited, knelt by her bed, and you know what I was thinking? When I should have been thinking about my mother? I was thinking about what kind of death was worse. Whether I would have coped if it had been that way with Graham – knowing it was coming. And you know what I also wanted? I wanted her to hold on, not for my dad, not for her. I just didn't want her to die on the anniversary of Graham's death. Seriously, Nora, what kind of son am I?'

She reached across the table. 'You're a wonderful son. Amrita was so proud of you.'

'I kept thinking I heard her try to say my name. I was almost sure I could hear it: *Gur*.' He shook his head. 'It was only the saliva in her throat. I should have visited sooner.'

'I'm sure she knew you were there.' Nora listened to the

platitude leave her mouth. Small lies of the right kind. The kind of lies that people now told her about Ollie.

As she walked home, Nora tried to shake free of Gurj's grief. The books all said she would grieve many times. The first stage, knowledge, was done. The next, grief for the smaller losses, the attrition of their lives, had already begun. Eventually, somewhere in the future, though probably earlier than she expected, Ollie would die.

Again she made up her mind to focus on the things they still had, to create as many good memories as she could so that when the time came, when all that was left was grind, she could take out these moments and use them for solace.

Back at the A-frame, the front door was open and her heart quickened. But inside she found Ollie taking a loaf of bread from the oven.

'I don't know what went wrong.' He turned the flat loaf over in his hands as if the answer to its inadequacy might become clear.

'Not to worry, babe.'

Ollie tore the bread in half and stuffed it into the chook bin. 'I'm going to have a bath,' he said.

From the kitchen, she listened for signals. Water plinking against the base of the bath then pooling, creaking pipes as Ollie turned off the hot tap. A long, low groan as he lowered himself into the water. She smiled. Ollie had made bread. His bread had never failed before. But Ollie had made bread.

She took out the *Foods of the World* cookbook. There was hope and she was going to do what she could to keep hold of this thread. She flicked through the pages, past images of sauerkraut and enormous fat sausages. At the beginning of the desserts section: an intricate house made of gingerbread. She tried to remember whether, as a child, she'd enjoyed or been afraid of the Hansel and Gretel story, whether she'd ever read it to the girls. She smoothed out the page for the next recipe. Primitive cartoon-like images of bees in the top corner and a list of ingredients that Nora ticked off in her mind then pulled from the cupboard and fridge.

She had everything for the bee stings set out on the bench when she read the part that said to rest the dough overnight. Deflated, she put the ingredients away and made a batch of gingerbread men instead, used the cutter that Ollie had used to make biscuits with the girls when they were young.

As she pressed the dough into shapes, she recalled that first morning she'd caught Lara eating banana bread at the table with Ollie. He'd had to work so hard to get her girls onside, Trudie especially, and in typical Ollie fashion he'd never once complained, never once made it seem an effort, or like a duty.

Nora had a tray of gingerbread men cooling on the table when Ollie emerged in a towel, steam from the bathroom wafting into the lounge like some kind of wraith.

'I used to make these with my grandmother.' He bit into a gingerbread man. 'Perfect.' He kissed her. '*Danke.*'

Nora, still covered in flour, felt her heart lift.

The night had been long. Ollie was unsettled, kept calling out in his sleep, woke at three and made himself breakfast. Five hours later, Nora was exhausted, was tempted to go back to bed when Ollie finally fell asleep again, but if she did that the day would be gone. If she slept, there'd be no time for anything but reaction to Ollie's disease.

She drove towards the shop but couldn't make herself go inside. Couldn't face the conversation about the demise of her life and – much as she relied on Sally's support, much as she appreciated it – she drove past. It wasn't until she got to Woodbridge that she realised what she'd done. It had been years since she'd taught art classes there, but somehow she found herself in the car park.

It was school holidays and the place was empty, so Nora decided to get some fresh air, bring some sense back into her brain. She climbed out of the car and walked between the buildings and down to the bottom oval. Lately, she'd begun to worry whether Ollie's condition might be contagious. It was a stupid thought, she knew that, and yet her memory kept failing her in ways that seemed perplexing and unreasonable.

She walked around the oval, weaving in and out of the poplars that surrounded it. It had been the same kind of day when she, Sally and Gurj first hit it off at the school fete. Gurj was wearing a lion's mane, had decorated the bookstall with posters inspired by *The Lion, the Witch and the Wardrobe*, and was doing his best to get kids engaged. He'd tried to interest Hannah, Rob and Lynn's daughter, but she'd told him books were for dickheads.

Gurj had introduced himself to Nora and Sally as the new librarian, then nodded towards the water-balloon stall where kids were shrieking as they threw balloons at staff. 'Impossible to compete with that.'

'Actually, we did okay on the cake and preserves stand.' Sally gestured to the empty trestle table. 'Hard to compete with sugar too.'

Gurj turned to Nora. 'I feel like we've met.'

'I help with the art program but I've only been in a couple of times this term.'

'Right. Wasn't sure if it was that or if it was one of those fate things.' Gurj pushed his mane out of his face.

'Probably both,' Sally said.

Lynn and Rob joined them, shared chocolate crackles they'd bought at the cake stand. Then Hannah and a couple of kids from Kingston High were found smoking and drinking a Cascade long neck in one of the school's sailboats, and Rob and Lynn had to haul Hannah off to their car.

Sally, Nora and Gurj stood around chatting for the rest of the afternoon; Sally supplying hedgehog slice, all of them lamenting the lack of booze.

Near the end of the day, Gurj introduced them to Graham. 'Graham's the principal at Kingston High, which is why he's spent most of the day talking to my boss instead of helping me,' Gurj said and smiled.

'I think you can hold your own,' Graham replied.

So much had happened in the years in between. Nora felt a surge of gratitude for the steady support of her friends, knew it was foolish to cut herself off. She drove back to the shop.

When Nora got home, Ollie was standing at the open front door.

She climbed out of the car. 'Good morning. How'd you sleep?'

'Do you know where my wife is?'

Her heart sank. 'That's me, Ollie.'

'I can't find my wife.'

She removed shopping bags from the boot.

Ollie's voice louder now, agitated. 'If you see my wife, will you tell her I've been looking for her?' He closed the front door on her.

Only yesterday he had seemed himself, and she'd been hopeful. Now hope felt like a cruel and pointless thing. Perhaps Gurj was right: maybe it was easier to lose your partner suddenly.

She let herself in and put the groceries on the kitchen bench, left quietly through the back door and stood by the smokehouse, summoned the will to pretend. Was reminded of the endless games of make-believe when the girls were small. Wished she could escape to Gurj's house or go for a walk with Sal; escape to the refuge of friendship.

This time she entered loudly. 'Ollie, it's me, Nora. I'm home.' And there she was, an actor in her own life.

'Oh, I've been looking for you. Did that other lady tell you?'

And although it had been days since she'd been able to convince him to clean his teeth, she forced herself to go over and kiss him. 'Yes. Yes, she did.'

⬩

They had a few good weeks, and Nora was buoyed. She and Ollie slipped into a semblance of their old routines, and when he put dishes in the wrong place, made coffee with cold water, she ignored it. On a rainy afternoon, he ran his hands down her back, and while they made love slowly she tried not to think it could be the last time.

The next evening, after Ollie finished washing the dishes, he sat in the sling chair. Nora knew he'd fall asleep soon and that she should stay with him till he did, enjoy what might be the last vestiges of normal, but the inevitability of relapse was wearing her down and she thought she might suffocate if she didn't get away.

'Have a good walk,' Ollie called after her as she headed out the door, and she almost turned around and changed her mind.

She was halfway to Gurj's place when the rain started. By the time she got there, her jeans and T-shirt were pressed flat to her skin, water snaking down her arms.

'Shit.' Gurj pulled her inside, closed them in the warm shell of his house.

Her whole body shook; her face was both hot and numb.

'Don't move.' Gurj brought towels, wrapped one around her back, used another to dry her hair. 'You're freezing.' He led her closer to the fireplace. 'Stand there. I'll get you a drink.'

He returned with a blue chenille dressing-gown and two glasses of cognac. She stripped to her underwear, left her soaked outer clothes in a pile on the hearth and tied Gurj's dressing-gown tight around her, then lifted the glass to her mouth with two hands and drank the cognac in one hit. She coughed. 'God, that's disgusting.'

Gurj pinched his nose and poured cognac down his throat. 'Want another?'

'Christ, no.' She laughed, felt tremors move under her skin, the twitch of her left eye.

Seeing Gurj notice, she ran her index finger across her eyelid. 'Always happens when I'm stressed. Since I was a kid.' She sat on the couch, reached forward and rubbed her hands together in front of the fireplace.

A gentle silence filled the room as the two of them were absorbed in the warmth.

'I'm sorry, Gurj. This isn't fair.'

'Don't be ridiculous. We've been friends for more than fifteen years. You're supposed to depend on me.' He added logs to the fire, moved them about to ensure there was enough oxygen to keep the flames alive. 'How's Ollie?'

'He's good. It's weird but he's been good for a few weeks now. As though something has happened to wind it all back.'

'That's great news.'

'Yeah. It won't last.'

Gurj smiled. 'It might, for a while.'

'Stupid thing is that I can't really enjoy it. I feel like I'm going mad waiting. Almost as if I'd rather that it was unequivocal. How fucked is that? How stupid am I? I should be thrilled, but all I can think about is how long it will last.' She picked up the poker and stabbed at the coals. 'And I'm complaining to you, of all people, right after you've lost your mum. Christ, I'm a selfish bitch.'

He put his arm around her.

'I'm so fucking angry with him. How messed up is that? As if it's his fault that he has this stupid disease. But I can't help it; sometimes I really hate him.'

'Do you want to get drunk?'

She shrugged.

'We should definitely get drunk.'

Gurj went to the kitchen, picked up the phone and called Sally, then he brought the cognac and a bottle of wine into the lounge.

Sally let herself in. 'Nice outfit, Nor.'

'What's wrong with it?' Gurj feigned offence.

Nora pushed herself up from the couch, paraded around the room and turned dramatically, flicking the ties on Gurj's dressing-gown.

'Very nice.' Sally drained her first glass and clapped. 'Gorgeous, darling.'

'Very bloody gorgeous.' Gurj was getting drunk already, had never been able to hold his booze.

Sally sat on the lounge chair opposite, put her feet on the coffee table and wiggled her toes at the fire. 'Where's Ollie?'

'Home.'

'Is that a good idea? I mean, is he okay?'

'I don't know. He's a grown man. It's not like he's gone shooting. Anyway, I slipped him a couple of sleeping tablets.'

'Okay.'

'We're getting properly shit-faced. Are you in?' Gurj asked, as though the three of them didn't have form.

It was late when Darren came to pick Sally up. By then Sally was wearing one of Gurj's sweaters and his ugg boots, and Nora had added a pair of Graham's football socks to the dressing-gown ensemble. There were three empty wine bottles on the coffee table, a fourth open.

'You three have given it a nudge.'

Gurj got a fresh glass from the kitchen. 'No beer, sorry, mate.' He poured a glass of red for Darren.

'Don't mind if I do.' Darren got the fire roaring, and the night rolled into itself as they drank, and talked over and around one another.

In the morning, Nora watched as Gurj brought the fire back to life. Her mouth was coated; she swallowed, tried to rid herself of the foul taste. He made them both coffee with condensed milk and they sat on the floor sipping. Darren was half hanging off the couch, his arm resting on the floor next to his wife. Sally opened one eye, groaned and rolled over.

Nora and Gurj finished yesterday's gulab.

'How are you not hungover?' she asked him.

'It's my institution. Graham always said I have a very good institution.'

Nora laughed. 'Constitution.'

'I know. It was our private joke. I still miss saying it.'

~

Nora was sitting at the table trying to decide whether to leave when Sally finally woke. Darren continued to snore on the couch and Gurj had gone back to bed.

Nora put a cup of coffee by Sally's head and shoes by her feet. 'Let's walk it off.'

'Fuck, really?' Sally blew across the surface of her coffee then sipped tentatively.

They walked up into the hills beyond Gurj's, past the place where an elderly couple from Melbourne had taken sleeping pills a year earlier and were found entwined in rigor mortis.

'Christ, I feel awful. How 'bout you? I mean, apart from the hangover. How are you really?'

'I don't know.' Nora dragged her hair back into a ponytail. 'Ollie's there then he's not. He's himself, then he's aggressive, then afraid, little-boy afraid. I can't imagine how it is for him. How frightening losing yourself must be. And I just want to go back to the way things were. To a time when the future wasn't so fucking terrifying.'

At the beginning of the trail, Nora stopped.

'Had enough?' Sally asked.

Nora looked up at her. 'Sorry?'

'Walking. I mean walking.'

'Right. Yeah. Of course.' Nora sat on the bitumen and hugged herself tight, chin on her knees. 'I feel so sick.'

Sally sat next to her and put her hand on Nora's leg.

'I always told myself I left Tom for me,' Nora said and laughed softly. 'But it's not true, Sal. I left him for Ollie.' She traced a love heart in the gravel with her index finger then scrubbed it out. 'I didn't want to admit I was that kind of a woman. I mean, it's weak, isn't it?'

'No, it's not.' Sally let her hand drop.

'It always seemed weak to me, the idea of needing someone else to make you whole. But now, after all this time with Ollie, it just seems normal.' She let tears run down her cheeks. 'I have no idea who I'll be when he's gone.'

Nora planned wallaby casserole, coq-au-vin style, like old times. She'd serve it with mashed potato and too much butter. Distract the girls from their interrogation about Ollie, assure them that everything is okay. She'd pour wine and bombard them with questions about Lara's new life in Puerto Williams, and Trudie's latest dating dramas. While they were talking, she'd whip gold into white, beat the potato until all sign of butter had disappeared.

When she opened the freezer there, between two packs of wallaby meat, was the missing key to the gun safe. Ollie must have dropped it there after the last shooting trip. Must have let the key chain slip from his fingers when he packed the butchered meat away. She told herself he hadn't done it deliberately, in the way he sometimes put his dirty socks in the oven. In the way he often peed in the laundry if she didn't manage to redirect him. She put those thoughts aside. At least now she could lock the gun safe, hide the key somewhere that he would never find it.

Ollie slept late as he often did now, as he'd never done in all of their years together. He climbed down midmorning. Nora was lying in the sling chair worrying and pretending to read.

On his way to the kitchen he stopped to kiss her forehead. 'Coffee?'

'Thanks.' She put her book down and turned on her side,

watched as he moved effortlessly across the floor, still so easy in his large limbs. His high arches bridging from one slate slab to the next. He lifted his arm as though it weighed nothing and filled the coffee pot. Everything tiny in his hands.

She watched him sawing through the loaf of sourdough. He took a knob of salami from the fridge, carved it, made the bread disappear beneath slices of cured meat, then moved to the table and poured their coffee into the soapstone espresso cups they'd bought in Africa. She smiled; he seemed fine. Today would be a good day.

They sat, the muted sound of Ollie's closed-mouth chewing a backdrop to their easy silence.

'I thought I might visit Agnes. Want to come?' Ollie asked.

She sipped coffee, gave herself time to think. 'Agnes isn't there.' She kept her voice even.

'Gone away?' Ollie looked up from his breakfast.

'Mmhmm.' Nora nodded, took another sip. She waited for the next question, not yet sure what her response should be. The books said it was often best to agree, better not to confront. Best not to cause distress. But what of her distress? Did that not count for something?

'Would you like more coffee?' Ollie asked, coffee pot hovering mid-air, ready to tilt, and Nora thought of Agnes buried last year.

When Trudie and Lara arrived, Ollie was at the top of the property. Nora was inside folding washing. She had not cooked, had been derailed by the question about Agnes, by the idea that Ollie did not remember her death, her funeral, helping one of her daughters clear out her house. Ollie had wrapped his arms around Agnes's daughter and she'd cried for more than an hour. How could his disease have robbed him of that memory? How could it be right that Ollie would go this way?

Trudie and Lara tumbled through the door, and Nora felt a surge of relief as Trudie carried in bags of groceries and commanded her to relax.

'Where's Ollie?' Trudie was unpacking groceries while Lara put coffee on.

'Chopping firewood.'

'I might go and help him,' Lara said.

'Maybe leave him for a bit.'

'I want to spend some time with him before I head off again.'

'Just wait till he comes in.'

'Right. Okay. Sure.'

'He needs to feel capable, Lar. It will only upset him if you try to help.'

'I understand. It's just that I've been looking forward to seeing him.'

It wasn't a cold day, but Nora, ignoring the pages ripped from novels she'd found in the kindling box, had lit the woodfire for the girls, and now the room was too hot. She turned the damper down and listened to their stories about Lara's research and the new person Trudie was seeing. More than once, Nora, staring at the flames, tuned out and had to force herself back into the present. Lara wouldn't be home for long and she should be enjoying having them all here together, but she felt like a guest in her own home, or an extra in a movie that she didn't have the script for.

Finally, the girls brought coffee and cake to the table.

'Can I go get Ollie now?' Lara asked.

Nora rolled out of the sling chair and stretched.

'Actually, he's working on the smokehouse.' Trudie was looking out the kitchen window.

'Let's eat. He'll come in when he's ready,' Nora said, cramming a hunk of cake into her mouth, licking cream cheese icing from her fingers.

'Have you and Ollie made plans?' Lara asked.

'Tell me about chilly Chile.'

'We're worried, Mum,' Trudie said, joining them at the table.

'I don't want to talk about it. Did you bring your photos, Lar? I want to see a million photos of penguins, and at least seven of you.'

Lara took packets of photographs from her bag and talked nonstop as she showed Nora image after image. Most of the photos were of penguins, some of a town hardly larger than Kettering, and a few were of Lara smiling and huddled with groups of people she worked with.

Nora marvelled at the life Lara had arrived at, what it might lead her to, who she might become. And yet somehow, there in the A-frame, with Ollie working outside and she and the girls by the fire, it seemed as though Lara had never left, as though she didn't now live in another country, another climate, another culture. As though she wasn't now another person. Nora felt the bite of jealousy. The sediment of her own life. She swallowed more cake, sipped coffee and tried to quell the anxiety that was rinsing through her body. She could hear Ollie banging around outside, the creaking of the rusting door hinges of the smokehouse. She was mid-swallow when it hit her, like a swarm of bees in her chest: her life with Ollie was over. She beat at her breastbone.

'You okay, Mum?' Trudie was on her feet, banging on Nora's back.

The swarm dropped into Nora's abdomen. All of the things that she should have done fell across her vision like rain. Squandered years. She'd been arrogant and wasteful with their time and now Ollie was past being able to teach her to do this simple task that was at the heart of their lives.

She could reverse the boat trailer down the ramp, launch the thing and, at the end of the day, winch the boat back on and tow it home. The handle of the small axe carried the impressions of her fingers. Imprints of Ollie's recipes – sourdough, dark rye, banana bread – were etched in her brain. But the smokehouse. She had always left the smokehouse to him and now he wouldn't teach her.

'Mum. Hello. Are you in there?' Lara touched Nora's arm.

Nora shook her head to clear the buzz. 'We need to help him.'

'Mum?'

She caught the girls exchanging a look, but neither of them said more. She closed her eyes and steadied herself, one hand resting on the bench, the other still at her chest. She tried to push calm through her body, settle the hive. 'We need to help with the smokehouse,' she said, and they both smiled at her in a way that seemed choreographed and unreal.

'Of course,' Lara replied.

'Hello there.' Ollie's grin was wide enough to capture them all.

He was dressed, as usual, in his clay-coloured overalls and a threadbare T-shirt that used to be white. He was using a kitchen spatula to press mortar into the cracks between bricks.

Lara and Trudie stood on tiptoes either side of Ollie, kissed him on opposite cheeks. Then Nora clasped her hands around one of his biceps, pressed her nose to his skin and breathed him in. He bent towards her, and she kissed his cheek. The faint smell of papier-mâché glue on his hands, stuck to his arms. Nora inspected the contents of the mortar bucket, knew it was flour and water. She bit her lip as he set about his work again, oblivious to the futility of his actions.

'Need some help?' Lara said.

Ollie turned. 'Finally she asks.' The flint of his old humour sparked. 'Just about finished here,' Ollie said, scraping the dregs from the bucket and pushing them into cracks. 'Next we will do the sealing but first this must cure. Two hours. Three hours.'

Nora gathered the twigs, bark and small branches that had found their way into the clear space that Ollie usually maintained around the smokehouse. As she crouched and grasped, she lamented the fickleness of Ollie's disease, the way he had become less fastidious about some things, more so about others. The girls joined in, and between them they created a pile of kindling next to the wood stack.

They worked – bending, twisting, placing. Nora paused to survey, realised that Ollie was no longer helping. He had backed away slightly, was resting against the trunk of the old gum. Nora went back to clearing, extended the tableau in the hope that the memory of it might linger in him, but in that moment she wasn't even sure he knew who the girls were. She hated the disease that snaked through his brain, indiscriminately stealing his past, their past, their future.

When she checked again he had disappeared.

'It's okay, Mum. He's in the house,' Trudie said.

Nora released her breath.

'I'll check on him,' Lara offered.

From the languid pace and length of Lara's gait as she returned, Nora knew that Ollie had gone again.

'He peed in the kitchen sink,' Lara said, shocked.

'Oh.' The sound emerged quietly, high pitched, as though from a tiny hole deep in her chest. All pretence of normality collapsed. She opened her mouth, and the bees fled the hive in a wailing swarm.

Ollie was asleep in the sling chair, and Nora let the girls put her to bed in the loft. She hadn't told them she and Ollie no longer slept up there, not since she'd woken one night to find him hovering by the edge of the ladder as though about to step off.

She was curious to know what the girls were talking about downstairs, how much they now understood about the way things really were, whether they were scheming to get her help with Ollie.

As she settled under the duvet, she worried that the girls would sleep in the study, closer to Ollie, where Nora often slept these days. For some reason, she wanted them to sleep in their old room. She stared at the knots and twists in the timber ceiling, for a long time thought over and over: *Nothing runs smooth. Nothing runs smooth.* She wished the sling chair were big enough for her and Ollie to sleep in together, wished he would come and join her, wrap his body about hers like a cocoon.

She woke early. When she climbed down, Ollie was snoring. He was on the floor, and the girls had thrown a blanket over him, pushed a pillow under his head. Nora imagined him waking disoriented, sitting, rubbing his eyes. Completely himself, or more likely not.

She made coffee and sat at the table. Ran her fingers along the wood grain, thought about the first time she'd seen inside the smokehouse. She remembered the sweet musty smell of applewood smoke, picking the splinters from her T-shirt afterwards. She wished they still slept in the loft together, wished they could wind back to the beginning and start again. She would do it all the same. Only the ending would be different.

She poured another coffee and watched Ollie's great chest rise and fall, listened to the rhythm of his breath – calm, measured, yet full. She felt him in her marrow, wondered how she would breathe when he was gone.

Later in the morning, the girls made breakfast and the three of them ate while Ollie still snored in front of the wood heater.

'You're doing a good job, Mum,' Trudie said.

'But we think you need help. Both of you,' Lara said.

'Thanks, girls. But I'm fine. We're fine.'

'There's nothing fine about this, Mum. And we don't want to interfere but we're worried about both of you.'

'Look at him, Mum. It's almost lunchtime and he's asleep.'

'It's just his body clock.'

'For Chrissake, Mum. He peed in the kitchen sink. When did that start?'

She felt her face go hot as if the shame of Ollie's actions belonged to her. Their lives laid bare; Nora was infuriated. 'I'm sure you both mean well but Ollie and I will make the decisions about our lives.'

'Come on, Mum. Ollie can't. We wish that he could. But—'

Nora got up, turned her back to the girls and started washing the dishes.

Right after the diagnosis, Ollie had asked her if she'd put him out of his misery. 'When things get really bad. Maybe a bit before.' He'd looked at her hopefully. 'I wouldn't ask you to shoot me, Nora, but we could get some pills. You could kiss me goodbye. Let me go to sleep.'

She had cried violently until she could hardly breathe, and then Ollie had wrapped his arms around her and promised he hadn't meant it.

Hands deep in scalding water, she thought about the time she'd gone shooting with him. Ollie was helping Harry with a cull on one of the farms on Bruny and she'd wanted to see what it was like. She remembered the cage-like rear of the ute, the spotlights. Roos, sliced through the ankles, hung off hooks on the purpose-built frame at the back of the vehicle. Flesh sliced open, testicles removed, then bodies carved down, entrails spilt.

The next morning they'd walked on the beach, the bracken crunch of dried barnacles underfoot. Small cliffs of grey and white stone, and trees bursting out of the sloping bank, somehow growing straight up, their roots wound across the earth, desperately holding on.

She hadn't asked to go again, but every time Ollie went shooting she would make a loaf of dark rye, and while it baked she'd beat the carpets over the wooden railing of the front verandah and try not to think about those fresh, warm carcasses hanging from the frame.

'Mum.' Trudie shifted into Nora's field of vision.

'We brought some information.' Lara held a pack of nursing home brochures in front of her.

Nora looked away.

'I'm sorry, Mum, but you've got to be honest with yourself. You need to make plans, for both of your sakes,' Trudie pleaded.

She walked towards the door and went outside.

Ollie ran his hand up Nora's thigh as she climbed down the ladder with a fresh duvet cover.

'Want to get crays near Tinderbox?' He smiled. 'Yes?'

Nora couldn't remember when Ollie had last put the craypots out, but she did recall the last time she'd tried to take him fishing. Today though, he seemed fine. He seemed Ollie. Against all logic, she let a wisp of hope take flight in her chest.

'Why not? Sounds great.' She threw back a coffee and returned up the ladder to put on warm clothes. She should move her clothes downstairs but that would feel too permanent, too much like an admission of defeat.

When Ollie went to the driver's side, Nora, on autopilot, climbed into the passenger seat then remembered the last time he had driven. She was about to get out and insist they swap places but she smelt toothpaste on his breath. It had been a long time since Ollie had cleaned his teeth unprompted. Maybe this disease wasn't all downhill; maybe there were flat stretches, meagre inclines.

She ran her fingers across the back of his neck as he started the car, watched closely as he drove: fluid gear changes; comfortable, confident cornering. She decided to relax.

They'd been driving for twenty minutes, had just passed Margate, when Ollie turned to her. 'I'm not sure how to get there. Can you tell me the way? Stupid, stupid, stupid.'

The wisp of hope withered. She rubbed the back of his neck again and tried not to calculate how many times they'd driven this route.

'Of course.'

Every couple of minutes when he looked at her for confirmation she told him to follow the road, to keep going. At Kingston he asked if she had brought wine then swerved into the supermarket car park.

'Did you bring wine? Did you? Did you?' Ollie took the key from the ignition.

'Of course,' Nora lied, and he started the car again and drove off smoothly.

They were approaching the junction where they needed to turn right towards Blackmans Bay when he became agitated.

'Which way now? Which way? Quick. Quick.'

'Turn right, Ol. Turn right.'

'Right, right.' He turned left.

'We needed to go right, Ol.'

'I know.' He drove on.

She was expecting him to find somewhere to turn around, go back, but he kept on driving. A couple of minutes along was the roundabout that took you towards Longley, on to the Southern Outlet or back into Kingston.

'Which way, which way?'

He had picked up speed and so, instead of telling him to go all the way round, Nora shrieked, 'Straight ahead. Straight ahead.'

They hit the rim of the roundabout hard, all three sets of wheels on the car and boat trailer clunking up, across and over the concrete edging.

Ollie stopped the car and got out. 'Well, that was a bloody stupid idea.'

She opened her door, rested against the boot of the car and breathed deeply. When her heart stopped hammering, she told him to get in the passenger seat and she drove them home.

Nora had spent the return trip planning how she'd hide the car keys, wondering what she'd do if he got aggressive about it.

'Home, home, home.' Ollie rapped his knuckles on the bonnet.

She led him inside. 'Are you hungry?'

'Hungry, hungry, hung, hung, hung.' He was trying to drag his trousers down.

'Do you need help?' She reached for his zip, and he pushed her in the chest. She fell hard, watched Ollie walk out the back door and pee against the old gum.

Later that night, bruised and feeling fragile, Nora chopped vegetables to make ratatouille. She didn't even like the dish, but Sally would have closed the shop by now so it was that or bread and cheese again.

She fried the vegetables in a pan, opened a bottle of shiraz and watched Ollie moving about the room touching walls, books, vases – tap, tap, tap – as though he needed to test their solidity. He was driving her crazy. He had a conversation in front of the mirror by the sideboard. Words in German, gesticulation. Grinning and head shaking. For now they were best mates. It would be like that until he'd had enough, tried to walk away and caught the bloke still staring, mimicking him.

She could hardly believe this was their life now. Could hardly believe she'd thought they could go out in the boat. The things she was telling herself. She was losing her fucking mind.

She ate ratatouille from the pan and sobbed. Poured a glass of wine. Bitterly, she watched the scene between Ollie and his reflection play out, snot and tears sliding down her face. She should probably take the mirrors down or turn them around, but what difference would it really make? What difference would anything make?

The nursing home told her it would be better just to move him in one go. Nora played the conversation over in her head – too hard when you ease them in, more unsettling for everyone, too confusing. She shouldn't be hard on herself. No-one could sustain it alone. She tried to believe the assurances but she felt ill. She was betraying him.

They'd given her the weekend to think about it, but she'd known the answer straightaway. Ollie would never do that to her. No matter how bad it got, she couldn't do it. But, over the weekend, she noticed the pacing, the pushing, the conversations Ollie had with his reflection – the way they seemed like the only thing he understood.

She thought of the times he'd peed in the corner, in the cupboard, in the kitchen sink, that one occasion when he couldn't work the clips on his overalls and a turd had slipped out, been squashed into the grooves in the floorboards, and she'd had to scrub it out with an old toothbrush. The day he'd shat himself in the sling chair and she couldn't get him up, had to turn him out onto the floor and the shit had gone everywhere.

Mostly, though, there was the absence of everything he used to be. She missed his strength, his capability, the way he'd always known when to get things done and when to stand back and let her be capable and strong. She missed the long, slow sex; the fast, desperate sex. She missed the feeling of being bound together, as if they were one body. She missed the presence of hope.

The nursing home had made it sound like a choice. But others were on the waitlist, and she didn't have his name down anywhere else.

Nora cooked the foods Ollie loved, bought his favourite wine, but it wasn't possible to turn the wheel back. Ollie paced, dragged books into towering piles and attempted to find items long gone.

She tried not to think about all of the things they wouldn't do again, how quiet and empty and impossible the house might be on her own. She wanted to make love one more time, but the last attempt, months ago now, was almost too painful to think about. Ollie had been fine that night, had seemed himself, and so when they went to bed she had straddled him, moved slowly, kissed his lips. He smiled and she was captured by both joy and sorrow, let tears leak down her face. Then he dropped his hands from her breasts, lay perfectly still.

'What are you doing?' he asked.

'It's okay, happy tears,' she assured him.

'Get off.' He pushed her aside.

Too wounded to move, she sat hunched, arms knitted around her knees.

Trudie had wanted to go with her to the nursing home, help Ollie get settled, but Nora told her it would be easier on her own, less distressing, though she wasn't convinced. She'd packed Ollie's suitcase days before, put it in the corner. Aware of its presence every time she moved in and out of the room.

She prayed that he would not be himself when they went. Prayed that he would. Tried to focus on the job. Tried not to think about all of the last times. Wished she had known them for what they were, then changed her mind, was glad that she hadn't.

The matron left them. Nora opened Ollie's suitcase on the bed while he stared vacantly.

She was surprised when the woman re-entered the room without knocking.

'Oh, you'll have to take those. He can't wear those.' The matron pointed to the overalls that Nora was packing into the drawers.

'It's all he wears.' She closed the drawer.

'Sorry.' The woman shook her head. 'No belts. No buckles. Nothing that doesn't work with incontinence pants.'

'But he's not …'

'You'll have to bring something else.'

'But he won't wear anything else,' Nora said.

The matron crossed the room and took Ollie's neatly folded overalls from the drawer, and pressed them into Nora's hands.

Nora stood there and remembered the first time she'd climbed the ladder in the A-frame, the first time Ollie had taken her out on the boat. He would never do this to her. He would shoot her before he would do this to her. She piled his clothes back into the suitcase and grabbed his arm, turned him towards the door. 'Come on, it's time to go home.'

Nora ignored the matron's protests, left the woman standing in the room with Ollie's open suitcase on the bed. His pocketknife hidden, tucked into a pair of thick socks.

'Come on, Ol. We're going home,' she repeated.

He shook his hand free, went back to the room.

'Come on, Ollie,' Nora pleaded.

The woman looked smugly at Nora.

Ollie moved to the bed, flicked the suitcase closed and zipped it with the kind of dexterity he'd rarely shown recently.

'Let's be sensible.' The matron grabbed Ollie's elbow, tried to direct him.

Ollie shrugged her off, picked up the suitcase and reached his other hand out to clasp Nora's. They walked together to the car.

'Let's talk about this.' The matron was almost shouting as she followed them. 'Let's start again.'

Ollie sidled up to Nora, chuckled conspiratorially as the woman continued her diatribe.

Nora opened the car boot, took the suitcase from Ollie and threw it in. She longed for the days when the boot was full of biscuits, their life together still ripe with promise.

'Bitch.' Ollie sat in the passenger seat.

Nora sat beside him, hands on the steering wheel. 'Stupid cow,' she said, and they laughed, long and hysterically, a team effort. Nora's laughter continued until it was a sob – a last time stuck in the moment, in the car of all places.

She gathered herself. 'You need to put your seatbelt on, Ollie.'

He looked at her blankly. He seemed afraid, confusion scored into the tiny lines about his eyes, laughter gone.

She reached across to gather the strap, yanked it taut. Just before the tongue clicked into place, she felt time stretch – this was where she got out of the car, where she took Ollie's hand, returned to the room, apologised to the woman. This was where she left him. But then the buckle locked.

She pulled into their driveway, a heaviness weighing down on her as though the air were laced with mercury. Ollie had fallen asleep, and she was not sure whether to leave him there or wake him. If she opened the windows and took the keys, he should be safe.

She touched his cheek, wove her fingers through the beard that had been growing since it got too difficult to shave him. If he were a dog or a roo, Nora would be working up to shooting him, planning when she might have to relieve him of the burden of his suffering. At least that's what Ollie would do.

She was still sitting in the car when Sally arrived.

'I thought you might need company.' Sally started talking before she was out of her car, before she noticed Ollie in the passenger seat. 'Oh. I didn't realise.' Sally dropped her voice to a whisper.

Nora's eyes filled with tears as she climbed out of the driver's side. 'What have I done, Sal? I don't know what I'm doing anymore.'

'I've put an ad on the noticeboard.' Sally frowned. 'I don't want you to be mad, Nor. Gurj and I talked about it and, well, we know it's not our place, but …' She turned her palms over, supplicated.

Nora stood in front of the board and read the words Gurj and Sally had put together, read the spaces in her life, the places where she was failing. She knew that Sally expected her to be angry, that in another life she probably would be, but Nora was flooded with relief, like a blood transfusion, a lifeline. *Kind, intelligent, attentive, patient.* They were the words she might have used herself. The sorts of descriptions she still aspired to but rarely achieved.

'Oh, Sal. What would I do without you two?'

'You'd stay sober, probably.'

They laughed, the kind of small laugh that you turn to when crying feels like the appropriate response.

'You're the best.'

The girl – whose parents Harry knew – climbed out of a beat-up orange Datsun, shielding her eyes from the sun. She slammed the door shut and strode across the driveway to shake Nora's hand.

'Rachel.'

Nora stretched her hand out, introduced herself. 'Come inside. I'll make us some coffee.'

It would be Nora's third cup and already her stomach was

restless, the back of her neck tight, but last night had been long. She'd only managed a scant few hours of sleep just before dawn.

She led Rachel into the house. 'My husband's asleep.'

The girl smiled at her. 'Harry told me he slept a lot.'

'During the day, yes,' Nora said.

'Would you like me to make it?' Rachel took the coffee pot from her, spooned in coffee and turned on the cooktop.

'Thanks.' Nora sank into a chair at the table.

While the coffee was brewing, Rachel made conversation. 'Great house. Did you build it?'

'Ollie did. Harry helped on some of it. Ollie's always been good with his hands.' How she wished that were still true.

Rachel brought the pot to the table and poured.

'I should tell you that I'm not sure about this. I mean, it wasn't my idea; my friends wrote the advertisement.'

'Don't worry. I'm not sure either. I mean, I've never done this before, not as a job. Actually, I haven't done many things as a job. I've got a linguistics degree and I spent a lot of time in Europe.' Rachel sipped her coffee. 'Long story short, I don't have any proper experience, but I've learnt to be good with people and I'd like to give it a go if you're keen.'

'Ollie's German.'

'Oh.'

'I don't suppose that matters, it's just sometimes he speaks in German and I don't really understand.'

'I speak a little Hungarian but not much German. Unless you count ordering beers. Sorry.'

'That's okay. I'm not sure it would make much difference.'

'I cared for my boyfriend's grandmother in Romania. Helped nurse her before she died.'

Nora looked over to where Ollie was sleeping in the sling chair.

'Shit. I didn't mean.'

'It's okay.' Nora refilled her cup.

'You should know that I live on Bruny. So I have to plan around the ferries.'

They talked then about logistics, organised for Rachel to do a trial, agreed that, if it worked for all of them, Rachel would do three days a week.

She watched Rachel drive away, wondered at her assuredness, the self-possession that had taken Nora years to come by. Wondered which of them had done the interviewing, worried that the girl might be ambivalent.

'Okay, what do you think I need to know? Are there things he likes? Things he doesn't like? Things you want me to do or not do?'

They were sitting at the table and Rachel, notepad in front of her, was chewing the end of a pen.

Nora wasn't sure what to tell her. 'I should have thought about this, shouldn't I?'

'You know Hugo – that's my boyfriend – his grandmother was terrified of strangers. She kept lunging for me with the poker and we had to take it away until she got used to me. Hugo and I slept with the bedroom door locked for weeks.'

Nora laughed. 'Most of the time Ollie's pretty placid, unless you try to stop him from doing something he wants. Really, I wouldn't ask you to be here if I thought he might be aggressive.' She wondered if she was being honest. 'It's more about the small things. Like getting him to eat. He'll usually eat the things he's helped to cook. But he can't be left to cook on his own.' Nora gestured to a deep burn mark in the table. 'And I know it sounds demeaning, but I take him outside to pee. On the big gum out by the smokehouse.' She tilted her head towards the back door.

'Okay.' Rachel made notes.

'He gets fidgety when he needs to go. You'll start to recognise the signs.' She shook her head. 'The whole house smelt like a urinal. I just couldn't do it anymore.'

'You don't need to explain.'

But she felt traitorous, as if she were describing a toddler or a puppy, not a grown man, not Ollie.

Rachel spent the next three days with Nora and Ollie. She helped to cook, talked to Ollie about books and followed him around the room feigning interest in his gibberish-spattered attempts at conversation.

On the third day, Nora let Rachel convince her to have a rest and she climbed up the ladder to the loft. When she came back down an hour later, Rachel and Ollie were eating banana bread and moving pieces around a backgammon board and, though Ollie's moves on the board bore no resemblance to the rules, he seemed more himself than he had in a long time.

'Were you able to sleep?' Rachel asked.

'No, but it was nice just lying in my own bed. It was nice to know that it was possible.' Nora laughed.

'I know what you mean.'

The following week Rachel had arranged to stay a few nights with a friend in Kettering, and Nora went for a pub meal with Sally and Gurj. Left Rachel with Ollie. Told her she'd be back in a couple of hours but Nora could barely swallow her food and, by the time she'd finished her meal, the anxiety was crushing.

Gurj put his hand over hers. 'Why don't you get home? We'll sort out the bill.'

'I'm sorry.' Nora kissed each of them on the cheek and left.

She was nervous when she opened the front door.

'Who's this then?' Ollie asked from the sofa.

Rachel was painting his toenails. 'This is a friend of mine. I think you'll like her.'

'She's got nice tits.'

Nora burst out laughing. It was not the kind of thing Ollie would ever have said. 'Thank you.'

'I'd like to take it further but I'm married. Sorry about that. Do you like the colour?'

'Ollie wanted red but I only had blue.'

'It's very nice.' The tension in Nora's chest fell away.

The next evening Rachel stayed until late, and they ate the lamb shanks she'd cooked. Afterwards she insisted on washing up while Nora tried to get Ollie washed and into something clean. But, once she'd gotten him undressed and sponged down, he refused to put clothes on.

'Stop. Stop. Stop.'

'Come on, Ol. You'll get cold.'

He sat on the sofa and stretched his legs out, seemed to be admiring his toenails.

'How about undies? Just undies. Maybe a T-shirt.'

Ollie turned away from her, bent down and ran his fingers across his toenails. He started humming.

In the end, she threw a blanket over him and accepted the glass of wine Rachel handed her.

'You know I could stay here overnight if you wanted. Let you sleep. I used to work dusk till dawn on Mykonos. So I'm okay with night shift.'

'Thanks. I'll think about it.' Nora was surprised she hadn't considered that kind of care.

After a couple of months, Nora started leaving Ollie with Rachel for longer stretches. She'd go for lunch with Trudie, meet her old boss Cara at Salamanca Market. To begin with, the hours away had seemed interminable and she made Rachel promise to tell her the truth. Needed to know that her absence didn't upset Ollie. But who was she kidding? Most days he didn't even remember who she was, not properly. She finally got used to leaving him.

As Trudie's birthday drew closer, Nora summoned up the courage to ask if Rachel would stay over alone so she could spend the night in Hobart. By then, Rachel was already sleeping over on the days she worked but, even when she went out, Nora had always come home for the night.

They celebrated Trudie's birthday with a movie at the State Cinema, had dinner afterwards at an Indian restaurant. When they got back to Trudie's, even though Rachel was holding the fort, Nora considered driving home.

'You've had too much to drink,' Trudie reasoned. 'Anyway, what good would it do? Ollie's probably asleep.' Trudie touched Nora's arm. 'You have to give yourself a proper break, Mum.'

They stayed up late talking. Remembering camping trips, the move to Kettering, so many good memories. Somewhere in the midst of reminiscing, Trudie got teary and said she was sorry for everything as though any of it were her fault. They were both crying then, Nora apologising for forgetting that Ollie's disease affected them all.

Finally, when Nora could barely keep her eyes open, Trudie fell asleep with her head on Nora's lap, and Nora sat there for ages, the way she had when Trudie was a baby, until she could no longer ignore her bladder. She gently lifted her daughter's head, went to the bathroom, then went to bed in Trudie's guest room.

In the morning, she got up early and fed Trudie's ridiculous hairless cat. She stroked its skin then stripped the bed and, like a guilty lover, left before Trudie emerged from her bedroom.

As she drove up the Southern Outlet, Nora felt stupid. Ollie wasn't a child. She wasn't expected home yet. She could go to the bakery, head back to Trudie's and pretend that was all she'd been doing. But Trudie might have seen her note, might already know that she'd planned to leave, so she drove on.

She was passing the market on the edge of Margate, the one they'd housed in old train carriages, when it came to her. She would park down the road and walk to the house. It wasn't that she didn't trust Rachel, not that she wanted to snoop, but it seemed like the only way to know if Ollie had really been okay.

When she arrived, she locked the car and walked along the gravel road towards the A-frame. Followed the side fence past the house then made her way over to the smokehouse.

The doors and windows of the house were all open. Midnight Oil's 'Beds Are Burning' album was blaring. Rachel had been a good choice. With no-one else applying, she'd also been the only choice but, for this, Nora let herself believe in fate.

She crept across the yard, as though it were possible her footsteps could be heard above the shouty Oils lyrics. Through the open back door she could see Rachel and Ollie. They were in the kitchen, almost close enough for Nora to reach out and touch, and they were making a batter. Ollie's tattered handwritten banana bread recipe was on the table. Briefly, the scene seemed normal, Ollie seemed perfectly normal.

She watched as Rachel took ingredients from the cupboard and fridge. Then Rachel tied an apron around Ollie's waist. He was wearing pyjama pants, was passive, uncomplaining. Saliva caught in Nora's throat, and she had to swallow hard to stop from coughing. She snuck around to the side of the house. A kernel of melancholy dropped into her stomach, burst and spread through her body. The man in the A-frame was not Ollie. He was a stranger, a non-man inhabiting Ollie's body, and she was repulsed. She had to turn the thought away. Felt the seamless guilt of betrayal.

Rachel had just arrived, was hanging her coat on the stand by the door, the smell of her perfume like the scent of orange jessamine on a summer evening.

'Hello, you.' Rachel took Ollie's arm, tried gently to guide him.

In recent weeks, Ollie had got serious about pacing again, brought his old fence-line habits indoors. For a few hours in the afternoon or evening, sometimes all night. Moving from kitchen to front door and back again. Mostly he shuffled, head tilted forward, chin almost to his chest, like a zombie in a B-grade movie.

Some nights Ollie examined his hands while he walked, as though they were a thing of mystery, as though all of the secrets of the world and the pathway back to himself might be there, written in his skin. His attention was so intent that on occasion Nora was drawn to inspect his hands with him, to check if the answers might all be there, right in front of them.

'How long's he been going?' Rachel asked.

'A while.' Nora tucked her feet under a cushion and curled into the sofa. She let herself drift; in her imagination the two of them were walking in a park somewhere in Germany, in the place of Ollie's childhood, where Nora had always thought they would go some day.

Nora started as Ollie tripped on the edge of the mat, fell into the back of the sofa and pressed heavily into her. The weight of him was too much. She pushed back hard, felt the shift from kindness to frustration, from patience to anger. Ollie's endless steps were wearing her down as though it were her body, her brain being ground away.

Rachel moved furniture, rolled the carpet and propped it in the corner. Things Nora might have done had she been capable of thinking straight, had she not been worrying whether she too might be losing her mind.

She had finished a bottle of pinot, begun a second. 'You know, Rach, it's a fucking heavy weight to bear – the memories of two people. D'you know that?' Nora had been rehearsing the line in her head, but it came out sounding staged and pretentious. She poured herself another wine.

'Maybe you should sleep downstairs tonight.' Rachel filled the kettle.

'I'm not that drunk. I could climb that ladder in my sleep.'

'Okay.'

'It's perfectly safe, you know. Ollie built it.'

Ollie was walking slowly now, dragging his feet.

'Of course.' Rachel made a pot of peppermint tea, let it steep then poured them a mug each.

'Thanks.' Nora was aware of the weight and warmth of the mug in her hands. She closed her eyes and breathed in the peppermint aroma. The two of them sat, sipping tea and observing Ollie on the move and, through an alcoholic haze, Nora felt solidarity with this girl who only months before had been a stranger. Wondered if anyone would ever know her better than Rachel did right now.

Nora undressed, dropped her clothes on the sheepskin by Ollie's side of the bed and climbed under the duvet, leaving Rachel downstairs to rinse their cups and keep watch on Ollie until he tired and fell asleep, or until morning, whichever came first. Nora lay on her back and stared at the apex of the A-frame, tucked the covers under her chin. The tension in her chest lightened a little as frustration dropped away. She placed her hand between her breasts the way Ollie used to, and she tried to feel the beat of her heart and hear Ollie's voice in her mind: 'Ba boom, ba boom, ba boom.' Her tears ran fast, carved a ravine in the hardness that remained beneath and carried her beyond fury to the dense matter of deep, deep sorrow. A sob caught in her throat and she coughed.

'You okay?' Rachel called.

She breathed slowly, gathered her voice. 'Just a hiccough.'

'Would you like this?' Rachel's upper body was visible above the top of the ladder.

Nora sat up.

'I don't think he'll miss one.'

Nora held out her hand as Rachel shook a single pill from the container of Ollie's sleeping tablets. 'Thank you.' She got back into bed.

As Rachel disappeared down the ladder, Nora listened to Ollie's incessant shuffling below. It was like he was erasing their lives step by step by step, and there was nothing she could do to stop it, nothing she could do to stop him.

She heard Rachel dragging the old brown lounge chair across to provide a visual block to the base of the ladder. She rolled towards the wall and buried her face in Ollie's pillow. Her body softened and her eyelids drooped as the warm blanket of the medication eased her into oblivion.

Ollie was in bed, sedated. Nora had returned from Trudie's the evening before and let Rachel go home for a break. She'd hoped for sleep, but Ollie had paced all night and the relaxation of a weekend at Trudie's was long gone. By morning she'd been desperate and exhausted, had given Ollie a double dose of his sleeping tablets. She should sleep herself but she needed some time to participate in life.

She made a batch of dough, left it proving in a bowl on the bench, and went out to the vegetable patch. Garden fork spiked into the earth. She was leaning on the handle, watching her reflection in the kitchen window: thin dress, Blundstone boots, dirt marks like patterns in bark, shadows on her legs. She'd propped the radio on a log by the edge of the path and she was gesturing with her right arm, broad open sweeps, as she mimicked the song, made strangled yodelling sounds. In between bursts of sound she laughed hysterically.

Then Rachel arrived, was at the back door, looking at her as though she was crazy. Nora beckoned her. Rachel shook her head.

'Come on.' Nora said, and Rachel walked across the furrowed earth to stand next to her. The two of them, clasping hands, bellowed and howled like wolves baying to the moon.

Later in the afternoon, Rachel drove to the shop for milk. Nora brushed the dirt from her legs and went inside, removed hunks of cheese and a stick of salami from the fridge, and put it on the table. She was taking salad greens from the crisper drawer when she saw the platter of smoked salmon pushed to the rear of the bottom shelf. It had been months since Ollie had fired up the smokehouse, perhaps more. When had he made it? How was it possible? She dropped to her knees, pressed her forehead to the cold slate floor. Time seemed to leach out of itself into nothing until all she could feel were the ridges in the slate, the chilled air from the fridge.

'Are you okay?' Rachel asked, standing at the open front door.

Nora should have been embarrassed but she didn't have the energy, was disconnected from reality.

She knelt and ran a finger across her forehead, traced the imprint of a cleft in the slate, felt a dribble of something running down her nose. She wiped the wetness across her cheek, saw the red smear on her finger.

'Is Ollie alright? Are you okay? Christ, Nora.'

'When did he do it?'

'Do what?'

'The salmon, Rachel.'

'It was meant to be a surprise. He had a good day when you were up visiting Trudie. It wasn't …'

The trickle of warmth moved down Nora's neck.

'We should get that checked.'

She stood up and leant against the kitchen bench. 'I'm fine.'

'Okay, I understand, but.'

Nora shook her head. Rachel held a clean tea towel under the tap.

Nora stood looking out the kitchen window. 'I'm not sure this is working. I mean, I don't know if I can do this anymore. Maybe it's time.'

'Do you want to use this?' Rachel hovered the damp cloth in front of her eyes and Nora took it without turning.

Outside, the solid form of the smokehouse had slipped inside the shroud of night as though it had somehow disappeared. Nora dabbed at her face, wiped her neck.

'Do you want me to leave?' Rachel asked.

'Yes. No. I don't know.'

'Have you eaten?'

'I can't.'

'How about I make us a snack and then you take one of Ollie's pills? We can talk about it later.'

Nora sat at the table as Rachel carried plates and a leftover loaf of rye bread over. Brought the platter of smoked salmon from the fridge.

'You were supposed to eat it together, but …' Rachel let the words trail off.

Nora tore a chunk from the loaf, stuffed it into her mouth and chewed, mouth half open. She stared into Rachel's face and lifted her glass, poured water into her bread-filled mouth and continued to stare as she chewed the sog down to nothing.

Finally she spoke. 'He is more himself with you. It's like he waits until I've gone.' She began to sob. 'I don't know how to do this anymore.' She wiped at her tears while watching Rachel serve slices of smoked salmon. 'I don't think …' she began. Then she held to the sides of her plate as though it might anchor her. She took another slug of water, swallowed a sleeping pill then lifted the salmon flesh to her mouth, tears dripping on the table. She sobbed with each mouthful, while Rachel awkwardly picked at her food.

She gorged on salmon and opened a bottle of wine, drank glass after glass, well into a second bottle until it felt as though Rachel wasn't really there, as though she was a prop or some kind of device to move Nora along through this, to stop her from collapsing completely. The skin on Nora's forehead felt tight, and she touched the crusted cut.

At last she pushed away from the table and climbed into the sling chair. She lay there sniffing while Rachel washed the dishes, and she thought about this girl who, for reasons she still couldn't quite comprehend, had become a fundamental part of her life.

Rachel brought Ollie's blanket from the sofa and placed it over her. She opened her mouth to speak. 'It's okay,' Rachel said.

She closed her eyes as Rachel smoothed her fringe against her forehead, wiped the tears that continued to slide down her cheeks.

'Go to sleep now.' Rachel's voice was soft, the weight of her hand comforting against the crown of Nora's head, and she let herself imagine it was her mother, breathing in her pain, pressing strength into her skull.

'Dad's moving back.' Trudie was sitting on the edge of the fountain at Salamanca Place, picking stones from the bottom of her shoes with a twig.

'Really? I thought he loved Sydney.'

'Gran's sick. Dad says she'll be alright, but he's actually moving. It has to be a lie, doesn't it?' Trudie looked up at Nora. 'She must be dying.'

'Maybe she just needs some help for a while.'

Trudie gave her a look. 'Gran?'

'You never know? Your gran always liked to keep everyone on their toes.'

'I guess. Anyway, I thought you'd want to know.'

Nora was at the shop, planning a movie night with Gurj and Sally. Gurj wanted to see *The Rose*, but Sal was lobbying for *The Life of Brian*.

The door creaked.

'Well, hello, stranger.' Sally moved around the counter, reached a hand out to Tom.

He embraced her. 'Hi, Sal. Good to see you.' He turned to Nora. 'How are you, Nora?'

Gurj put his hand to the small of Nora's back.

'I'm alright. How's Marjorie? Is there anything I can do?'

'You know Mum. She won't go down without a fight.'

'No, I don't suppose she will.'

Nora was surprised at how easy it felt between them, was comfortable in the ensuing silence, then the mood shifted and Tom took his wallet from his pocket.

'Just need to pick up some basics.' He went towards the fridge.

'When did you arrive?' Sally asked.

'Last week. I've been staying on the sofa at Mum's. Had to give the tenants some time to move out. They've been bloody great about it.' He put a carton of milk and a loaf of bread on the counter.

'You're moving back into the house?'

'Mum's new place is too small.'

'Want to start a tab?' Sally asked.

'Thanks, but I might as well give you the cash.' He went to the door. 'I'm bringing Mum down next week. You should come visit,

Nor. She'd like that.'

'I'm not sure she would.'

'Think about it. For old times' sake.'

'Okay.'

For much of the next fortnight Nora was preoccupied, found herself wondering which of the girls' old rooms Marjorie was sleeping in. One afternoon she left Ollie with Rachel and walked up to the top of the property but couldn't bring herself to climb through the fence. Walked back down and drove there instead.

At the entrance to Tom's property, she had to stop once to open the gate, then again to clip it shut behind her. She remembered the day with the padlock, how that day had cemented it for her, reinforced the rightness of her decision to leave. But now Ollie was disappearing, the life they had was surging in and out of reach, and the person she had become with Ollie was slipping beneath the surface.

Tom opened the back door and kissed her warmly on the cheek. 'It's good of you to come.'

Marjorie was sitting on an unfamiliar lounge chair, looking out at the view across the bay, blankets over her lap and an open book on the coffee table beside her.

'Hello, Marjorie.' Nora stood by the chair.

'Well, isn't this a blast from the past.'

The three of them sat and talked about the old house in Bellerive, about the lives the girls had now: Trudie in her apartment in North Hobart, and Lara still in South America.

Marjorie said they'd been lucky to have such good girls. 'I thought the divorce would ruin those two. But credit to you both.' She raised her glass of water as if in toast.

'And Ollie. Ollie did his fair share. More than his fair share really,' Tom said.

Nora smiled gratefully at him.

'How is Ollie?' Marjorie said.

Nora shrugged. 'It's not easy.'

'Anything I can do?' Tom asked.

'Probably not. But thanks for offering.'

Tom filled her glass. 'I've been checking the fences and I'm thinking of redoing the one between our places. Would that be okay?'

'Actually, it'd be great to get rid of the barbed wire. Some days Ollie gets a bit fixated on the fences. He keeps cutting himself.'

'Okay if I just get in and do it? I'm feeling like I need to be outside.'

'Am I boring you already, Tom?' Marjorie asked.

'Never, Mum. Never.'

Nora couldn't help thinking about how she might have responded to Tom's offer of help in the past. Ironic that his assistance now seemed like a life raft rather than a show of superiority.

She looked at the man who she had once loved and was sorry that life with him had been so suffocating, had felt so small. She tried to picture herself in this house, standing in the kitchen, sitting by the fireplace drinking wine with Tom. She tried to imagine how life might have been if she'd stayed, but in her mind she saw the day she'd met Ollie, the way her heart had thumped in her chest and the muscles in her stomach had clenched. She'd wanted him from the moment he bent down to slip off his boots.

But the life she had with Ollie now was something new, something different again. It was something neither of them would have chosen.

~

Coming down Wiggins Road, Nora noticed the ferry making its way across the bay from Bruny Island. Rachel was with Ollie, and Nora wasn't ready to go home, so she drove through town and stopped at the end of the queue of cars for the ferry, wound down her window and waited.

It had been fine seeing Marjorie, and Nora wasn't sure what to make of it. Her ex-mother-in-law looked frail but she didn't seem unwell, and there'd been none of the thinly veiled judgement Nora had been sure Marjorie would supply. Weren't people meant to become meaner and less forgiving as they aged? Maybe, she thought, if you begin by being judgemental and harsh, the norm is inverted.

When the ferry reached the island, Nora drove straight to The Neck, parked and climbed the steps to the viewing platform. Wind whipped across the vantage point at the middle of the isthmus. For a few minutes, she took in the view.

She closed her eyes and tried to save the image in her mind but she was distracted by the sharpness of the wind on her face, the bleak outlook of Ollie's prognosis. Her life was headed the way it was headed and, unless she was going to abandon Ollie, there was nothing she could do about it.

Rachel was having a few days off. Some friends from Hungary were visiting, and she'd promised to show them around.

'Sounds great,' Nora had said, wondering how she'd cope, how she'd become reliant on Rachel so quickly.

But then on that first morning, right around the time Rachel would normally arrive, she heard a car in the driveway, felt the shift in equilibrium as she allowed herself to fully exhale. She turned away from the toaster to see Trudie letting herself in the front door. 'Oh, it's you.' She smiled.

'Thought I'd escape the madness at work.' Trudie grimaced at her phrasing. 'Sorry. How is he?'

'You know.'

'Not really, Mum.'

'No, me neither. Want some crumpets?'

Ollie, having been awake for much of the night, slept well past breakfast. When he finally rose, Trudie and Nora had finished folding the washing and were about to reward themselves with coffee.

Ollie was wearing his favourite Midnight Oil T-shirt. He'd been wearing it for days by then, and Nora had given up trying to persuade him to change or bathe, to clean his teeth. Trudie raised her eyebrows at Nora as Ollie moved about the room, his penis swinging below his T-shirt. Nora shrugged and sliced large pieces of carrot cake, cream cheese icing almost thicker than the cake itself.

'Are you hungry, Ollie?' Nora held a plate of cake out towards him.

He moved instead to the dresser and began pointing at things. 'There's this. And this.' He looked at Trudie for acknowledgement, and she left Nora's side to stand next to him.

'This, and this.' He picked up a stone paperweight then an old Burda pattern that Nora had bought at the Margate market for no other reason than it reminded her of her mother.

'I liked that one,' Trudie said, as Ollie flipped a book over in his hands, held it by the spine and shook it as though the pages were designed to fall out like confetti. Trudie reached for the framed photograph of her graduation.

Ollie put his arm out. 'Don't touch that. That's my daughter.'

'Sorry,' Trudie said.

Ollie picked up the sheep's skull. 'Poor, poor, poor.' He cradled the skull in his arms.

'Time for cake.' Again, Nora held the plate in front of him. 'Mmm, smells good, doesn't it, Ollie?'

He moved towards her but, just as he was about to take the plate from her, he walked out the back door, pulling his T-shirt up to wrap it around the skull.

'Christ,' Trudie said.

'You get used to it.'

Nora and Trudie sat on the sofa, Nora with a clear line of view out to Ollie, who was in the vegetable patch now, digging up the seedlings she'd planted last week and tossing them into a pile under the big gum.

'Did you hear what he said?'

'Which bit, hon?'

'He said the photo was of his daughter.' Trudie ran her fork across the top of her cake, scooped a mound of icing into her mouth. 'He called me his daughter.' Trudie bit her lip, eyes shiny with tears. 'Do you think he knows who I am?'

'He's been calling you and Lara his daughters for years.'

'Fuck, Mum, I don't know how you do it. It kills me to see him like this. I always thought he could do anything. I mean really, there wasn't anything Ollie couldn't make or fix. And to see him now. I mean, he'd hate it, wouldn't he?' She shook her head. 'He'd fucking hate it. And much as I want him to know who I am – to know who all of us are – I just don't think he does anymore.'

Trudie's foot was resting on the coffee table, and Nora put her hand out to touch it.

Midafternoon, and Ollie was sleeping in the sling chair. Nora and Trudie had spent twenty minutes trying to get his underpants on without waking him or tipping him out of the chair. Minutes of lifting, wriggling and silent full-body shaking laughter. In the end, they'd given up and left the underpants pulled halfway up his thighs.

'High enough not to trip him,' Nora announced, and they headed out to the vegetable patch.

Nora dug while Trudie gathered twigs with twisted gumleaves to take home for the vases she liked to keep about her flat.

'I don't mind living in town as long as I have the smell of the bush. It makes me feel like I can breathe properly.' She took a long, leaf-laden branch and swept it across the gravel by the edge of the vegetable patch.

Nora was halfway through turning the soil when Ollie strode out the back door wearing her slippers, underpants almost to his armpits, and walked across to the side fence. Nora took a deep breath.

'Shall I go?' Trudie asked.

'No. Your dad replaced the top wire. He's fine.'

'Seriously?'

'Yep.'

'Geez.' Trudie exhaled as if she were blowing out a candle.

Nora listened to Ollie's gibberish and tried not to feel annoyed as she replanted the seedlings. Trudie swept long arcs with her branch, made swirling patterns in the gravel under the old gum.

Nora picked up the garden fork and worked it deep into the soil at the bottom of the vegetable patch. Turning it over, again, again, again.

'Maybe it's a good thing he doesn't know us. Maybe it's better than the in-between part,' Trudie said.

Nora stuck the tines of the fork deep into the earth and peeled off her gardening gloves. 'I don't understand how you could say that. Do you actually have any idea what you're saying?' Nora sensed her anger rise. 'The day he can't tie his shoes, the day he can't remember the word for egg, every day, every tiny little thing he loses, he's a step closer to gone. Do you actually understand that?'

Trudie froze.

Nora crouched and dug little holes with her hands and pressed plants into place, compacted the earth around them. When she stood, she saw there were tears streaming down Trudie's face. She touched Trudie's arm – couldn't manage more – as she walked past her into the house.

It seemed like hours before Trudie came inside, long after Ollie had ventured back from his incessant laps and fallen asleep again on the sofa. Nora was chopping shallots for pasta with spinach and pine nuts.

Trudie walked straight through the house and out to her car and, when Nora heard the car door open, she thought about following her, but she couldn't make herself do it, the hum of frustration still vibrating through her nerves. Then Trudie reappeared with an overnight bag and a small box of half-a-dozen wines, poured two glasses and handed one to Nora. She got a sheet from the linen press and threw it over the sling chair.

'That should do it.'

'Great idea, Trudie. Let's hide the chair, treat him like a toddler. He'll really appreciate that.'

'Come on, Mum. I'm trying to help.'

'Then treat him with some bloody respect.'

'I just don't want to him to get stuck again.'

Nora took their plates of food to the table, sat and wound her fork in pasta. She heaped it into her mouth. Then she drained her glass, held it out for a refill. 'I'm sorry, Trudie, sometimes I forget to be kind.'

Trudie reached across the table and held her hand and they sat like that, drinking and eating pasta and salad. They finished the first bottle, started a second, flicked through photo albums and talked about old times.

Later, Nora tucked Trudie into bed in her old room and settled into her bed in the study. She tried to sleep while she waited for Ollie to wake and begin all over again.

On the way home, tears blurred Nora's vision. She pulled into the emergency lane on the Southern Outlet and rested her head on the steering wheel and memories flooded her mind. The shape of Ollie on the slate floor at the bottom of the loft ladder, the weight of his head in her lap, the shock of sirens and a kaleidoscope of strobing lights against a black sky; the antiseptic smell of the hospital.

It had been almost two days since she'd called the ambulance, her heart thundering in her ribcage. The urgency of the early hours in hospital had passed in a blur, Ollie rushed into emergency surgery to relieve the pressure on his brain then, after what felt to her like an interminable wait, he was admitted to the intensive care ward. She was only allowed to stand by his bed for a few minutes before relegation to the critical care waiting area, where she sat on a hard, vinyl-covered chair, the nausea of worry folding the edges of her world until she felt hemmed into herself. She hadn't called anyone, didn't know what to say.

Just earlier, a nurse had told her to go home and get some rest, have a shower. Nothing would happen tonight and now, in the car, the questions they'd asked at the hospital were playing in her mind. How did he climb up there? Why wasn't he in care? Where had she been?

Nora cried until she was empty, until she was not sure she had the energy to drive on.

Ollie had been agitated that day: aggressive and manic. He couldn't settle anywhere, navigated the living area of the house like a maze or some kind of unstructured orientation course. Nora had wondered if he was looking for the sling chair, thought briefly about uncovering it, letting him drop into the familiarity of the animal-skin sling, but she couldn't bear the idea of trying to drag him out of it, couldn't face the thought of cleaning up his piss and shit when he couldn't roll out. He hadn't been up the ladder in months; it hadn't occurred to her that he'd climb it.

Grief rushed through her veins. This was her fault. This was not her fault. She still felt in her marrow the man Ollie had been. Hard as it was, she could not bear to be separated, could not bear the thought that he would live, breathe, sleep in another place. That he might not do any of those things for much longer.

That night, she lit the fire, pulled the sheet off the sling chair, climbed in and drew Ollie's blue mohair rug across her body. She tried not to think about him in that place.

'Don't put me in one of those homes, and I don't want to go to hospital.' He'd said it early on and he'd meant it, but what could she do? Since then, she'd hovered the pillow above his face more than once, and every time her inaction had made her feel weak. Ollie would have done it. He could kill and gut; he could skin. He would have done it for her.

Instead, she'd left him unconscious in that unfamiliar room, bound to a single bed by thick, greyed sheets, while she lay in the home he had made, in the chair he had built, warmed by their fire.

She took one of his sleeping tablets, closed her eyes and remembered their life in a slide show. The silken sweetness of Ollie's salmon. The rungs of the loft ladder on the soles of her feet. The depth and width of his chest. Sheepskin rugs. Scant wisps of hair on his torso. Making bread. The trips they'd taken. And, through all of it, the strong, calm constancy of Ollie. All of it. She couldn't imagine how they had come to this. Salty tears like the juices from his salmon slipped down her cheeks and she hoped it wouldn't be long.

Ollie was the kind of man who'd have been clear about his funeral. He'd always known his own mind but, in the early stages of the disease, when he wanted to talk about how she might help him along, Nora had shut the conversation down. She'd been unable to consider his death, could only focus on delaying his decline. Later, when she wanted to know his preferences, Ollie's mind was already addled. Nora would have to decide for him. She would have to choose whether to put him in the ground where his flesh could wind its way into applewood, or feed him into flames and let the essence of him drift away in smoke.

She lay in the sling chair and tried to get comfortable. Lara and Trudie had been no help, were divided. Trudie had lobbied for cremation; Lara – over a crackling phone line – for burial. Or was it the other way around? Nora couldn't remember. She couldn't remember much, her mind saturated with the memory of Ollie bound tight to the bed then those few manic days in the hospital.

Signing the 'Do Not Resuscitate' forms with no idea they would be relied upon so soon.

'Hello?' Harry opened the front door, and Nora walked into his open arms and wept properly for the first time since Ollie had been taken away.

Later, she watched as Harry filled the kettle, lit the stove.

'Tea?' he asked. Then: 'You know, I think he's still here.'

Nora's nose tingled and she let tears she'd thought were finished run down her face. She wasn't sure if Harry was right, wasn't sure she wanted him to be.

Harry motioned for her to come to the table, dragged out a chair and, as Nora sat, he rested his hand on her shoulder, as though solidifying her into the space, brought a lemon and the small chopping board to the table.

Ollie had made the board; she had watched him cut the shape with the electric saw, then hand-plane and sand it. Afterwards, he'd rubbed it with linseed oil.

Nora waited as Harry deftly sliced the lemon in two, watched the halves roll away from one another, rock and teeter on the timber. When they came to rest, the edges of skin touched in one place.

The kettle's shrill whistle dragged her attention from the lemons. Harry poured boiling water into mugs. Standing with his back to her, she could almost imagine he was Ollie.

'I want to ask you how you are. I know that's stupid. I'm sorry. I don't know what to say. What not to say.' Harry was wringing his hands. Behind him, through the frame of the window, Nora could see the smokehouse. Still, empty, dormant.

'Tea.' Harry handed her a mug.

'I didn't know we had any.'

Harry smiled then. 'You don't. It's just hot water and lemon. I don't know why I called it that.'

Nora stepped into the smokehouse, closed the door behind her and stood in the dark. She laid her palms on the bench, pressed her nose to the timber and breathed in the sweet applewood aroma, let it fill the empty space in her chest.

'Ollie.' She whispered his name, felt a rippling sensation move across the surface of her heart.

'What now then?' Tom had asked when he'd dropped in the day after the funeral.

'I don't have a clue,' she'd replied. But the truth was something else. The truth was pins in a map, it was articles ripped from magazines, the sign in the window of the travel agent in Hobart, an overheard conversation between a couple of the nurses at the hospital. It was Ollie's ashes scattered at the edge of the Black Forest.

'I'm thinking of going away for a while.'

In the end, she'd agreed to a small farewell dinner at Tom's. Marjorie, having recovered, cooked, and they sat around the table sharing stories and Marjorie's chicken baguettes with caramelised onion. Gurj brought gulab and Sally made bee stings, and the night was warm and welcoming.

After dinner they stood around the fireplace, and Nora admired the view, the catalyst that had drawn her to live in Kettering. Lights rippled on the bay the way that shivers of sadness lapped in the cavern of her chest. She put her hand to her breastbone and thought of Ollie counting out her heartbeats. Swallowed the sob before it swallowed her whole.

Then Trudie's arms were around her, a warm cheek against hers.

'See you and Lara in Chile,' Trudie whispered into her ear.

'Can't wait, love.'

At the airport, Gurj cried.

'You promised.' Sally punched Gurj on the arm.

'You know me.'

The two of them embraced her, and they huddled together.

'They're calling my flight.' She pulled away.

As she passed through the security check, Nora blew kisses to Gurj and Sally. 'Look after each other.'

When she walked up the stairs to the plane, she didn't turn back. Ollie's ashes secure in a vial in her hand luggage. She looked out the window as they rose into the sky. Clouds like a plume of smoke leading towards whoever she might become next.

Acknowledgements

The stories in *Smokehouse* were written and edited at desks and in studios granted to me through fellowships. I am grateful to Writers Victoria and the Grace Marion Wilson Trust for a studio at Glenfern; to the Wheeler Centre for the gift of a Hot Desk Fellowship; to Varuna for a Residential Fellowship; and to Bayside City Council for a studio in the beautiful Billilla mansion, as part of the Bayside Artist in Residence program.

To ACT Writers Centre, in particular Nigel Featherstone, and my fellow 2016 Hardcopiers, thank you for the gift of the HARDCOPY program. To Nadine Davidoff, deep gratitude for your erudite editorial input. Your skilful insight on early drafts of stories (provided through an ASA Emerging Writers' Mentorship Program, funded by the Copyright Agency Cultural Fund) was utterly invaluable.

To Carrie Tiffany, thank you for being an early and unflagging champion of my writing, and Robbie Arnott, Mark Brandi and Jennifer Down for reading and responding to this manuscript before it hit copyedits.

To the many excellent teaching staff and fellow students of RMIT's Diploma of Professional Writing and Editing, much appreciation.

I've been incredibly lucky to workshop with some amazing people whose writing talents I admire greatly. To Jennifer Down, Thomas Minogue, Yasmine O'Sullivan and Kieran Stevenson, thank you for your excellent critical feedback, your loose boundaries, and for being among my favourite humans.

To the Chickens: AJ Collins, Ara Sarafian, Kathryn Moore and especially Jo Burnell, workshopping and becoming friends with you has been a joy.

Thanks to the Varuna Five: Steven Amsterdam, Rachael Mead, Margaret Morgan and especially Harriet Gaffney for your writerly support and friendship.

Immense gratitude to the C Collective: Christopher Breach, Tim Byrne, Alex Fairhill, Melissa Ferguson, Stephen Samuel and Jennifer Porter for always turning up to argue and defend your critical responses, for boozy weekend workshops – may there be more – and for your staunch support and friendship.

To the terrific team at UQP: I feel so very fortunate to have found my way to you. Every one of you has been a dream to work with. In particular, thanks go to my publisher, Aviva Tuffield, for very early and unwavering interest, and big-picture vision for what the manuscript could be. To Felicity Dunning, for bringing such deep understanding of the stories to the fore; at times it felt like you were in my head. I am immensely grateful for your sensitive and skilful eye. To Josh Durham, for my stunning cover design; I can't express how much I love it.

To Grace Heifetz of Left Bank Literary – what can I say? Grace, you're a star and I'm so thrilled to have you on my team.

Acknowledgements

Love and thanks to my friends and extended family for your support, particularly to my sister, Krysta Fox, and my niece, Chloe (Chloe, you are such an inspiration); to Claire Brooks for wonderful company and excellent editorial suggestions; and to my children, Zoe, Josh and Charlie, for being yourselves, and for putting up with my frequent distraction.

Finally, to my husband, Paul, to whom *Smokehouse* is dedicated. Thank you for everything.

Versions of some of the stories in *Smokehouse* have been published elsewhere: 'Woodsmoke', which won the *Overland* Story Wine Prize and was published in *Overland*, was the inspiration for 'Smokehouse'. 'Boy' won the Tasmanian Writers' Prize and was published in *Tasmania 40° South*. 'Stone' was published in *The Big Issue* (Fiction edition).